Deceiver on the Levels

ALSO BY DAVID HODGES

DETECTIVE KATE HAMBLIN MYSTERIES
Book 1: Murder on the Levels
Book 2: Revenge on the Levels
Book 3: Fear on the Levels
Book 4: Killer on the Levels
Book 5: Secrets on the Levels
Book 6: Death on the Levels
Book 7: Poison on the Levels
Book 8: Witch Fire on the Levels
Book 9: Stalker on the Levels
Book 10: Venom on the Levels
Book 11: Watcher on the Levels
Book 12: Storm on the Levels
Book 13: Diamonds on the Levels
Book 14: Shadows on the Levels
Book 15: Deceiver on the Levels

STANDALONE NOVEL
Slice

DECEIVER ON THE LEVELS

DAVID HODGES

Detective Kate Hamblin Mysteries Book 15

Joffe Books, London
www.joffebooks.com

First published in Great Britain in 2025

© David Hodges

Cover art by Nick Castle

ISBN: 978-1-80573-274-7

*This book is dedicated to my wife, Elizabeth,
for all her love, patience and support over so many
wonderful years and to my late mother and father,
whose faith in me to one day achieve my ambition
as a writer remained steadfast throughout their lifetime
and whose tragic passing has left a hole in my life
that will never be filled.*

AUTHOR'S NOTE

Although the action of this novel takes place in the Avon &
Somerset Police area, the story itself and all the characters in
it are entirely fictitious, without any intended connection to
real events or persons living, or dead. At the time of writing, there is *no* police station in Highbridge. This has been
drawn entirely from the author's imagination to ensure no
connection is made between an existing police station or any
personnel in the force. Some poetic licence has been adopted
in relation to local police structures and specific operational
police procedures to meet the requirements of the plot. But
the novel is primarily a crime thriller and does not profess
to be a detailed police procedural, even though the policing background, as depicted, is broadly in accord with the
national picture. I trust that these small departures from fact
will not spoil the reading enjoyment of serving, or retired
police officers for whom I have the utmost respect.

David Hodges

BEFORE THE FACT

Tammy Robinson walked out of the school gates with a spring in her step. It was a sunny Friday afternoon and school was over, with the weekend to look forward to, and she felt on top of the world. Tonight was the night when it was all going to happen. In just under three hours she was going to meet him at last. Gerry! For over a month they had corresponded via the internet, ever since she had been contacted by him on the social media chat line. She had sent him her photo, and he had sent her his, and he looked absolutely gorgeous. Eighteen, with jet black hair, lovely brown eyes and a tan to die for. Okay, so he was a bit old for her — well, quite a bit really, but who cared? She would be fifteen in a couple of weeks, and anyway, age was relative, wasn't it? She had always been told that she was mature for her age and as girls were said to be two years ahead of boys in that respect, really the gap wasn't so great when you thought about it. She couldn't wait to introduce him to the gang at school. They would be green with envy.

Mum and Dad didn't know about Gerry, of course, and they wouldn't have approved if they had known, that was a fact. But they didn't need to know, did they? It was none of their business, and Tammy was old enough now to see who

1

she wanted to see. They had been treating her like a little kid for far too long, cramping her style, and now she was going to show them that their "little angel" had grown up. She stared down at herself and smirked. Oh, she'd grown up all right. She just hoped Gerry liked what he saw.

'Have fun tonight,' someone called out to her, and she turned and waved back at Mandy Williams, who was talking to a group of other girls, blowing her a kiss.

Home was just a short distance from the school, and she took a deep breath before turning into the driveway. No car there, which meant her father was out somewhere, probably at his sports club, as usual. One problem less to deal with, she thought. Her mother was in, though, bustling around, starting to get dinner prepared. She bypassed the kitchen and headed straight upstairs, keen to avoid any small talk that might arouse suspicions. Well, when you were about to do something you shouldn't, it was hard not to look guilty and then the questions would start, wouldn't they?

She dumped her schoolbag on the bed and went straight to her secret hiding place to retrieve her diary. Sitting on the edge of the bed, she opened it and sat for a moment, thinking.

'That you, Tam, is it?' her mother called from the bottom of the stairs.

She jumped. 'Er, yes, Mum,' she shouted back. 'Just got home.'

'Dinner's on the go, but Dad's likely to be late. Some meeting or other at the sports club.'

She breathed a sigh of relief. At least the "chief interrogator" wouldn't be there to harangue her about everything.

'Okay, but I think I'll take a shower, and I'll skip dinner. Going round to Gabrielle's to revise.'

'You never said before, and you'll be hungry.'

Tammy raised her eyes to the ceiling. 'I'll be fine, honestly. Gabrielle's mum will give me something there.'

There was no reply, but she heard her mother muttering to herself as she returned to the kitchen. First hurdle over!

Returning to her diary on her lap, she wrote: *Hi, Diary. Big date with Gerry tonight. Wish me luck!*

Taking care to return the book to its hiding place, she stripped off her school uniform, slipped on her dressing gown and headed for the bathroom with her cosmetics bag.

An hour later she was back in the bedroom, doing her hair and putting on her make-up. Then, dressed in a denim jacket over a skimpy nylon top, plus a very short skirt, high heels and a personalised silver anklet, she crept to the bedroom door and peered out. Her mother was singing, and she heard the clink of a saucepan on the hob. Now for the really hard part. Escaping "Colditz" without detection.

Slipping off her heels, she crept along the corridor in her new fishnet tights and began the descent to the hallway, wincing at every creak of the treads.

The front door opened easily and, pulling on her heels in the porch, she left it ajar to avoid the sharp metallic "crack" she knew it always made when it was being shut. Clenching her teeth, she crept quietly towards the open gate, lifting her feet carefully at every step to attract as little attention as possible. The street outside was deserted. Great! No sign of her father's car yet and no nosy neighbours in evidence, thank heavens. Just a hundred yards of tree-lined tarmac. Hesitating for just a second, she took a deep breath and set off with a rapid tap of her high heels to the far end, swinging left on to the footpath that cut right through the village to the other side, away from prying eyes. Her heart was thumping wildly and there was an excited tremble in her legs, but she didn't care. She had made it. Now for the best bit: Gerry!

The so-called recreation ground where they had agreed to meet was a half-acre field on the very edge of the village, with a country pub and a collection of houses opposite. The rec boasted football goalposts in the middle and the usual swings, roundabout and slide on a square of hardstanding at one end, close to a small copse. She could see, even as she approached, that the rec was completely deserted, the playground equipment standing idle. She'd thought that would be the case at this time in the evening. The older kids would be having dinner before gathering later in the evening for football and so forth, and the tots would be in the process of being bathed and put to bed. She spent a few moments walking up and down on the hardstanding, glancing at her watch. The plan had been for Gerry to wait by the entrance to the copse. When she saw him, she would then follow him into the trees. But he was at least ten minutes late. Surely, he hadn't stood her up? That would be the end. Frowning and chewing her lip, she propped herself on one of the swings, staring around the recreation ground with mounting frustration.

Another five minutes passed, and she was about to get up and leave altogether when her mobile rang.

'I'm in the copse,' a male voice said. 'Come and join me.'

She was on her feet in a second and heading across the grass towards it. A narrow path had been made through the trees by the local children and some ropes hung over a thick bough on one side. Ducking her head under it, she picked her way carefully towards a small green space she could see ahead, then stopped uncertainly in the middle of the clearing, looking about her.

'Gerry?' she called anxiously. 'Where are you?'

'Right here, Tammy,' a voice replied and, turning, she stared with a sense of shock at the man standing feet behind her.

'You're — you're not Gerry,' she exclaimed, backing away.

'No,' the man said from inside his sinister black hood, 'I know I'm not. But life is full of disappointments, isn't it, Tammy?'

* * *

Tammy awoke, as if from a nightmare, shouting and screaming — only to find that the nightmare was real. She was in a poorly lit, windowless room reminiscent of a cellar, a single lightbulb flickering fitfully from the ceiling above her head.

She was lying on a smelly mattress on a concrete floor under an equally smelly duvet and, even in the poor light, she could see that she was not alone. Horrible black spiders and other creepy crawlies seemed to be flitting about everywhere. If that wasn't scary enough, it suddenly dawned on her that she was shut inside some sort of steel cage, like the one her friend, Mandy, kept in her kitchen for her boisterous Labrador dog. Only this one was very much bigger.

She shook her head several times, trying to break through the mist that seemed to have enveloped her mind, trying to make sense out of what had happened to her. Who had put her in the cage and why? She remembered going into the copse at the recreation ground to meet Gerry — when was it? Friday? Yes, that was it, Friday evening, but then what? According to the luminous dial of her wristwatch it was now eleven thirty the same evening, so she must have been unconscious for just a few hours. But what had happened between going into the copse and now? She just couldn't remember. Everything was so hazy.

Then abruptly something seemed to click into place, the mist began to dissipate, and her memory clawed its way free. But clarity did not bring relief. Gerry hadn't been in the copse, waiting for her, had he? But someone else had. A terrifying hooded bogeyman, who had come up behind her and seized her in a vice-like grip. She remembered struggling against him and becoming entangled in some brambles, which had ripped into her legs through her tights. But then there had been that sharp stabbing pain in her neck, and, after that, nothing. Not until she had woken up in this foul cage, feeling confused, sick and giddy, with very sore legs, no doubt from the brambles, and absolutely terrified. And there was something else too. Her denim jacket was gone and with it her mobile phone, while her shoes and tights had been removed and the flickering light above her head revealed that there were four large plasters affixed to her bare legs.

Desperately trying to hold back the panic that was rising up again inside her, she threw off the duvet and scrambled up on to her knees to peer around her. The cage seemed to be about five foot square and was constructed against a wall, in front of a wooden door. Grabbing hold of the steel bars on one side of her, she hauled herself to her feet and made her way unsteadily towards the door. She found it opened easily enough, and a light snapped on automatically as it swung inwards. But then her spirits sank. There was just a small toilet smelling of disinfectant on the other side equipped with a low-level bowl minus a seat, an old-fashioned high-level cistern and a small wash-hand basin with a soap dispenser and a towel on a hook beside it. There was no other door in there and not even a window.

What was this hideous place and why was she here? Swinging round, she stumbled to the other end of the cage and found another steel door made of the same material as the cage, which appeared to open outwards into the cellar. But as she was rattling it to see if she could open it, she saw the business-like padlock fixed to the other side and realised she was wasting her time.

Sinking back on to her haunches, she started to shake and then to hyperventilate. Inevitably, more screams followed, welling up in her throat again as the sheer enormity of her situation got through to her. But only echoes greeted her, bouncing off the walls of the cellar in gleeful mockery, and eventually, exhausted and totally defeated, she was only able to produce a weak, strangled whimper.

The soft chuckle issued from the semi-gloom nearby moments later.

'No point screaming, Tammy,' a strangely distorted voice said. 'No one will hear you down here.'

Reanimated by the presence of the speaker, she pulled herself back up on to her knees. Then, reaching forward with her head against the bars of the cage, she gripped the padlocked door in front of her and shook it again in desperation, sobbing her fear and frustration.

'Let me out of here!' she shouted. 'Do you hear me? Let me out!'

'Sorry, Tammy,' the voice replied. 'No can do — not until you have acknowledged the error of your ways and redeemed yourself.'

'Redeemed myself?' she choked. 'What are you on about?'

There was a heavy sigh. 'The fact is, you are not a very nice person, Tammy, and you are a bad influence on others. Your friends, Mandy and Gabrielle, for instance, who will end up just like you unless something is done about it.'

'What do you know about me and who my friends are?'

'Oh, I know a lot about you, Tammy. I have been watching you for some time now, and Mother and I have come to the conclusion that punishment is the only way to change your behaviour.'

'Punishment?' Anger suddenly burst through Tammy's fear. 'Who the hell do you think you are? You can't do this to me, you arsehole.'

The voice sounded unperturbed by her outburst. 'Oh, but I can, Tammy, and I will. Now is not the time to discuss it, though. We will talk later when you are less aggressive. Till then, I suggest you catch up on some sleep. You have some big days ahead of you.'

Tammy gulped. 'Days? You . . . you're not going to leave me in here?'

There was a noticeable sneer in the voice when he replied. 'And why not, Tammy? You have a nice comfortable bed and ensuite facilities for your sole use. What more could you wish for?'

A shadowy hooded figure crossed the room from a corner and a door opened to the right of the cage, admitting a much brighter light, which framed him in its glare.

'But-but why have you shut me in a cage?' she shrieked after him, her panic returning. '*Tell me!*'

'Why?' he said, half-turning. 'Well, it's quite simple really. Animals belong in cages, don't they? So, as you have proved yourself to be an animal, you are in the place you should be.'

Then he was through the door, which slammed shut behind him, leaving Tammy alone with just the flickering bulb and the creepy crawlies for company . . .

* * *

It had to be daylight outside, going by Tammy's wristwatch, which put the time at just after six in the morning. It was also Saturday, and she knew that by now her mother would be climbing the walls over her disappearance. What would she do? Obviously contact the police, but then what? No one knew where her daughter was, so how could they ever find her?

Despite the ordeal she had suffered, Tammy must have drifted off into a deep exhausted sleep for several hours after her hooded captor had left. Now, awake but still feeling weak and groggy, she heard the sound of heavy footsteps close by. The door of the cellar opened a few minutes later, and what looked like the same hooded figure appeared carrying a tray, sunlight streaming down a staircase through the gap behind him.

In her continuing traumatised state, she immediately felt like screaming again at the sight of him. But common sense won the day, and she controlled herself with an effort. Screaming hadn't got her anywhere before and she guessed it wouldn't now. She had no idea where she was, but he'd told her no one would hear her anyway and she had no reason to doubt him. Furthermore, though only fourteen, she was mature enough to realise that she had to force herself to stay calm if she was ever going to get out of this awful place. After all, he hadn't hurt her yet, apart from sticking what she guessed was a needle in her neck to drug her, so maybe he wasn't intending to. She'd seen a film once where a kidnapper had kept his mask on and, because of that, the victim hadn't been able to identify him, so she had survived. It gave her some reassurance to see that her own captor had also stayed hooded. The time to worry, she told herself, was if he took the hood off.

But hood or no hood, why had he abducted her at all? What did he intend doing with her now she was locked in his cage? From what he'd said to her about being punished and having to "redeem" herself, it sounded like he was some sort of religious freak, whose marbles were not too secure. But on the other hand, it could be that he was a nasty brand of paedophile with some sort of sexual perversion in mind. She wouldn't stand a chance against a man his size. The very thought turned her blood cold, and she shuddered involuntarily.

Then there was the question of his identity. He said he knew her well and had been watching her for quite some time, but, seeing as he had been hooded since he had snatched her, she hadn't the faintest idea who the hell he could be. Even his voice had sounded strangely distorted, as if he had done something to disguise it, so there had been no clue there. Yet she couldn't fathom why anyone she knew would have gone to so much trouble to deceive and then kidnap her the way he had. The whole thing was not only terrifying but made little sense.

She watched as her captor set the tray down carefully on a stool beside the cage and stared down at her, returning his gaze with a look of defiance that was in stark contrast to the fear she felt.

'I thought you might like an early breakfast, Tammy,' he said quietly.

'What, so you can drug me again, then touch me up while I'm out of it?' she said chancing her arm with as much cultivated aggression as she could muster. 'Some kind of perv, are you?'

He tutted. 'No, I'm not a pervert, Tammy,' he replied, 'and that's a very insulting thing to say. If I were such a creature, I would have had ample opportunity to take advantage of you while you were unconscious earlier, but I didn't.'

'So, who took my tights off then?' she demanded.

'I did, but I had to. You had quite nasty cuts on your legs from the brambles. I had to wash them and put on some clean plasters to stop the wounds getting infected.'

'And why should you care about them getting infected?'

'Because you are my guest, Tammy, and I am responsible for your welfare.'

'Welfare, bollocks! And what else did you do when I was out cold? Have a quick feel, did you?'

He tutted again and shook his head. 'You really are a most unpleasant young . . . I won't call you a lady — and you have a very twisted mind for a fourteen-year-old girl. But I feel we can work on your recalcitrant tendencies when we start the programme tomorrow.'

Her bravado faded and she felt her fears return. 'Programme? What programme?'

'You'll see tomorrow. It's something Mother and I have spent quite a bit of time putting together.'

'Stuff your mother!'

A little unbalanced giggle. 'Oh you really are going to be a challenge for us, aren't you, Tammy? A real challenge. But then we are used to challenges, Mother and I.' Suddenly he raised his voice to a shout. 'We are used to challenges, aren't we, Mother?'

Unsurprisingly, there was no reply and Tammy found herself shrinking back into the cage, an icy chill taking possession of her as her worst suspicions were confirmed. She hadn't been kidnapped by some money-motivated criminal seeking a ransom; she was in the hands of a madman!

'Now,' he said quietly, 'do you want some breakfast or not? It's your choice, and I haven't got all day while you decide.'

She swallowed hard and glanced quickly past him at the half-open cellar door, her brain already working on the possibilities. 'C-course I want breakfast,' she replied in just above a whisper.

'Good. Then move back further into the cage and I'll put the tray down on the floor for you. But don't do anything stupid. It would only end badly for you.'

Unlocking and removing the padlock, he picked up the tray from the stool and put one knee against the cage door after opening it halfway. Then he bent down to place the tray on the floor just inside, keeping his eyes on her the whole time. She tensed, despite his warning not to try anything, weighing up her chances of success in making a break for the cellar door while he was in a semi-crouched position. But then she decided against it. That was exactly what he would be expecting her to do and she was sure he would be ready for her, however vulnerable he might look in his semi-crouched position. Furthermore, fear of what a madman might do to her if she failed dominated her thinking. So, she forced herself just to sit there and say and do nothing, trusting in luck that, armed with a proper plan, there might be a better opportunity later on — provided, of course, that she managed to survive that long!

* * *

Tammy had always seen Sunday as the traditional "old folks" holy day, but there was nothing holy about the particular Sunday that greeted her when she opened her eyes at just after six the following morning. She was still locked in the nightmare cage, she felt even rougher than the day before and, for some reason, her head felt cold and sore, as if in a constant draught. Feeling also dizzy and nauseous, she rolled over on to one elbow, convinced she was going to be sick, but, apart from a series of long, retching gags, nothing happened.

Falling back on to the mattress, she lay there for a few seconds with her eyes tightly closed, trying to get herself together. Her brain seemed woolly, just like it had when she had first regained her senses on the Friday night after her abduction. She only remembered the hooded man bringing her tea the previous evening, nothing else, and she had no idea whether she had slept the whole time after that or what. Then the next second the realisation hit her. The bastard had drugged her again, hadn't he? She recognised the after-effects only too well. The stuff must have been in the tea or the sandwiches he had given her and, like an idiot, she had fallen for it. But why had he done it at all? There was no way she could have escaped from the locked cage, so what had he hoped to achieve? She thought about the first day when he had drugged her with the needle and the suspicions that had dominated her mind afterwards, despite his denials. They crowded in on her now as she agonised over what he might have done to her while she had lain there, drugged and helpless, and her stomach churned in revulsion at the horrific images her fevered imagination conjured up.

In fact, her suspicions turned out to be way off beam, yet that proved to be of little comfort when in the next instant his cruel motive for drugging her was suddenly brought home to her. Prompted to raise a hand to her temple in an instinctive reaction to a sudden stabbing pain, she found with a sense of shock that instead of long, silky brown hair, her fingertips were rubbing against smooth, bare skin. Scrambling up into a sitting position with a loud gasp, she ran her palm over the rest of her head — then, in horrified disbelief, immediately followed this up with a further examination to confirm what her previous check had already revealed. It was now abundantly clear why he had drugged her again — and it had had nothing to do with committing some form of sexual abuse. The beautiful brown hair that had once tumbled down over her shoulders in almost riotous profusion was not there anymore. While she had been insensible, he had calmly sat her in a chair and meticulously cut the whole lot off, before completely shaving her head and leaving her totally bald!

The scream this time was one of tragic loss, rather than fear. A high-pitched, heart-wrenching cry of misery that went on and on for several seconds before ending in plaintive sobbing. But there was no sympathy in the voice that responded from the corner of the room, and its tone was hard and unrepentant.

'Your hair will grow again, Tammy,' her captor said, 'but you must learn that bad behaviour has consequences. Based on your previous conduct, this is your first lesson. Other lessons will follow until I am satisfied you have changed your ways for good.'

Raising her head, Tammy peered venomously into the gloom through her tears. 'You bastard!' she choked. 'You filthy, stinking bastard. I hope your guts rot inside you!'

There was a sharp hiss of breath. 'My, my,' he retorted, 'what a nasty little horror you are. So abusive and without any respect at all for your elders, despite having already been punished for your misbehaviour. Well, so be it. Perhaps forgoing breakfast, and possibly lunch as well, might help you to give some thought to your future conduct, and, as I always believe that meditation is best achieved when there are no distractions, I will switch off that irritating flickering light for you.'

Then he left the room, plunging the cellar into total darkness.

* * *

The toilet light didn't work. Obviously, it only operated when the main cellar light was switched on. Tammy might have known that that would be the case in Mr Hoody's personal "torture chamber". Okay, at fourteen, she didn't like the dark and she didn't like spiders and other creepy crawlies either, but she was determined he wouldn't break her. Returning to her mattress, she sat down on it with the duvet pulled right up to her chin, trying not to think about the creatures that she'd seen running about on the concrete floor, but jumping every few minutes as she fancied she could feel tiny legs creeping over her bare feet and up her legs as she sat there.

In the end, her resolve simply collapsed, and she resorted to shouting and screaming again and shaking the steel bars of the cage in a desperate attempt to attract attention. But there was no response. Either her tormentor couldn't hear her, or he was ignoring her.

As he had threatened, breakfast never arrived and by mid-morning she was starting to feel very hungry. By lunchtime she was ravenous, but still he did not put in an appearance, and it was not until early evening that she heard the footsteps and then the sound of the cellar door opening. Moments later the flickering light was back on, and he was standing in front of the cage with a tray of something hot in a bowl, together with a plate of crusty bread and a mug of tea.

'Anything to say to me, Tammy?' he asked. 'Or would you rather I ate your dinner myself? Be a pity, that, as it smells so nice.'

She bit back the retort that had formed on the end of her tongue. In the nine to ten hours she had sat there alone in the hideous darkness, she'd had plenty of time to think and, though she hated to admit defeat, she had come to realise that losing her temper and insulting him would get her nowhere. He held all the aces and, until she could think of a way of escaping from this place, her only option was to swallow her pride and appear to give in to him — but not too willingly so as to arouse his suspicions.

'S-sorry,' she muttered grudgingly.

'What did you say?' he goaded. 'I couldn't quite hear you.'

'I said sorry!' she shouted.

He emitted a hard laugh. 'What got to you first? Hunger or the spiders?' he mocked. 'Although I don't really believe you are truly sorry, saying it is a first step that we can build on, so I'd better let you have your beef stew before it gets cold.'

He went through the same performance of setting the tray down on the stool outside, unlocking the cage door, then putting his leg against it as he opened it halfway and handed her the tray.

'Eat up,' he said. 'Lots to do tomorrow, when we'll see if you really are as contrite as you would like me to think or are just playing me along so you can fill your belly. *Bon appétit.*'

Tammy looked at the food on the floor in front of her for several minutes after he had gone, hungry yet reluctant to eat after the drugging episode she had experienced the night before. What if the stew or the tea were drugged this time as well? What he might do to her while she was uncon-scious didn't bear thinking about, and it could be a lot worse than the loss of her hair. But finally, after much deliberation, hunger won the day, and she tucked into her dinner without further hesitation. Only time would tell if he had slipped something extra into it and she wouldn't know that until the following morning. All she could do was hope and, probably for the first time in her life, pray.

* * *

Tammy awoke at just after six on the Monday morning to find that the cellar light had been switched on, suggesting he was on his way down to her. She had none of the symp-toms she had suffered the previous two mornings, and she felt a tremendous sense of relief that nothing seemed to have happened to her, despite her fears over the possibility that her dinner had been tampered with the previous night. In fact, she felt more alert and focused than she had ever been since her abduction, which was probably why she spotted the metal nail almost straight away. It was lying on the concrete floor by the side of her cage, and it took her only minutes to thrust her slim hand in between the bars to retrieve it and conceal it under her mattress before her captor delivered her breakfast.

The moment he left, and the cellar door had slammed shut behind him, she retrieved the nail and examined it closely. It was about six inches in length and bent slightly in the middle, with a sharp rusted tip at one end. Ever since her abduction, she had watched how her meals had been deliv-ered each day, and a desperate escape plan had been building slowly inside her head. But it had lacked one thing for its success — something small and sharp instead of the thin, plastic spoons that came with the hot meals — and now, by a sheer stroke of luck, she had found exactly what she needed.

She spent the rest of the morning working on the details of her plan in her head. What she contemplated would be very risky and depended on so many things falling into place, but it was her one hope of getting out of the place and she knew that she would only get one crack at it. If she failed, she would never get another chance.

The morning seemed to last for ever and she was soon in a state of nervous agitation desperately hoping that, as he had brought her breakfast, he would deliver her lunch at midday, like on the Saturday, or all her planning would have been for nothing.

It hadn't been easy pulling off two of the four plasters covering the long bramble cuts to her legs and deliberately opening up the crusted wounds with her fingernails to make them bleed, but she had gritted her teeth with grim determination and carried on, knowing full well that it was her only chance. She had been surprised by just how much blood had flowed from them, but it had at least enabled her to have sufficient to spread over her mouth, neck and the skimpy top she was still wearing. Now lying down, completely covered by the duvet, all she had to do was wait for him to come, knowing that she would have just seconds to get herself into position the moment she heard the cellar door being unlocked. She just hoped that the flickering light in the cellar was strong enough for him to see what she wanted him to see at the crucial moment.

Midday came and went and then one o'clock. Once again cold and shaky, she clenched her right hand tightly over the bent nail she had found as she stressed over what she was about to do. Where the hell was he? What if her previous fears were justified, and he had decided not to bring her lunch at all? And maybe that meant dinner as well? She had been to the toilet already, but the more tense she became the more she felt she wanted to go again.

Now 1.15 p.m. and still no sign of him. There were tears of frustration in her eyes as she thought of all the planning and preparation she had gone into what looked like for nothing. But it was plain he wasn't coming, so she had no choice but to give up altogether — and it was at that moment that she at last heard the approaching footsteps on the stairs and the jangle of keys.

She just had time to throw off the duvet and spread herself out on her back close to the front of the cage before she heard the cellar door open.

She held her breath until she thought she would burst. Where was he? Surely, he had brought her lunch on his tray and was not just going to sit in the corner of the room and mock her, as he had twice before. But he was actually closer than she had thought and the next instant his horrified yell right beside the cage nearly made her jump out of her skin.

'Bloody hell, what on earth—?'

She heard the noise of the tray being dumped on the stool outside and something falling off it. A second later, a powerful torch lit up the interior of the cage and she heard the snap of a key turning in the lock. She forced herself to remain completely motionless until she could feel his breath on her face when he bent over her, and it was then that she acted.

As her eyes flicked open, and her lips curled into a vengeful snarl, her right arm flew up with the bent nail gripped tightly in her hand. He had no chance to defend himself and the sharp, rusted point tore into the hood he was wearing with a force born of absolute hatred and desperation. Whether it caused him any real injury or not, Tammy had no way of knowing, but she heard the fabric of the hood rip and had the satisfaction of seeing him stumble backwards through the doorway of the cage with a loud cry, cannoning into the stool and pitching the tray and its contents all over the floor. Then, losing his balance, he fell heavily on to the concrete floor, shouting and swearing.

She was up and out of the cage even as he tried to regain his feet, and moments later she was through the cellar door and scrambling up the flight of stone stairs beyond, heading for the light blazing from another open doorway at the top.

It seemed that she was going to make it too, for he was some way behind her, but then, within two to three steps of her objective, she tripped, pitching backwards down the staircase and slamming into him as he raced up after her.

Still very angry, he made to grab hold of her before she could regain her feet, only to stop short when the wrist he had seized settled limply in his hand and she remained where she had fallen, strangely inert. At first, he thought she was just play-acting, trying to hoodwink him into thinking she had knocked herself out so that she could suddenly turn on him again when he least expected it. But with a sense of shock, he saw blood creeping out from under her head and trickling down over the edge of the step it was resting on. Panic gripped him and he quickly felt for a pulse in the wrist he was holding, but he couldn't find so much as a flutter. Immediately he checked the artery in her neck, but again he could find nothing.

'You silly little cow!' he gasped, rising slowly to his feet and staring down at her, his whole body shaking and his head swimming. 'Why the bloody hell couldn't you just do as you were told?'

But Tammy Robinson was in no position to reply. Whether she had fractured her skull or broken her neck in the fall was immaterial. Either way, it was quite obvious to him that she was dead!

Gathering her small body up in his arms, he carried her to the top of the stairs and crossed the tiled floor of a small kitchen into the hallway that lay beyond. There was a sitting room to one side of the hall and, pushing the door open with his shoulder, he gently laid her body on a shabby, old-fashioned settee set against one wall. Then, white-faced and trembling, he started up a wide oak staircase by the front door to the corridor above and knocked on another door.

'Mother,' he called in a voice filled with emotion, 'A really bad thing has happened . . .'

* * *

Tammy's captor had been lucky in one way. His hood, though quite thin, had prevented the point of the rusted nail

18

from causing him serious injury. While it had ripped open the flimsy material and caused quite a long cut down one side of his face, after washing and disinfecting the injury he didn't envisage the plaster he had stuck over it staying on that long. Furthermore, he was too shocked by Tammy's death to waste time worrying about it, and, after a long conversation with Mother, he had regained his confidence and was clear in his mind that the most important thing he had to do was to get rid of the girl's body.

He had a job getting her into the boot of his battered, old Volkswagen Passat saloon, however. She seemed a lot heavier dead than when he'd loaded her into it alive, but insensible, at the village rec. He was glad that he had left the job until it was dark when there was less risk of him being seen, and he was relieved that he had heeded Mother's advice. Nevertheless, once the girl was in the boot, he still covered her with an old blanket he always kept in there for emergencies.

He took his time driving across the Levels. The last thing he needed was to be stopped by the police for speeding, and he felt sick at the thought. The evening was warm and dry, and the road ahead brilliantly lit by a full moon, which was ideal for his purposes. Fortunately, the Somerset Levels were more sparsely populated than a lot of other areas, and there were any number of really remote places suitable for the disposal of Tammy's remains, without the risk of running into anyone, but he had selected one particular spot that he felt was far enough away from his home to avoid any possible connection to him in the unlikely event that her body were ever to be discovered.

He had been genuinely mortified at the girl's accidental death, not from any sense of remorse, but because it should never have happened that way. But Mother had soon calmed him down, as she always had after other unfortunate mishaps in his life, and his survival instincts had kicked in to replace his feelings of anger and frustration within no more than twenty minutes. It was Tammy's fault that she had died anyway. She had chosen to disobey him when he had only been trying to turn her from her wicked ways, and she had inflicted quite a nasty scratch on his face in her bid to escape. *He* hadn't killed her after all. She had done that to herself through her own misbehaviour.

Not that the police would see it that way if he was ever found out. They would lock him up and throw away the key — and what would Mother do then, with no one to look after her? He couldn't and wouldn't allow that to happen over the accidental death of such a wretched child. So, he had to make sure that Tammy Robinson disappeared completely, and then he and Mother would be safe.

With this thought uppermost in his mind, he turned off the main road shortly afterwards, crossing over a narrow drainage ditch, or "rhyne", through an open gateway and on to a rutted, bumpy track, still wet and muddy from heavy rain the day before. The headlights of his car picked out a sign just inside the entrance, indicating that he was entering the Holcroft Nature Reserve, and after a few yards the track opened out into a tarmacked parking area, encircled by trees and dense undergrowth.

He reversed into a marked bay to one side of a path that burrowed into the woodland behind the VW and cut the engine and lights. For a few moments he simply sat there, staring around the moonlit car park, taking deep, trembling breaths as he tried to pluck up the courage to get on with what he had to do. Then, finally forcing himself out of the car, he opened the boot to grab a torch and a spade and took the path into the woods, looking for a suitable spot. He found one almost immediately. A small gap among the trees to the right of the path. A quick check with the spade revealed that the earth there was soft and peaty. It would be fairly easy to dig. Returning to the car, with some difficulty he hauled Tammy's body, minus the blanket, out of the boot, and hoisted it over one shoulder, with her head and arms hanging down his back and her legs and feet gripped tightly against his chest by one arm.

He had actually closed the boot, picked up the spade again and was turning towards the path to finish the task he had set himself when he heard the sharp intake of breath.

A young woman with a camera slung round her neck had emerged from the path into the moonlight just feet away from him and was standing there, seemingly frozen to the spot, her face transfixed with a look of horror and her mouth gaping open.

What she was doing there, he had no idea, although it was likely that she was some kind of nocturnal twitcher. But he was not interested in finding out. Instead, his instinct for self-preservation kicked in and he reacted on impulse. He had expected her to scream, just like women always seemed to do in films when they were terrified, but to his relief this one didn't. It was as if her vocal cords had suddenly become paralysed. But her legs certainly weren't and, as he dumped Tammy's body unceremoniously on the ground and went for her, she took off like a hare, disappearing back into the woods in panic-stricken flight.

The girl was young and, by the look of her, quite fit. In normal circumstances she would probably have outstripped him, but she was no match for his stride, or the desperation of a man who had so much to lose if she got away, and he overhauled her, before she had gone more than a few yards. Then, slamming into her and sending her sprawling, he flipped her over on to her back and jumped on top of her as she lay there in the mud, his hands tight around her neck.

It wasn't the first time he had strangled someone, and, possessed of a fear of the consequences if she were to survive and subsequently identify him to the police, he made sure there was no mistake about the outcome. Afterwards he dragged her into the bushes and left her there while he raced back to where he had been forced to dump Tammy, acutely conscious of the fact that other twitchers might be in the wood and could be making their way in his direction.

As it turned out, the good news for him was that the car park was still empty, with no sign of anyone else, twitchers or otherwise. The bad news was that Tammy was no longer lying on the ground by the boot of his car. She had completely disappeared . . .

CHAPTER 1

It was eight thirty on a busy Monday morning in the old Somerset market town of Bridgwater and the traffic was in full flow. The sun was out again, promising to deliver a warm, cloudless day by lunchtime instead of the grey, rainy conditions of the previous weekend. It brought a bit of welcome cheer to the shoppers thronging the streets.

Up in the plush office on the second floor of Bridgwater Police Station, cheer was sadly lacking, however, as two old foes faced each other across the modern, steel-framed desk.

A sour-faced Detective Chief Inspector Toby Ricketts sat behind the desk in a deep, leather, executive-style chair, with his back to the half-open window. Twirling a gold-coloured fountain pen between his long fingers, he stared at the person sitting in front of him in a black and orange plastic chair, which by force of habit he always made sure was lower than his own so that he could intimidate whoever he summoned before him.

Approaching forty, tall and thinly built, Ricketts' once debonair appearance had taken an unmistakable hit. His silky, blond hair was now thinning, the luxuriant matching moustache beginning to show signs of wear and tear and there were definite wrinkles at the corners of his tired blue eyes. Nevertheless, he was dressed, as usual, in an expensive-looking Italian-style, blue suit, and he wore a gold Rolex on his wrist, which he made sure was clearly visible by tucking the cuff of his silk shirt under the strap. A former graduate-entry, "company" man, Ricketts had originally been starred as a future high-flier — one of the chief constable's blue-eyed whizz-kids — and he had been fast-tracked to his present position. But, for some reason known only to the top hierarchy of the force, he had fallen out of favour somewhere along the way, and his career seemed to have come to a halt on the third rung of the promotion ladder. Desperate to regain his former status, he showed little interest in the welfare or careers of those under him, keen only to impress those in the gilded cages at the top with his suitability for the next step up. Therefore he was seen by the rank and file as totally untrustworthy, or, as one wag had put it, "about as reliable as a broken wristwatch".

The slim, auburn-haired woman in the neat grey trouser suit who was sitting in the plastic chair opposite was a little younger than Ricketts and was also a former graduate entrant with a similar amount of police service. But she was an entirely different proposition to her boss. Dynamic, courageous and impulsive, with an enviable detection record to her credit, Detective Inspector Kate Lewis was a no-nonsense practical copper, who was liked and well respected by those she worked with. But at the same time, she was inclined to be impulsive, outspoken and a thorn in the side of the more senior ranks because of her unorthodox approach to the job and her tendency to sometimes act as a lone wolf and to disobey orders she didn't agree with. This had earned her the nicknames "Maverick" and "Go it Alone Kate", and, as a detective sergeant, it had cost her many career opportunities in the past. Her promotion out of the blue to DI at Bristol a year ago had surprised her as much as everyone else — none more so than Ricketts, whose hatred of her and what she represented had developed into something akin to vengeful paranoia, which he was not afraid to show.

'So,' the DCI said after a deliberate period of silence, 'you made inspector in the end then?'

Kate nodded, treating him to a cold smile. 'I certainly did, guv. DI on Bristol CID, and it was quite an experience.'

'And I suppose you're looking for congratulations and a warm welcome back?'

She shrugged and shook her head. 'I know I won't get either,' she said. 'You've made your opinion of me abundantly clear over the years.'

He leaned forward across the desk. 'Exactly right, Mrs Lewis. You see, I have never rated you, and I regarded your promotion to DI as a big mistake. In fact, I believe those who made the decision will ultimately come to regret it.'

His comments really stung her, but she wasn't surprised by them after all the aggravation he had dished out to her during her time as a DS at Highbridge, and she forced herself to remain impassive, only just managing to hold back the caustic reply that was on the tip of her tongue.

'Unfortunately, despite my best endeavours,' he went on, evidently not picking up on her stony silence, 'I was unable to put a stop to your undeserved elevation to the next rank and now, like a bad penny, you have come back to Highbridge as head of the department. Astonishing after your previous lamentable conduct there as a DS.' His face twisted into a sneer. 'Well, let me say this, *madam*, I don't know how you managed to wangle your transfer after such a short time, but I will be watching you very closely from now on, just waiting for you to step out of line, remember that.'

Kate had had enough. Jumping to her feet, her blue eyes blazing, she placed both hands on the front of his desk and stared him down. 'And you remember this,' she grated, 'I'm a DI now. Not a sergeant you can boss about when you feel like it. Furthermore, I am my own woman and the head of my own department. You may have overall administrative responsibility for the area's CID, but operationally, I run things my way and I will not tolerate any interference from you or anyone else. Is that clear, *sir*?'

Then, turning on her heel as he sat there gaping at her open-mouthed, she stalked from the office, making the middle-aged secretary sitting at her desk almost jump out of her skin as Kate slammed the door shut with full force behind her, rattling the windows and sending the picture of the King on Ricketts' office wall leaping from its hook and smashing on the floor.

* * *

Kate felt good as she drove out of Bridgwater and headed for Highbridge. She had been desperate to bring Ricketts down a peg or two for so long that it had become a running sore, and now at last she had done it. And the beauty of it was, he could do nothing about it, first because there was no corroboration of what she had said and, second because he had been well out of order with his snide remarks to start with.

But she forgot all about Detective Chief Inspector Toby Ricketts when she finally drove into the car park at the rear of Highbridge police station, the sight of the three-storey, red-brick building opening doors in her subconscious and bringing back a multitude of memories, some unpleasant, some poignant, but all still there.

Memories of past investigations. People she had worked with, the ups and downs, the successes and the failures, all supposed to have been consigned to the past and yet all with the capacity to be relived in the present. She could still vividly remember the case of the murderous funeral director, who had taken his calling to a whole new level by wasting prospective clients himself rather than waiting for them to die, and who had come back for her after she'd exposed his gruesome crimes. The nightmare investigation where, as a committed arachnophobe, she had endured the worst possible scenario with the escape of a deadly poisonous spider into the shadows of a rambling old house. The surreal affair of the psychopathic novelist, who had chosen her as his opponent in a lethal, twisted game of cat and mouse, where the penalty for losing was death.

She remembered the colleagues she had lost along the way, from her old boss, Detective Inspector Ted Roscoe, to her more recent friend and colleague, Detective Constable Indrani Purewal — good, decent officers who had died trying to bring about a better society — and, on the other side of the coin, the two renegade coppers, who had turned out to be the perpetrators in the homicides she was investigating. It was all there, indelibly etched on her memory, and now, after a year of blood and gore as a DI at Bristol, complete with other unsavoury memories to lock away, she was back on her old patch, about to do the same thing all over again.

She had to be some sort of weird masochist, she reasoned. She had already come close to one nervous breakdown a few years back, when the stresses of the job and the mental traumas she had suffered had culminated in a spell in a psychiatric clinic. This should have served as a gipsy's warning, which any sensible person would have heeded, and in fairness, she *had* attempted to do just that by packing it all in and retiring to quieter coastal pastures. But sadly, things had not worked out as planned, for the job had come calling on her, rather than the other way about. So she had been tempted back into doing what she did best, despite the odds that always seemed to be stacked against her, including a vengeful DCI whom she knew would always be lurking in the background, waiting for her to mess up. Still, what was it her cynical colleagues always said: if you can't stand a joke, you shouldn't have joined?

Maybe they had a point, she mused as she pulled into the parking bay reserved for the detective inspector, close to the back door of the police station. Then, climbing out of her car with her briefcase, she paused for a moment to throw a glance at the sky. The sunny day appeared to be clouding over. She just hoped that wasn't a bad omen.

Her first port of call, once her security card had let her into the building by the back door, was the office of the local intelligence officer, or LIO, as he was known. She wasn't surprised to find it empty, and even less surprised to find the present incumbent, who had only recently been appointed to the post after the retirement of his predecessor, sitting at a table in the canteen, with a couple of currant buns and a mug of coffee in front of him. After all, it *was* approaching mid-morning and, as she knew from painful experience, it was more often the case that her husband, Hayden, would be found where the food was and where the work wasn't!

She had been married for most of her service to the big untidy lump, with his mop of thick, unruly, fair hair, posh, pompous manner and resemblance in appearance and style to the former British prime minister, Boris Johnson, and he had always been the same. Highly intelligent, perceptive and knowledgeable, he had a first-class, analytical brain, which in the past he had used to brilliant effect in solving a number of complicated criminal cases. But at the same time he was an infuriating eccentric, proudly calling himself a free spirit, which in her book meant nothing more than an admission to being a lazy, arrogant sod, and his laissez-faire approach to everything had become almost legendary.

But despite all his faults, she thought the world of her lovable, good-natured and intensely loyal other half and she couldn't repress a smile when she saw him there, practically overflowing on to the table with a mouthful of bun and his eyes firmly fixed on the newspaper in front of him. Hayden, she had long ago had to accept, was Hayden and he would always be a mess. He just couldn't help it and even Armageddon wouldn't change him. Furthermore, the successful application he had made to transfer from CID to the uniform role of LIO with the retirement of the previous post-holder was perhaps the most sensible thing he could have done. He may not have been the most dynamic, go-getting detective, but, with his intellectual qualities, he was most certainly of more use to Highbridge nick as a backroom boy than wearing out shoe leather on the street — provided, of course, he spent more time in his office than in the canteen.

Grabbing a coffee and a sandwich from the service counter, she strolled over to join him, and was mildly impressed to see he had actually taken the trouble to tuck a serviette into the collar of his crumpled uniform shirt to protect it from the collateral damage his shirts usually suffered on such occasions. His attempt to promote a better image of himself had not been entirely successful, though. His thatch of thick blond hair had obviously still not seen a comb recently and, even from where she was sitting, Kate could see that his ample stomach had forced open a lower button of his shirt, so that an off-putting patch of hairy skin had thrust itself into view. Furthermore, despite his precautions with the serviette, he had still managed to collect coffee stains in two places on his shirt cuff.

Made aware of her presence when she pulled out a chair and sat down opposite him, he looked up and grinned. 'Heard you leaving the house when I was in the shower,' he said through a mouthful of bun. 'How did the interview with old misery guts go then?'

'You could say I received hearty congratulations and a warm, friendly welcome back,' she replied, 'but that would be a gross overstatement.'

He chuckled. 'So, it was a *Kojak* moment of "Who loves ya baby", was it?' he said in a poor imitation of the catch-phrase of Telly Savalas.

'Something like that,' she agreed. 'Busy this morning, are you?'

He nodded slowly. 'Er, you know, this and that, but holding my own.'

'I bet,' she retorted. 'Holding a currant bun anyway. Maybe I'll be able to get you some work now I'm back.'

He looked mortified. 'Hey, steady on, old girl. Don't overdo things. The job is taxing enough as it is.'

'Taxing?' She snorted. 'You wouldn't know taxing if it jumped up and bit you. You are without a doubt the laziest sod I've ever known.'

He affected a hurt expression. 'That's not fair. I'm . . . I'm just a free spirit, that's all. I do what is necessary when it's necessary.'

'Exactly. Which is almost never.' She glanced at her watch, then unwrapped her sandwich. 'Anyway, a quick bite with my lovely husband and then I have to meet my new crew upstairs.' She nodded towards his plate. 'Oh, by the way, you've got butter all down your sleeve now . . .'

The CID general office on the first floor was empty. Everyone appeared to be out, but, as it was now ten thirty, that was hardly surprising. The mickey-taking wags had been busy before they had left, though. Big cardboard arrows had been affixed to one wall, pointing down the room to a separate glass-walled office at the end, carrying the words, *This Way to DI's Domain*, and there was another very large cardboard sign hanging on two cords from a strip light over a desk on the left-hand side, which read, *Out of bounds for DI!* She stared at it and gave a whimsical smile. It was the detective sergeant's desk she had sat behind in her previous life, the "in" tray still choked with buff-coloured files, as it had been in her day. She'd heard that it now belonged to her former colleague, Jamie Foster, who had gained his stripes shortly after she had left for Bristol. The job couldn't have gone to a better person.

Her gaze wandered across to the desk opposite. It was bare, the computer on top switched off and unplugged. She felt a cold hand clutch at her heart and was conscious of the tears brimming in her eyes. That desk had special significance for her. It was, and always would be to her mind, Detective Constable Indrani Purewal's desk. Poor Indi, who had died at the hands of a ruthless killer in one of Kate's last cases. She quickly dried her eyes on her sleeve. Maybe it had been a mistake to apply to come back here, she thought. Maybe she was still carrying too much baggage from the past? But it had seemed like the right thing to do. After all, the cottage in the village of Burtle, where she had lived for so many years with husband Hayden, was just down the road and the trek to Bristol every day, particularly on call-outs at night, had been a real pain. Not to mention the fact that, as a DI, she needed to be near her workplace, so she was available at a moment's notice. Anyway, whether her move was a good one or a mistake, it was too late to do anything about it now. She was here and that was that.

The door to the DI's own tiny office was shut and another notice had been stuck on the glass door, saying, *God's World!* The buggers had certainly been busy, she mused, and she wondered what DCI Ricketts would have said if he had seen it all. She could imagine him walking in and tearing everything down in a fit of fury.

The desk inside what she'd always referred to as the "inner sanctum", with its familiar battered swivel chair, was unchanged — the force was never too keen on spending money if it didn't have to — and there were yet more notes in evidence, saying, *DI's desk,* and *DI's chair.*

Propped against the desk's nest of three plastic file trays was an A5 manila envelope addressed to her and marked, *Strictly Confidential.* Tearing it open, she found a small pewter hipflask inside, with a yellow Post-it attached, bearing the words, *Stress Beater,* plus a congratulations card with a picture on the front of a cartoon policeman with his trousers round his ankles. The message inside was short and sweet.

> *Hi Kate,*
>
> *Sorry I couldn't be here to hand over to you. Full brief in top tray. Currently en route to the Smoke and my new post with NCA. But congratulations on your promotion! It's well deserved. The manor is all yours now. Just keep taking the tablets!*
>
> *Very Best Wishes,*
> *Charlie Woo*
> *PS. Give Toby Ricketts a big wet kiss from me, will you?*

'Good old Charlie,' she murmured aloud. She would miss the man she had worked under for so long. But as the DI now, she was the one in the hot seat and, as she had quickly learned during her time in Bristol, from now on the buck stopped with her.

A soft voice cut through her reverie. 'Congratulations, Kate. Good to have you back.'

A dapper, tousle-haired figure was standing by the open door, smiling at her. Jamie Foster, now her DS. Behind him, the civilian office manager, Ajeet Singh, beamed and waved at her from his desk. Kate hadn't been aware of either of them entering the general office. She had been so absorbed with Woo's note. Two familiar faces from the old days and neither seemed to have changed a bit.

She left her office and shook hands with them both. 'Great to be here again,' she replied. Then she said pointedly to Foster, 'Congratulations to you on your promotion too. You've certainly earned it.'

'Thanks, but sometimes I wonder what I've taken on.'

Kate looked surprised. 'You mean they still haven't filled the vacancy for a second DS?'

He shook his head. 'No, we have to rely on Bridgwater when I'm not available, just like you did when you were here as DS. Charlie Woo did his best to get it sorted, but he said it was like banging his head against a brick wall.'

'Surely the DCI is fighting your corner on this?'

He laughed. 'You're joking, aren't you? The last thing he wants to do is to cause ripples in the system and queer his own pitch with Headquarters, so he just goes along with whatever they say.'

Kate sighed. 'Doesn't surprise me — but what about the team? I expect there are some new faces here now.'

He nodded. 'Not enough, though, I'm afraid. Fred Alloway has finally retired, and we lost poor Indrani, of course. Ben Holloway is through his probation and is now a fully-fledged DC, and we still have Danny Ferris. Part of the furniture, I reckon. We've got two new additions — Lucy Templeton, who's transferred to us from the Met, and Jimmy Barker, another import, from South Wales. You'll be able to get to know the new 'uns once you're settled in.'

Kate smiled. 'Look forward to it. So, where is everyone now then? Place was like a morgue when I walked in.'

He grimaced. 'Bit up against it at the moment. Ben Holloway and Lucy Templeton are out at a farm the other side of Mark Moor, investigating the theft of a couple of quad bikes from a barn, and Jimmy Barker has drawn the short straw by being lumbered with an alleged ABH on one of our well-known "tea-leaves", who was caught screwing a woman's car by an angry boyfriend at a picnic spot near Westhay. As for me, I've been attending a house fire near Wedmore with Danny Ferris. Place gutted, though no one was hurt. We think it might be an insurance job, but not a lot we can do until the fire service investigators have done their bit. I left Danny with it and came back to see you. He knows what he has to do.'

At this point, the buzz of his mobile abruptly interrupted their conversation and he turned away for a few moments to answer the call, grabbing a pen and paper from a vacant desk behind him and scribbling something down before ringing off.

'No peace for the wicked,' he said. 'Fourteen-year-old girl reported missing from home. I'd better get over there.'

She dumped her briefcase on top of her desk. 'Want some company?'

'Who am I to refuse?'

CHAPTER 2

The house was detached and situated in a quiet residential street in the centre of the village. There was a sleek BMW parked in the driveway and a medium-sized caravan beside it brushing the laurel hedge that separated the house from a similar property next door. There was a marked police patrol car parked outside, and Foster parked the CID car behind it. As Kate climbed out of the car, she saw two uniformed police officers, a sergeant and a constable, neither of whom she knew, emerge through the front door of the house, followed by a man wearing a dark suit. The man seemed aggressive and was waving his arms angrily at the two officers.

Walking briskly up the short gravel drive, she met the officers halfway as the man on the doorstep shouted after them, 'Bloody disgraceful. I won't have it!'

'Detective Inspector Lewis and DS Foster,' she said, flashing her warrant card. 'Problem?'

'Ted Morris, and Bob Stevens, ma'am,' the sergeant replied, and nodded briefly towards the constable. 'We've got a fourteen-year-old girl, Tammy Robinson, AWOL since Friday. Father's a bit irate at the moment. Doesn't like the idea of his place being searched.'

Kate shrugged. 'Has to be done, skipper, I'm afraid. Standard procedure.'

Morris sighed. 'Agreed, but, with respect, I think you'd better tell him that yourself. Won't listen to me.'

Kate nodded. 'I'll give it a whirl. Can you both wait in your car for a few minutes?'

A faint smirk. 'Delighted. Best of luck.'

Robinson was a tall, athletic-looking man, with balding fair hair and a military-style moustache, and he bristled at Kate as she approached.

'And who are you?' he snapped, his hazel eyes glaring at her through gold-rimmed spectacles.

Kate introduced herself and Foster, and showed him her warrant card, which he studied closely.

'Detective inspector, eh?' he said. 'Maybe now we'll get things done at last.'

'Can we come in, sir?' Kate asked. 'We won't keep you long.'

He hesitated, and a woman's voice from inside called out in desperation, 'For goodness' sake, Tony, stop your nonsense.'

He scowled and reluctantly stepped aside to allow the two detectives through. A thin, middle-aged woman with short, blonde hair and very red lipstick was waiting at the end of the hall, smoking a cigarette between trembles. She showed them into a comfortably furnished sitting room and waved a hand towards a couple of fully upholstered armchairs next to each other. The man Kate assumed to be her husband hovered uncertainly in the doorway while she dropped on to a settee opposite them, taking a sip from a glass of something on a little card table. Kate guessed it was brandy.

'Sorry for the intrusion, Mrs, er . . .' Kate began.

'Robinson,' the woman said. 'Helen Robinson.'

'It's your daughter who's missing then, is it, Mrs Robinson?' Kate began quietly.

'Well, it's hardly the pet cat!' her husband exclaimed. 'And it's about time you lot did something about it.'

'Pack it in, Tony,' his wife wailed, her eyes welling with tears. 'You know how upset I am.'

'What's your daughter's name, Mrs Robinson?' Kate asked.

The distraught woman wiped her eyes with her handkerchief. 'Tammy,' she said, 'Tammy Robinson.'

'And when did she go missing—?'

'We've already answered all these damned questions,' Tony Robinson cut in again. 'Why aren't you out there looking for her?'

Kate didn't answer and, resisting the temptation to shut the door on him, waited for Helen Robinson to reply.

'Friday night,' his wife said. 'She-she came home from school while I was getting dinner ready, and-and told me she didn't want anything, but was going to take a shower, then go along to a friend's house to revise.'

'What time was this?'

'About four in the afternoon. Then she went up to her room and-and that was the last time I saw her.'

'You didn't see her leave?'

'No, when I called out to her a bit later, she didn't answer, so I went upstairs to her room to-to find she was gone.'

'What time was this?' Foster put in.

'I don't know. Maybe just after six thirty.'

'And this friend,' he went on, 'do you know her name?'

'Yes, it's Gabrielle, Gabrielle Wiseman. She lives a few doors down the street.'

'Have you spoken to Gabrielle to see if she is still there?'

'What a daft question,' Tony Robinson snorted. 'Of course she's not there. Think we're stupid?'

Neither Kate nor Foster chose to express an opinion on that one.

'So, you *have* been in touch with Gabrielle?' Foster continued.

Helen Robinson stubbed out her cigarette in an ashtray and nodded. 'Joan Wiseman, her mum, said she never went there.'

'Are there any other friends she could have gone to?'

'Only Mandy Williams. She lives on the other side of the village. Tammy's been over there once or twice. But I've rung her mum, Jenny, too and she hasn't seen her either.'

'Does Tammy have a boyfriend?' Kate asked.

'She'd better not,' the voice snapped from the doorway again. 'She's far too young for that sort of nonsense.'

'I don't know,' Helen Robinson said, taking another gulp from her glass, then going into a brief fit of coughing and wheezing the rest of her reply. 'She never talks about things like that. She's a very secretive girl.'

Hardly surprising with the father she's got, Kate mused. Then she asked, 'Can you think of anywhere else she could be — with a relative perhaps or at a place that is particularly special to her?'

'Not that I can think of. Both her grandparents are gone now and I can't think of anywhere else she would have gone to.'

'Has she done anything like this before? You know, stayed away overnight with someone without telling you in advance?'

'What are you implying?' Tony Robinson blazed. 'That she sleeps around or something at just fourteen? Damned impertinence!'

Kate turned slightly in her chair to give him a cold stare. 'I'm not implying anything, Mr Robinson. I'm just trying to get to the bottom of Tammy's disappearance, which means I have to cover every possibility. Your constant interjections are not helpful.'

'The inspector is right,' his wife agreed sharply. 'Why don't you go and make a cup of tea or something. You're getting on my nerves.'

Kate waited for him to shuffle away, muttering to himself, then turned back to his wife, with a heavy frown.

'You see, the thing that I find rather concerning, Mrs Robinson,' she explained, extrapolating on her previous unanswered question, 'is that, according to what you're saying, Tammy failed to return home on Friday night, yet you are only reporting her missing today, Monday. Why didn't you report this before?'

Helen Robinson went into another choking fit, then quickly emptied her brandy glass. 'Tony,' she blurted, glancing nervously at the door. 'My husband, he said she'd turn up again just like she'd done before and-and he was worried what the neighbours might think if-if they heard . . . It's a very close community here, you see, and he is a very well-respected figure at the local church . . .'

Her voice trailed off and she lit another cigarette and hid behind the smoke for a few seconds, no doubt out of embarrassment.

Kate raised her eyebrows in astonishment at her appalling admission but carefully avoided voicing any outright condemnation of such negligent conduct, as that was not only an issue best dealt with by social services at a later stage but could have been counter-productive to their enquiries if the frightened woman then clammed up altogether.

'You say she's done this before?' Kate said instead.

Robinson nodded. 'Twice. She just stayed away overnight . . .' There was a moment's hesitation. 'The thing is, she doesn't get on very well with her dad. She's always been outspoken and rebellious, and he is very old-fashioned and dictatorial. Ex army major, you see. Acts like he is still serving—'

'Where did she go on those two previous occasions?' Foster said.

She gave a brief, wan smile. 'She took her sleeping bag with her the first time, and she later told me that she'd spent the night in our shed at the bottom of the garden. I-I never told Tony where she'd been, and he still doesn't know.'

'What about the second time?'

'In the bus shelter on the village green apparently. Look, they were just acts of defiance really when she was a bit younger, but this time . . .'

'How much younger?'

'Twelve, then thirteen, if I remember rightly.'

'So, this time is different?'

She nodded again and the tears were back, streaming down her face. 'I'm worried to death that . . . that something bad might have happened to her.'

'You say you're worried, yet, as we've already established, you didn't even report her missing for three nights,' Foster pointed out brutally.

Kate threw him a warning glance, but it was too late.

'I told you, it was Tony,' the woman sobbed. 'It's always been Tony.' There was a sudden look of venom on the pale face that stared at them through the tears. 'He's never liked her, never wanted her. We . . . we had her late in life; a bit of an accident, you see. Now we're both retired and in our sixties, and he . . . he resents her. Always on at her, day in, day out. She-she hates him and now she's gone . . .'

'So, you think she *has* run away again then?' Kate asked, trying to quieten her down.

She shrugged. 'How do I know? She told me lies about where she was going on Friday, so what am I supposed to think? But even if she did run away, she could still have come to harm out there on her own in the dark. You hear about these things all the time, don't you?'

Kate didn't confirm or deny the fact, but tried to steer her away from speculations about what may have happened to her daughter.

'One of the uniformed officers will take down a description of Tammy shortly, Mrs Robinson,' she said. 'Do you know what she might have been wearing when she left home?'

'I'm sorry, I've no idea. She has lots of clothes she's bought herself with an allowance I give her every month. I think it's important she has a bit of independence. Naturally, Tony doesn't know about that any more than he knows about lots of things. Spends most of his time down at the pub or at the bar of the local sports club.'

'Well, we shall need a recent photograph of her anyway.'

'You can have that one on the sideboard, if I can have it back when you've finished with it. The school photographer took it last year.'

She climbed unsteadily to her feet to pick up the silver-framed photograph, then handed it to Kate.

It was a head and shoulders shot of what looked like a woman of eighteen or nineteen. Kate scanned it quickly. The fourteen-year-old had long, brown, shoulder-length hair framing pale, porcelain-like features and was undeniably very pretty. But the large brown eyes and the tight, unsmiling set of the thin lips portrayed an expression of stubborn defiance, which Kate read as "trouble", and she suspected that, attractive as the girl was, she could be a real handful to deal with. She didn't pass on her concerns to her mother, though.

'Excellent,' she said instead. 'Now, I know your husband was not happy with the request by the uniformed officers to look round the house and garden, but it is standard procedure in missing person cases like this, so it has to be done before we can do anything else.'

The woman snorted. 'Don't worry about him, he's never happy,' she replied bitterly. 'Just do what you have to do. I want Tammy back. Safe.'

There was no sign of Tony Robinson when Kate beckoned their uniformed colleagues back into the house, and Kate saw through an upstairs window that the car was no longer in the drive. He'd obviously had enough of it all and, like the good, caring parent he wasn't, had driven off somewhere, maybe to the pub or the sports club to drown his sorrows.

That suited her fine. Giving Sergeant Morris and PC Stevens the job of searching the downstairs area, including the large back garden, with its jumble of sheds and a single garage at the bottom, she and Foster concentrated on upstairs. Kate didn't expect to find anything significant in the two large bedrooms, or what was obviously a study, complete with desk, computer and printer, just along from the bathroom and toilet. That didn't surprise her; she hadn't expected to. But she did nurse hopes of learning something about the missing girl from her own bedroom. As a woman herself, she knew that teenage girls often kept secret material in their bedrooms, safe from the scrutiny of their parents. Diaries and mobile phones, for example.

Initially, though, it seemed that she was going to be out of luck this time. The bedroom, with its posters, mirror stickers and weird keepsakes, was surprisingly neat and well-ordered for a fourteen-year-old. The whitewood wardrobe contained nothing but a selection of tight trousers that looked as though a shoehorn would have been required to fit into them, as well as some very short skirts, jumpers, skimpy tops and piles of shoes. The five-drawer dressing table held only tights, underwear, an assortment of teenage magazines, plus some cheap jewellery, perfume and personal toiletries. In short, there appeared to be nothing of any relevance to their inquiries.

Then, as Foster was on his hands and knees checking under the single bed, Kate said, 'Have you noticed something?'

He straightened up and brushed his trousers down with his hands. 'Well, for a start, there's no sign of a laptop, which you'd expect every kid to have nowadays, nor a mobile phone either, although she probably took the phone with her, and I can't see a charger anywhere?'

'True, but I'm talking about something else.'

'What?'

'A diary.'

He made a face. 'So what? They're hardly the in-thing for fourteen-year-olds in this modern digital age?'

'Maybe not, but in my experience a lot of girls still keep diaries. I know I did when I was fourteen.'

'Yeah, but, with respect, that was a very long time ago.' He grinned. 'And I expect Walkmans were a fashion accessory then too.'

Kate scowled at him. 'You cheeky sod, I'm not that old, and you've just earned yourself your first black mark.'

He didn't stay in her bad books, though. Just fifteen minutes later he completely exonerated himself. She had returned to checking inside the wardrobe and was just closing the double doors when he let out a loud 'Whoop!'. Swinging round, she saw that he'd pulled the dressing table out from the wall and was holding an A5 notebook with a fancy psychedelic cover up in one hand.

'Behind the mirror,' he said. 'Inside an A4 envelope taped to the back. Seems you were right. Some girls do still keep diaries.'

Kate smiled her satisfaction and took the book from him, propping herself on the edge of the bed and flipping open the cover. 'So, let's see what secrets Tammy had been harbouring,' she said. 'It might save us a lot of time.'

There was silence in the bedroom as Kate flicked through the pages of the diary, speed-reading the entries at first, while Foster went through the drawers of the dressing table again to ensure he hadn't missed anything. Tammy seemed to have started keeping a diary at the beginning of the year and her first page on 3 January stated it was her New Year's resolution. Much of the content, which was full of dramatic exclamation marks, related to family and school. The frequent rows she'd had with her father, whom she called the *Obersturmführer* after the German Nazi rank (but with the wrong spelling), and spats with teachers and pupils, including those she liked and disliked. There were particular references to her studies and her hatred of discipline and homework, and it was plain that she was very much the rebel her mother had claimed. There were some comments about boys she fancied, but overall she was dismissive of them as "immature and stupid" and there was no mention of any actual boyfriends, only her two girlfriends, Gabrielle and Mandy.

It was not until Kate got to the spring that a more interesting entry jumped out at her.

Saturday 10th May
Hi Diary. Done it at last! Joined this new chatroom site.
Cool move, or not? Sent them pic and profile. Maybe some
fab guy will see it and get in touch. I wish . . .

The site was not named, but she referred to it again a week later.

Saturday 17th May
Hi Diary. Loads of wannabes from chatroom I joined —
most of them stupid bitches or deadbeat tossers, but it's a
start.

Two further entries a couple of days after this were more exuberant.

Monday 19th May
Hi Diary. Can't believe it. There's this real cool guy, Gerry,
who raved about my pic and profile and sent me his. Looks
a real hunk and, wait for it, he wants to keep chatting. I
say, bring it on, dude! WOW! Who's the lucky cow then???

Friday 23rd May
Hi Diary. Gerry says not to tell anyone about us, especially
not parents, as they will put a stop to it. Dead right there!
Obersturmführer would have a fit! Gerry asked if he can
PM me from now on, so we can keep things between the
two of us. How cool is that? Our own private space. Sorry,
diary. No more sharing. Everything PM now. Ha! Ha!

There were no further references to Gerry over the next week and a half, just the usual school and family gossipy things. Then, early on the following month, Gerry's name came up again.

Wednesday 4th June
Hi Diary. Get this! Gerry wants to meet up. I can't wait.
He'll let me know when and where! I'm so excited!

Thursday 5th June
Hi Diary. WOW!!! Seeing Gerry tomorrow night — at
last. This the best day of my life!

Finally, there was an entry on Friday 6th June.

Hi Diary. Big date with Gerry tonight. Wouldn't you like to know where? Wish me luck!

'Found anything of interest?' Foster asked at Kate's elbow, having finished his recheck of the drawers.

She gave a grim smile. 'You could say that, but not something I wanted to find. It seems Tammy has been in contact with some guy, calling himself Gerry, in an internet chatroom and she was meeting him somewhere last Friday night.'

'Oh shit!'

'Exactly. Trouble is, she doesn't say what chatroom, except that it was on private messaging, which means we've got virtually no way of following this up — unless our technical team can work miracles I don't know about — and she doesn't say where she was meeting him.'

He grimaced. 'Maybe Gerry is a genuine guy and has nothing to do with her disappearance?'

'Yeah, but we can't take that chance, can we? Time, I think, to have more words with Mrs Robinson.'

CHAPTER 3

Helen Robinson was still sitting on the settee, and Kate observed that the brandy glass was half-full again and there were several cigarette butts in the ashtray. Husband Tony was once more nowhere to be seen.

'Have you found anything?' she asked, looking up hopefully, when they walked in.

Both detectives sat down again.

'What did you expect us to find, Mrs Robinson?' Kate asked.

A weary shrug. 'I don't know. I just wondered.'

'But maybe you can help us with a couple of matters.'

'I'll try.'

'We noticed that your daughter has none of the usual things most youngsters seem to have in their bedrooms these days, a laptop computer and a printer, for example.'

Robinson nodded. 'Tony wouldn't allow her to have a computer. He said she would only sit up there on her own, looking at dodgy material.'

'What about her schoolwork? Most schools use computers as part of the teaching process nowadays,' Foster said.

'She uses Tony's computer in the study when she needs one. He says that way she's under proper supervision.'

'And what about a mobile phone?' Kate asked.

She started and glanced quickly at the door, lowering her voice. 'Tony wouldn't let her have one of those for the same reason either. Said she was too young. But I gave her some money to buy one and she hides it when she's at home, so Tony doesn't see it.'

'We didn't see a charger in her bedroom.'

'No, she has one of those pocket battery charger things that she always takes with her in case she runs out of power.'

'Do you know her mobile number?'

Robinson shook her head. 'No idea, I'm afraid. I would never ring her in case Tony found out. He'd go mad.'

'What about the make of the phone?'

She shook her head again. 'I let her do it all. I just gave her the money for it. She knows what she's doing with those things, but I don't. I haven't got a mobile phone of my own. Don't want one.'

'But how does she pay for her subscription? Do you not foot the bill? After all, as a schoolgirl, she isn't earning a wage herself.'

'Tony and I have separate bank accounts. He pays for all the major bills, like the mortgage and so forth, and I pay for housekeeping, food and the rest. As I told you earlier, I give her an allowance, which Tony knows nothing about, and she has an occasional Saturday job at a local shop too. When I let her have the upfront money to buy the phone, I told her she would have to fund its use herself from the allowance. She has her own bank account and debit card, and handles everything herself — online I think it's called.'

'But surely she would need adult approval to open a bank account or subscribe to an internet site?' Foster said. 'She *is* only fourteen.'

She shrugged. 'I just signed the papers she put in front of me and she went and did the rest. She's a bright girl and I trust her.'

And look where *that's* got you, Kate thought grimly, but kept the thought to herself.

'So, you don't even know which social media platform she uses? Snapchat, Instagram, X . . . ?'

'Sorry, I can't help you.'

'What about her bank? Do you know who she is with?'

'Barclays, if I remember correctly. It was quite a while ago when I signed her up.'

'Do you know her account number or have any copies of her bank statements?'

'I never see them. She has everything sent to her online so Tony doesn't see it. Why do you ask about that?'

'They might tell us who she pays her internet subscription to,' Foster explained.

Kate released her breath in a loud hiss, her frustration finally boiling over. 'For goodness' sake, Mrs Robinson, this is beyond incredible. You're her mother, yet you seem to know hardly anything about her and what she is doing. How to contact her when she's out, who she's mixing with, who she might be talking to on her phone — you do realise the danger you could have put her in, don't you?'

The woman almost dropped her glass as she went for another drink, once more coughing on the harsh spirit.

'You don't understand what it's like in this house,' she almost whispered. 'Tony is so strict and intolerant, and he drinks heavily. I'm half-scared to say anything to him in case he loses his temper, and Tam and him are always at loggerheads. So, I say nothing and try to keep the peace by placating Tam behind his back. I-I'm a bundle of nerves.'

'The perils of being married to a gaslighter,' Foster murmured drily, half to himself.

'A gas what? I'm sorry, I don't know what that is.'

'A controlling person,' Kate said quickly. 'But never mind that. Do you know anyone called Gerry?'

A look of bewilderment. 'Gerry? No. Where did you get that name from?'

Kate produced the diary from under her coat. 'Your daughter had this hidden behind her dressing table,' she explained. 'It's a diary, and in it she talks about someone she met in an internet chatroom, called Gerry.'

'Good heavens, I've no idea what an internet chatroom is and I've-I've never heard of anyone called Gerry.'

Kate's face was grim. 'Well, she was apparently meeting him Friday night,' she said. 'But we don't know who he is or where the meeting was taking place — and that is a very big problem.'

* * *

'What do you reckon then?' Foster queried when he and Kate returned to their car. 'Do you think she's as dumb as she appears?'

'More likely pissed out of her mind,' Kate replied. 'She was knocking back enough liquor while we were there and it looks like she's at it most of the time.' She shook her head. 'I've come across some dysfunctional families in my time, but this one really takes the biscuit. Helen Robinson is plainly an alcoholic and way off the grid where the real world is concerned. She has absolutely no idea what her daughter is up to, and it's obvious that our Tammy has been playing her for quite a while now to get her own way. As for the old man, from what I've seen of him and what his wife has said about him, he's plainly a relic of the 1950s — a classic gaslighter, as you tactlessly pointed out — who still believes children should be seen and not heard and wives are chattels, created solely to serve and obey.'

'What's wrong with that?'

She gave him a hard stare. 'Careful, Detective Sergeant,' she said, manufacturing a stern expression. 'You are treading on very dangerous ground.'

He chuckled, but didn't push his luck any further, commenting instead, 'The thing is, from the info we've gathered so far it seems pretty clear that our misper went to meet this guy, Gerry, on Friday evening. The key question is, was Gerry legit or some pervert posing as a kid of the same age, and did she go off with him voluntarily or because he gave her no choice?'

'There's something else to consider too. Did she get to the rendezvous in the first place, or did she fall foul of someone else en route?'

He shrugged. 'Good point, and we also have to bear in mind that she's done this sort of thing twice before. So, is she actually missing at all, or maybe off on her toes again?'

Kate nodded. 'Yes, but, according to Helen Robinson, on the previous occasions she was only away overnight. This time she's already been AWOL for three whole nights. We can't afford to take a chance on this being just another strop on her part, especially after what was in that diary of hers. This has got to be a full-blown vulnerable misper inquiry.'

'Then we'd better get some more troops on the job. Local door-to-door inquiries, area search, that sort of thing. Sergeant Morris and his oppo, PC Stevens, seem to have finished their search of the outside area and are back in their car. They could make a start on the close neighbours.'

'Agreed, which will free us up to pay a visit to the school to see if we can turn up anything there. After that, we need to have a word with Tammy's two friends, Gabrielle Wiseman and Mandy Williams, to hear what they have to say. I can't believe Tammy wouldn't have said something to them about Gerry. Girls of Mandy's age would usually be boasting about hooking a good-looking boyfriend. With a little coaxing, one of them might be willing to tell us where she is. Then we can return her to her parents safe and sound and bring things to a swift end, without the need to send the balloon up prematurely.'

Foster looked unconvinced. 'Let's hope you're right and instead we don't find her lying in a ditch with her throat cut,' he said, voicing Kate's own unspoken thoughts.

* * *

It was shortly after school lunch break when Kate and Foster arrived at the Windmill Academy that afternoon, and the prickly head teacher was not exactly welcoming when they were shown into her study by her secretary. A rotund lady in her late fifties or early sixties, Jane Turnbull's cherub-like smile vanished when Kate told her the reason for their visit.

'Tammy Robinson?' she snapped. 'Well, I must admit I'm not surprised. That young lady has always been trouble, and I knew something like this would happen one day.'

'What do you mean by "trouble"?' Kate asked.

The head tutted. 'Tammy is one of those children who are always at the centre of any disruption or misbehaviour but can never be tied into any wrongdoing,' she said. 'One can never prove anything against her. She's far too cunning for that. She's always the innocent bystander—'

'A bright girl then?' Foster suggested.

'Oh, highly intelligent, yes, but also irritatingly precocious. Too advanced for her years, you know, with a rebellious, anti-authority attitude. Someone who sees all rules and anyone who has the task of imposing them as a challenge to be overcome. She's had to be reprimanded on numerous occasions, particularly about the provocative way she dresses. She wears far too much make-up even when the rules expressly forbid it, her skirts are much too short and she has a habit at every opportunity of flaunting herself in front of workmen and deliverymen visiting the school, like some, er, well, you know what I mean.'

'Did you speak to her parents about her conduct?' Foster put in.

Turnbull frowned and shook her head. 'I didn't have to. My deputy, Jeremy Greatorex, is also the school's safeguarding team lead, and I know he's been to see the parents on several occasions. He has, of course, kept me informed of all developments, and I gather Tammy's mother, in particular, has been made aware of every reprimand and breach of the rules that has occurred.

'And her father?'

Another frown. 'I understand that Mr Robinson is not very easy to deal with and at times can be quite offensive.' Kate smiled faintly at her understatement, but said nothing.

'Mr Greatorex has told me that, as a result, he has tended to deal more with Mrs Robinson, who seems to be more amenable and willing to address the problems in a sensible manner.'

'And has she?' Foster went on. 'Dealt with them, I mean?'

A humourless smile. 'I have no idea, but I suspect not, because the same things have continued to occur. It is, er, my belief that there is some sort of disconnect between Tammy's parents, which the child has been able to exploit, but I may be wrong.'

You're not, Kate mused. *You're right on the ball.* But again, she didn't voice her thoughts aloud.

'Would it be possible for us to speak to Mr Greatorex?' Foster continued.

'I'm afraid not at the moment. He's on long-term sick leave. Stress, you understand. His role dealing with recalcitrant children and broken homes is quite an exacting one and I'm afraid he takes things to heart, which has affected his mental health — though I must emphasise that that is in the strictest confidence.'

Kate nodded. 'Which goes without saying, of course. But it is a pity we can't speak to him, since, having dealt with Tammy on a more personal basis, he might be privy to important information that would help us to find her.'

Turnbull noticeably stiffened, her mouth tightening in apparent umbrage at the suggestion that her deputy might know more about the girl than herself. 'I believe I am fully cognizant of all matters concerning the pupils at my school, Inspector,' she snapped.

Kate flashed her a brief smile. 'I am sure you are, Ms Turnbull,' she replied, 'but it would nevertheless have been useful to speak to Mr Greatorex to obtain any personal observations he might have — bearing in mind the serious nature of this case.'

Turnbull's face twitched as the shot went home. 'It's Mrs, not Ms,' she corrected. 'I am a widow, not a spinster. And as regards Mr Greatorex, I'm sure he would be willing to talk to you in these exceptional circumstances. I will ring him and ask if he would be prepared to see you at home.'

'That would certainly be appreciated,' Kate almost purred. 'But in view of the in-depth knowledge you evidently have of all your pupils, are you able to say whether Tammy had a boyfriend at the school?'

Turnbull seemed to miss the sarcasm loaded into the question. 'Not as far as I am aware,' she replied, 'and I would have thought her precocity among her peers would have precluded her from fraternising with any boys of the same age—'

'Meaning older men were more to her liking?' Foster suggested.

Turnbull flushed. 'Really! I didn't mean that at all. She was, after all, only fourteen, and still a child.'

'We are just trying to establish whether she could perhaps have been abducted by someone she had met before, either at the school or outside the school gates,' Kate explained, trying not to rile her anymore.

'Well, put it like this, Inspector,' Turnbull replied tersely, 'I never saw her talking to a stranger, either on the premises or outside, and I always see the children off at the end of the school day. Most are picked up by the coach transport that is provided, but a few living locally walk home. I pay particular attention to those pupils and I would notice if anything like that ever occurred and intervene accordingly.'

'Have you ever heard her or any of her friends refer to someone called Gerry?'

An immediate shake of the head. It was plain that the head teacher was still annoyed about her comments being taken out of context.

'Do you have any male staff with that name?'

The flush was back on Turnbull's face and her eyes glittered. 'What on earth are you implying?' she snapped.

Kate was losing patience. 'I'm implying nothing, Mrs Turnbull,' she snapped back. 'It is just a name that has come up. It's very possible Tammy struck up a friendship with an older man and either went with him voluntarily, or was abducted. She has been missing now for over three days and it is vital that we find her before she comes to harm.'

Turnbull got off her high horse and nodded a little sullenly. 'There is no one at the school with the name Gerry, or Gerald,' she confirmed.

'What about the other pupils?'

'I know them all and there is no Gerry among them.'

'Thank you! Now, would Tammy have a personal locker here?'

'Yes, all the pupils have their own lockers. I'll show you. We keep spare keys in my secretary's safe in case any of them happen to lose their own key. I'll get you Tammy's key now.'

Several youngsters who passed them, no doubt heading from one lesson to another, glanced at them curiously as they followed the head with her key along the main corridor. Turnbull nodded to a tall, thin man, dressed in a pink, open-necked shirt and a blue cardigan a size too large for him, who walked by as she paused by a line of grey metal cabinets next to the school hall.

'Pop and see me, after your next lesson, would you, Emrys?' she said, then quickly turned to Kate to add, 'Tammy's form teacher, Emrys Parry. I will speak to him later about this matter to see if he is aware of anything that could assist you with your inquiries.'

'We would rather speak to him ourselves, if you don't mind,' Kate said, 'and we would also like to have a look around the school grounds — sheds, changing rooms, sports pavilion, that sort of thing — before we leave.'

Turnbull nodded. 'As you wish, as long as it doesn't disrupt the smooth- running of the school.'

The locker she used Tammy's key to open appeared to contain very little. Just the anticipated PE kit, white trainers, some sweets, teenage magazines and a tobacco tin half-full of loose change, all packed on to a single shelf at the top. Underneath, there were just a pair of tracksuit bottoms and a light anorak hanging from a hook. Kate checked the pockets of each but found nothing of interest in them.

'No mobile or charger, then,' Foster commented, reading Kate's mind.

Turnbull overheard him. 'Pupils are discouraged from bringing mobiles to school, as they are a distraction to learning,' she said. 'If they do, the phones have to be deposited with my secretary and placed in a secure lockbox. They are returned to them at the end of the day.'

'Can we see?' Kate asked.

Turnbull clicked her tongue. 'Oh, very well,' she said, 'if you must.'

Relocking the cabinet, she took them back to the secretary's office, where they found the young woman they had first met on their arrival, seated back at her desk in the corner behind a laptop and a tray full of paperwork. She was talking to a muscular, dark-haired man in his thirties, wearing tracksuit bottoms and a vest, who turned inquisitively towards them as they entered the office.

Kate glanced at him briefly. Sharp blue eyes met her stare with uncomfortable directness and a crooked smile formed on his thin lips, as if he were fully aware of the fact that she found his gaze disconcerting.

'My son, Peter,' Turnbull said, almost as a formality and without any obvious sense of pride or emotion, which Kate was beginning to realise was a hallmark of the head teacher's character. 'He's our sports teacher.'

'Hi,' Kate said with a quick smile.

His own smile broadened, but became more sardonic, and he nodded, but said nothing.

'Tammy Robinson is missing,' the head said abruptly. 'She hasn't been seen since she got home from school on Friday. These police officers are here to make inquiries. They are concerned that she may have been abducted by someone.'

'Is that so?' he drawled. 'Well, best of luck to whoever's got her, that's all I can say. He'll probably be desperate to give her back by now.'

The head hissed her disapproval of the flippant remark and Foster immediately took him up on it. 'What makes you think anyone has got her at all?' he asked. 'She could have had an accident and be lying injured somewhere.'

The other shrugged. 'Well, Mother . . . er, the head . . . has already intimated that this is a possibility and, knowing Tammy as we all do, I'm merely saying that she's not the sort of youngster who would be easy to snatch. She's probably off with a boyfriend somewhere.'

'Let's hope you're right,' Kate said. 'Are you aware of anyone she could be with?'

He shook his head. 'I wouldn't have a clue. I know virtually nothing about her, and wouldn't want to know either. It's just that she can be a right handful when she goes off on one . . . Now, I have to be gone. I have a rugby match to referee.'

'And I have work to do,' the head said irritably. 'So, can we get on with what we came in here to do?'

'Of course,' Kate agreed, watching the head's son striding past the window in the direction of the school playing field. 'We've taken up quite enough of your time already.'

As it transpired, however, the phones turned out to be another dead end. Just three mobiles in all, each phone in a plastic bag, bearing the pupil's name, and slotted into one of a number of slots in a polystyrene block inside the lockbox. Tammy Robinson's name was not on any of them.

The school grounds didn't take long to search. They amounted to little more than a tennis court, a large playing field with unlocked changing rooms adjoining it, and a wooden shed nestling among shrubbery in a corner, which from the oil stains on the wooden floor, they assumed housed the groundsman's mower and other equipment, but now contained just tools and petrol cans.

A man in stained green dungarees rode up to the shed on his mower as they were peering through the open door. He was about sixty years of age, with short grey hair, stern blue eyes and a lugubrious expression on his lean face that suggested he wasn't entirely happy with life, but went with the flow anyway.

He nodded, seemingly unsurprised, when Kate introduced them both, and gave a crooked grin when Kate asked him if he was the groundsman.

'I can see why you're a detective,' he sniped sarcastically, leaning back against the seat of his mower and lighting a cigarette. 'Pretty shrewd deduction there.'

She rewarded him with a tight smile, knowing she had asked for that. 'And your name is . . . ?' she went on.

'Tom,' he replied through a puff of smoke, 'Tom Merchant. I'm kind of the caretaker, groundsman and general dogsbody.'

'Worked here long?'

'Long enough. Did twenty-two years in the Royal Navy, then joined British Steel till I was declared redundant. Got this job and been here ever since. Anything else you want to know?'

Kate sensed just a touch of resentment in his tone, as if he wasn't too happy with his lot. 'Do you know why we're here?' she asked.

'You tell me,' he replied, 'then I'll be as wise as you.'

She studied his worn, leathery face for a second. His sarcasm was starting to irritate her. 'One of the female pupils from Year Nine is missing from home,' she said. 'A girl named Tammy Robinson. She's not been seen for almost three days.'

'Not surprised,' he replied. 'The way some of these kids behave, I knew it would only be a question of time before one of them did something stupid.'

'Why do you say that?' Foster put in.

Merchant shook his head slowly. 'Cheeky little minxes, some of them, that's why,' he said. 'Need a damned good clip round the ear, I reckon. Don't know what their parents are playing at. If I'd behaved like them when I was a kid, I'd have got a real good hiding. No discipline, that's the trouble. They think they can do what they like.'

'So, what sort of behaviour are we talking about?' Kate said.

He snorted. 'Skirts up to here,' he replied, demonstrating with the palm of one hand edge-on to his thigh, 'flashing their belly buttons at every Tom, Dick and Harry that passes once they're outside the school gates, using every bit of foul language they've a mind to and even smoking weed behind my shed with some of the young lads when I'm not around—'

'How do you know they're doing that if you're not here?' Foster interjected again.

The older man gave him a contemptuous glance. 'I've got eyes, haven't I? Time and time again when I've been working on the other side of the playing fields, I've seen them scooting round the back of the shed, and I've found the joints they've left behind too.'

'Does the head know about all this?'

'Of course she does, but she just pretends it isn't happening. Doesn't want the governors or OFSTED poking their noses in, does she?'

'Haven't you told her about it?'

'Nothing to do with me, is it? I just keep out of the way and get on with what I'm paid to do.'

Kate pulled out the photograph Helen Robinson had given her of Tammy and held it up in front of him. 'This is the missing girl. Her name's Tammy Robinson. Know her, do you?'

She watched him closely as he stared at it, but he showed no emotion, simply shrugging, and taking another puff on his cigarette.

'May have seen her,' he said. 'But I can't really say. I see so many of them parading about lunchtime and in the breaks.'

Kate nodded and slipped the photograph back into her pocket. 'Ever noticed any suspicious-looking characters loitering outside the school gates?'

A sneering laugh. 'Suspicious characters? What time do you think I have to check on who's hanging about out there? I've got enough to do in the school without worrying about what's happening outside it.'

He dropped the butt of his cigarette on to the concrete path they were standing on and ground it under the toe of his boot. 'Now, if you're done, I've got things to do before I finish here today.'

Kate nodded to Foster. 'Fine, Mr Merchant. Thanks for your cooperation. Where can we reach you if we need to speak to you again?'

'House next door to the school. Comes with the job. That's why I stick it out here.'

Then he was manhandling his mower up the ramp into the shed, giving the detectives no choice but to leave him to it.

'What a nice tolerant soul,' Foster commented sarcastically, as they headed back to the school across the playing field.

Kate nodded, a thoughtful look on her face. 'You can say that again, and he seemed to have quite an axe to grind against the schoolkids.'

'Typical old-school type, if you'll pardon the pun,' Foster said. 'You know, spare the rod and spoil the child.'

'Maybe, but he could also be something else.'

'Oh, come on, Kate, you don't suspect him of having anything to do with Tammy's disappearance, do you? I can't see him pretending to be her boyfriend, then waylaying her to mete out some form of deserving punishment — he probably doesn't even know what a chatroom is.'

'Oh, I'm sure he does, probably more than us. He was in the Royal Navy, wasn't he? He's likely to be technically proficient. Anyway, I think we'll keep him in mind. After all, he's in the ideal place to set up something like this, and he certainly has a thing about the bad behaviour of the young girls. We don't know what they've said or done to him. Taunted him perhaps?'

Foster opened the rear door of the school for her. 'I take your point, but, assuming for the moment that Merchant is nothing more than a crabby old dinosaur, we seem to have wasted half the afternoon talking to him. Let's hope Tammy's form teacher has something more useful to tell us.'

But he hadn't. In fact, Emrys Parry was no help at all as far as Tammy was concerned, and it was plain from the answers he gave that he knew as much about her as he did the rest of his class, which was not a lot.

In his open-necked pink shirt, loose oversized cardigan and rumpled fawn corduroy trousers, Parry was a tall, slightly stooped individual of about thirty, with a weak, almost non-existent chin and a mop of ginger hair, which flopped in untidy curls over his forehead, ears and shirt collar, as if it had a mind of its own. His dark eyes blinked owlishly at the detectives from behind tinted, horn-rimmed spectacles, as he struggled to answer the questions put to him about Tammy in a quiet, hesitant voice, and Kate couldn't help wondering how someone so obviously lacking in confidence managed to survive in a class full of boisterous, unruly fourteen-year-olds.

It was plain that he had been briefed by Turnbull while they had been looking round the school, and he nodded when he was shown Tammy's photograph, but his opening comments immediately told the detectives that they were wasting their time.

'I haven't been here long,' he said. 'I was only recently selected to fill a vacancy for an English teacher, but it's an excellent school and I only live a few miles down the road in the next village, so it's ideal for me. I have to admit, though, I am only just getting to know the pupils in my class.'

'Can you tell us anything about Tammy Robinson?' Kate persisted. 'Her friends, who she hangs around with, what she's like to teach?'

He looked embarrassed. 'I-I know her face, of course,' he said, 'but I can't honestly say she stands out any more than any other pupil.'

'But from all accounts, she's trouble,' Foster put in, 'a regular pain in the backside.'

Parry made a face and at once disclosed his liberal outlook. 'No child is ever a pain in the, er . . .' he replied, looking slightly affronted. Then he smiled. 'But some can be more *challenging* than others. Although I can't say Tammy is any more or less of a problem than the rest of the pupils in her year.'

'The other kids say anything to you about Tammy?'

'Not to me.'

'Did you ever see her talking to a stranger outside the school gates?' Kate asked, not expecting a helpful answer.

He shook his head. 'By stranger, I suppose you mean a man. Not as far as I can recall, no.'

'Have you ever spotted any strangers hanging about outside the gates?'

'I can't say I have, but I suppose I haven't been here long enough to know who is a stranger and who isn't.'

Kate sighed, realising she was getting nowhere. 'Well, thanks for talking to us anyway. As the school day is over, we'd better let you get home. Can I just have your home address in case we need to contact you again out of school hours?'

He shrugged. 'I can't see I would be of any help to you in the future any more than now, but yes, no problem.'

Kate wrote the details in her pocketbook, then handed him her card. 'And give me a call yourself if anything occurs to you later, will you?'

'Of course.'

'What a waste of space he was,' Foster commented as they made their way back towards the car park. 'Talk about wishy-washy. No wonder teaching standards are as low as they are.'

Kate sighed. 'Bit of a wet, I agree. One of the modern, woke-inspired candidates, I would think. A total contrast to the head teacher anyway. She looks to be a right tartar. But maybe, as a newbie, Parry just didn't want to stick his head above the parapet by saying something about Tammy that could be construed as derogatory. You know the way things are going these days. Mustn't refer to anyone as fat, thin, short, ugly, good, bad — and in some quarters even girl or boy.'

'Even if that jeopardises a child's safety?'

'Probably not allowed to call them a child now either.'

He shook his head. 'Total bollocks!'

'Welcome to the "brave" new world, Jamie.'

Jane Turnbull caught Kate and Foster just as they were walking along the school's main corridor to the front doors.

She called after them shrilly, waving a piece of paper in one hand.

'Jeremy Greatorex would be happy to see you, Inspector,' she said, breathing heavily as she reached them. 'He will be in all afternoon.'

'Excellent,' Kate responded, taking the piece of paper from her and glancing at the address written on it. 'That would suit us fine, wouldn't it, Jamie?'

Foster nodded without enthusiasm and, as they walked out into the car park, he made a face. 'Without wishing to sound like Hayden,' he said, 'having forgone lunch, do you think it might just be possible to cram a meal of some sort in somewhere along the line?'

She grinned. 'Sorry, I didn't hear your stomach rumbling. So, pub first and *then* Jeremy Greatorex, followed by Tammy's two school chums — and I'm buying. Happy now?'

'Sounds a good plan to me,' he said. 'Especially the last bit!'

CHAPTER 4

Jeremy Greatorex was wearing an open-necked blue shirt and grey flannels when he answered the front door of the smart Georgian-style house to Foster's tug on the bell-pull. In his late forties to early fifties, and about five foot nine in height, he had pale, gaunt features and blue eyes framed by rimless spectacles. His mop of flaxen hair was swept back in an extravagant wave, and he displayed even white teeth in what seemed like a tired, haunted smile.

Inviting the detectives into an immaculate hallway with a wave of one hand, he gesticulated down the hall.

'Second door on the left,' he said. 'But could I ask you to keep your voices down, as my elderly mother is in bed with a nasty cold and fast asleep, I hope.'

Stepping into a neat, ordered sitting room, they glanced about them curiously. The room was furnished to a high standard, with a thick, patterned, wall-to-wall carpet and a double and triple settee placed at opposite corners. A large coffee table occupied the centre of the room and there was an ornate glass cocktail cabinet set against one wall and a bookcase, with shelves boasting three neat lines of extravagant-looking bound volumes against another.

Obviously someone not short of a bob or two, Kate mused, as she hung on to the smile she had automatically produced.

'Jeremy Greatorex,' the man said, extending a hand towards Kate in greeting.

'Detective Inspector Kate Lewis and Detective Sergeant Jamie Foster,' she replied, waiting while he shook Foster's hand too.

'Do sit down,' he said, 'but I might have to leave you for a few moments if Mother wakes up. She panics sometimes if she finds herself on her own.'

'No problem, sir,' Kate acknowledged. 'Your wife not here then?'

'Wife?' he echoed, then released a hard, ironic laugh. 'Not got one of those, I'm afraid. Never married. Too interested in a career in education, I suppose. Didn't seem to have the time to consider anything else. Now I'm what you might call a home carer for the old lady upstairs, a task I fit around my school responsibilities.'

'Quite exacting, I would think,' Kate commented.

Another laugh. 'Well, she is a bit of a tyrant, I must admit, but we all have to get old, don't we? Now, what can I do for you, Inspector? Jane Turnbull has already filled me in on Tammy Robinson's disappearance. You haven't found her yet then?'

Kate shook her head. ''Fraid not and, in view of the amount of time she's been missing, we are becoming increasingly concerned for her welfare.'

He frowned. 'I can understand that. But I always feared that something like this might happen one day.'

'Why do you say that?' Foster put in.

Kate mused that he wasn't the first person that day to have said exactly the same thing.

Greatorex sighed. 'Tammy has always been a problem,' he replied. 'I'm sure Jane Turnbull will have told you that, as well as my role as deputy head, I also lead the school's safeguarding team and, sadly, Tammy has been one of my many challenges — her and another pupil called Mandy Williams. Both children seem to have made a conscious effort to be as insolent and disruptive as possible, and this has detrimentally influenced the behaviour of some of the other pupils in their class. They've led Mr Parry, their form teacher, a merry dance, with rowdyism, practical jokes and suggestive sexual innuendos towards him to make him feel embarrassed, and I must say that, as a newly appointed teacher, the manner in which he has handled it all is deserving of a medal—'

'Oh?' Foster cut in. 'But he led us to believe that he didn't regard Tammy as any worse than any other pupil in his class.'

Greatorex laughed. 'That's typical of Emrys Parry,' he said. 'He always thinks the best of his pupils and, unlike some members of staff, he won't hear a word against them.'

You mean he's a soft touch, Kate mused wryly. *Weak and spineless*. But she said nothing.

'The trouble is,' Greatorex went on, looking a little more worried, 'Tammy never seems to appreciate that there is a thin line between naughtiness and some things that are a lot more serious, and there have been a couple of occasions where her misconduct has crossed the line of acceptability and I have had to refer matters to her parents.'

'What sort of things?' Foster demanded.

Greatorex hesitated, looking as if he regretted his comments.

'It would be breaching the rules if I were to be more specific,' he said. 'I have a duty of care in my safeguarding role, which includes maintaining absolute confidentiality in my dealings with both pupils and parents.'

'Mr Greatorex,' Kate said sharply. 'We have a fourteen-year-old girl who has been missing for three days, and could be at serious risk. To put it bluntly, your duty of care should also include full and open disclosure of any information you have that might assist us in our investigation!'

'But-but I don't think the information in question would be of any relevance to—'

Kate cut him off. 'With the greatest of respect, sir, it is up to us to decide what is and what is not relevant.'

He thought for a second, head bowed and staring at the carpet. Then he made up his mind and nodded. 'A few instances do come to mind,' he said. 'One was directed at Mr Parry, who is a committed Christian. Emrys likes to spend his morning coffee break in the staff room, reading a chapter from one of his collection of classic novels. Somehow Tammy got hold of one particular novel he had left on his desk in the classroom and scrawled profane comments over many of the pages with a felt-tip pen. It ruined the book, which was apparently a very expensive first edition. At first, she denied despoiling the book, but two other girls came forward and said they'd seen her do it, so she had to admit to it in the end.'

'How did Mr Parry take it?' Foster asked.

Greatorex shrugged. 'True to Emrys' nature, he forgave Tammy and refused to take any further action against her, simply accepting her grudging apology and insisting on the whole thing being dropped, though, of course, I had to bring the matter to the attention of her parents.'

He paused a moment, before continuing. 'Then there was another incident involving our sports teacher, Peter Turnbull, who is the head's son. Peter happens to be gay. It's not something he hides, but Tammy sprayed homophobic insults around the walls of the sports hall, seemingly in an attempt to cause him maximum embarrassment. But if there is one thing about Tammy, it is that she is not that clever. Peter caught her literally red-handed, and she was excluded for three days as a punishment.'

He sighed. 'Unfortunately even that had little effect in the long run and there were a couple of other incidents involving our school groundsman, Mr Merchant. Tom Merchant has been a particular target of Tammy's ire for some time because of his old-school attitude towards what he regards as the "ill-disciplined behaviour of modern youth".' He smiled slightly. 'His words, not mine. There was an occasion when he caught Tammy and her friend, Mandy, smoking cannabis with a couple of boys behind his shed and ticked them off.

One of the boys got cheeky and he gave him a well-deserved, if rather unwise, clip around the ear that got him an official reprimand, I'm afraid. Not satisfied with that, Tammy retaliated a couple of days later by pouring sugar into the petrol tank of his mower.'

'Ouch!' Foster remarked.

'Exactly! It destroyed the engine and cost the school a new one. Once again, she was seen doing the deed by another pupil, who reported what he'd witnessed shortly afterwards.'

'Funny Tom Merchant didn't happen to mention this when we spoke to him a short time ago,' Kate commented. 'How did he take it?'

A short laugh. 'Not well, I must admit. He went into overdrive a bit, telling the head that Tammy needed to be given a sound thrashing, or thrown into a police cell. But fortunately none of us took him seriously. He's often prone to outbursts like that, so we're used to it. He's a good, honest worker, though, and we'd be sorry to lose him.'

'Were the police informed about the criminal damage?'

Greatorex shook his head. 'Tammy's parents agreed to reimburse the school for the engine and it was decided to leave it at a week's exclusion, as we didn't want Tammy to end up with a criminal record before she'd even reached adulthood—'

'Or for the school to face adverse publicity,' Kate finished for him cynically.

He frowned. 'That honestly wasn't a consideration, Inspector.'

'Nevertheless, it seems Tammy was trouble with a capital T?' Foster said.

Greatorex shrugged. 'She has certainly been problematic,' he admitted, 'but I believe — and please treat this as very much off the record — that poor parenting has been the cause of it all. It is patently obvious that Tammy's father has no time at all for her and thinks that physical punishment and bullying are the answer to everything. As for her mother—he shrugged again — 'I fear she is an alcoholic, who appears to be in a world of her own and to be incapable of exercising any control over her daughter whatsoever.'

'Which suggests,' Kate summarised without disputing anything he had said, 'that far from this being a case of a silly, impressionable girl deciding to run off with her new boyfriend, it could be that there is a more sinister motive at play here with someone recognising her obvious vulnerability and capitalising on it for their own ends?'

He nodded. 'You obviously know more about the circumstances of her disappearance than I do, but yes, I suspect that that could be a real possibility, which is very worrying indeed.'

'When did you last see her?'

'Must be a fortnight ago. When I was signed off on sick leave. Stress, you understand.' He nodded towards the ceiling. 'My circumstances here as well as the heavy workloads at school. It's taken quite a toll on my mental health, I have to admit.'

Kate smiled. 'A problem for all of us in these demanding modern times, sir,' she sympathised, thinking of her own near breakdown a few years before. 'But can you tell us if Tammy had a boyfriend at the school?'

He pursed his lips, then shook his head. 'Not to my knowledge, no. I would have thought she'd be too much of a handful for the boys of her age she mixed with.'

'Ever hear her mention someone called Gerald or Gerry?'

'Can't say I have.'

'During your time at the school, have you ever noticed any strangers loitering about outside the school gates, or talking to any of the pupils?'

'Not at all. I'm usually around in the car park with the head when the kids arrive and when they are leaving in the afternoon. I would have noticed. Do you yourself really think Tammy could have been abducted then?'

'We don't know yet. It's all hypothesis, but we are actively investigating all possibilities. We believe she left home voluntarily, allegedly to meet a boy she had met on an internet chat site, but that's all we know. We have no idea who that boy was, or where she had arranged to meet him.'

'Or if the boy she thought she was meeting was actually someone else who had set her up?' he suggested.

Kate studied him for a second. 'You have it in a nutshell, sir,' she said quietly. 'And the question then would be for what purpose did he set her up in the first place?'

Greatorex's face twitched under her hard stare. 'I dread to think,' he replied.

'You and me both,' she agreed.

* * *

Gabrielle Wiseman lived a relatively short distance from the school and, following a quick bite in the village's quaint but pricey hostelry, the two detectives pulled up outside her house an hour or so after the school day had ended.

Short and plump, with curly ginger hair and large round spectacles that gave her an owlish look, she was every bit the spotty, awkward teenager and not at first sight the sort of girl who Kate imagined would have been befriended by someone like Tammy. She guessed that Gabrielle was actually Tammy's "insurance". Someone her parents would readily approve of. The friend she could use to give her an alibi when she was up to her tricks.

Joan Wiseman was a little taken aback when Kate introduced herself and Foster on the doorstep, but she recovered immediately Kate told her why they wanted to speak with her daughter. But like the enquiries at the school, it was a waste of time. It was apparent from the start that Gabrielle had not seen Tammy on the Friday she disappeared and had no idea where she might have gone. As for the mystery "boyfriend", Gerry, it was obvious from the look on Gabrielle's face that she knew nothing about him. Tammy, it seemed, had not risked imparting any confidences in that quarter.

Mandy Williams was an entirely different proposition to Gabrielle and Kate felt a quickening of interest in her when they got to the house on the other side of the village and were invited in by her bubbly mother.

Mandy was a slim, pretty blonde with sharp, intelligent blue eyes and a flawless, pale complexion, similar to Tammy's. Out of her school uniform and into slacks and a skimpy T-shirt by the time they got to her, as with Tammy she also looked a lot older than her years, especially as she was now wearing red lipstick and blue eyeshadow, a fact that her mother appeared to be quite happy about.

Curled up barefoot on the sofa in the lounge, she regarded her visitors warily when they were shown in and invited to sit down in armchairs opposite her and her mother. Then she slowly pulled herself upright with her back against the cushions when Jenny Williams explained who they were.

'Isn't it dreadful, Mand,' she exclaimed, her eyes wide with excitement. 'Tammy's disappeared.'

The wary look in her daughter's eyes seemed to change to alarm. 'What do you mean, disappeared?' she asked.

Kate studied her for a moment. 'She went out Friday night, saying she was going to see Gabrielle to do some revision,' she explained. 'She hasn't been seen since. Gabrielle says she never went to her house, and we are here to ask you if you have any idea where she might have gone?'

The jerk of Mandy's Adam's apple was an immediate giveaway, which, as experienced interviewers, both detectives recognised as a nervous reaction, usually indicating guilt.

Mandy stared at them wide-eyed. 'Er, no, why should I?'

'Because you are a close friend of hers, Mandy,' Kate replied, 'and close friends usually tell each other everything.'

Mandy tried to affect a casual shrug as she looked down at the floor, avoiding Kate's stare. 'We aren't that close,' she said. 'We just hang about together at school sometimes, that's all. She never said anything to me about going anywhere, and I have no idea where she could have gone.'

Kate nodded, as if accepting her answer. 'Could she have gone to meet Gerry, do you think?' she said, resorting to a shock tactic.

Mandy gaped at her. 'Ger-Gerry?' she echoed. 'I-I don't know any Gerry.'

The swallow in the middle of her reply was pronounced and Kate smiled. 'I think you do?' she said. 'She told you all about him, didn't she?'

Mandy shook her head fiercely several times. 'No, no, she didn't tell me anything about anyone. I don't know what you mean.'

'Now don't you go getting yourself all het up,' Jenny Williams said from her place on the sofa beside her, and she patted her daughter's knee. 'If my Mandy says she doesn't know anything, then that's fine with me,' she said. 'So, you must have got it wrong, Inspector.'

Kate felt the frustration rise inside her. 'Mandy,' she said, ignoring her mother's interjection, and crouching down in front of her, 'this is a very serious matter. Your friend has been missing now for three nights and she might be in real danger. We know from the diary she kept that she has been on an internet chatroom site, talking to someone who calls himself Gerry, and that she was due to meet him somewhere Friday night—'

'I don't know anything about any Gerry,' Mandy cut in angrily.

Kate sensed she was on to something and kept going. 'Listen, Mandy, it is very possible that Gerry is not the young man Tammy thinks he is, but someone much older who may have tricked her. We need you to tell us what you know about Gerry and where Tammy was supposed to meet him so we can make sure she is safe.'

The tears came immediately, and Mandy buried her face in her hands. 'I-I don't know any-anything,' she sobbed. 'Tam said she had a date with some cool guy and . . . and she was meeting him somewhere that night. She . . . she made me promise not to tell anyone.'

'Well, I'm blowed,' her mother breathed. 'These silly girls.'

Kate glanced quickly across at Foster, then said gently, 'You're not in any trouble, Mandy. We just want to find

Tammy. Have you any idea where this meeting place was? Any idea at all? I mean, is there somewhere you and Tammy liked to go to sometimes — somewhere special no one else knew about?'

The girl shook her head again several times. 'I don't know,' she moaned.

Kate changed tack. 'Do you know what this internet chatroom was called?'

A further desperate shake of the head.

'Can you even tell us what social media sites she was on?'

'I don't know *anything else*,' Mandy shouted, her voice abnormally high-pitched and close to hysterical. 'Leave me alone, will you?'

'I think Mandy has had enough!' her mother said sharply. 'She's already told you she knows nothing else.'

Kate's mouth tightened. It was obvious that Mandy was still holding something back, but she couldn't make the girl tell her what it was, and it was evident that any more pressure was likely to be counter-productive and also turn her over-defensive mother against them.

'Okay, Mandy', Kate said, straightening up, 'we'll have to leave it there then. It's just a pity you aren't able to tell us anything that could help us before it's too late.'

Nodding a thank-you to Mrs Williams, Kate turned for the door, with Foster reluctantly following her. Almost immediately both came to a sudden stop, as Mandy screamed after them.

'She *made* me promise not to say!'

Kate wheeled round. 'Promise not to say what?' she asked quietly, though her heart was beating faster now.

'To-to tell on her. She-she said her dad would throw her out if he knew.'

'That's not true, Mandy. Tammy's mum and dad are as worried about her as we are. No one is going to do anything silly like that. They'll just be relieved that she's safe. Now, what have you got to tell me?'

Another big swallow and Mandy wiped the tears out of her eyes with the back of her hand. 'Tam said she was meeting a boy called Gerry at the-the rec on the other side of the village,' she mumbled. She took a deep, trembling breath. 'A gang of us always used to hang out there when we were little. There's-there's swings and a roundabout at one end and a sort of copse next door we used to play in we called Witch Wood. Tammy said Gerry would . . . would be meeting her in there where they couldn't be seen by anyone . . .'

Kate nodded quickly, conscious of the fact that Foster had already left the room, pulling his personal radio out of his pocket as he went. 'Thank you, Mandy. You've done the right thing, really you have. And there's nothing else you can tell us?'

The girl shook her head miserably. 'Only that . . . that Tammy said Gerry is about eighteen and has black hair and brown eyes. She . . . she said he's really nice . . .'

I bet he is, Kate mused grimly as she followed Foster's exit into the street.

* * *

Two police patrol cars were already pulling up by the village recreation ground when Kate and Foster arrived, and a couple of young women stopped pushing their youngsters on the old wooden swings to stare in astonishment at the two uniformed police officers striding past them towards the copse and disappearing among the trees.

Kate and Jamie Foster were not far behind them and, following the narrow path into a small clearing, they saw both uniformed officers stop and stare around them, frowning. It was the same team who had assisted in the search of the Robinson house.

'What are we looking for?' Sergeant Morris asked. 'Control room just said you needed some backup in a check on the rec. This missing girl, Tammy Robinson, is it?'

Kate nodded. 'We think this is where she may have come to meet her boyfriend. We need to search the copse thoroughly for any trace of her.'

Morris raised an eyebrow. 'Not a lot here to search, is there? But we'll give it a go.'

Separating the copse into two halves, with Morris and Foster covering one half and Kate and PC Stevens the other, they split up and pushed slowly through the trees and under-growth, their gazes fixed firmly on the ground underfoot, hoping that they wouldn't stumble on what they half-ex-pected to find.

But there was no sign of a body, or any clothing, and it was only as they retraced their steps that PC Stevens suddenly called out from a few feet away and bent down to retrieve something from a tangle of brambles.

'Hey, what have we here?'

'Don't touch it!' she snapped back. 'This might end up as a crime scene.'

She was too late — he had already retrieved it — but at least he had had the good sense not to handle what he'd found and had hooked it up on the end of a biro, from which it was now dangling.

'Looks like a small necklace of some sort,' Stevens said. 'The chain seems to have broken.'

'It's an anklet,' Kate corrected, 'silver by the look of it, with some charms attached—' She broke off and felt a stab of acid in her stomach as she subjected it to closer scrutiny. The name that had originally formed part of the chain between two hearts had snapped in the middle, but it was not dif-ficult to see what that name would be when fully joined: *Ta . . . mmy*! As Kate had feared, this was now a crime scene.

* * *

'So, he snatched her then?' Foster commented sometime later as he watched the scenes of crime officers taping off the front of the copse.

Kate gnawed at her lip, a characteristic mannerism of hers when under stress. 'But not without a struggle by the look of it. That's when the anklet was broken,' she said. 'The brambles had been trampled and, as you saw, there appeared to be bloodstains on some of the leaves. He must have dragged her into the trees, which was when she put up quite a spirited fight. Problem is, where did he take her, and why take her at all if he intended killing her? He could have done the job quite easily in the copse.'

Foster nodded. 'And how did he get her away from here without being seen on a sunny summer's evening, with people about? He must have had a motor of some kind, but he would still have had to force her into it, or carry her to the damned thing even if he'd rendered her insensible.'

'Let's have another look round now we've set up the crime scene with SOCO,' Kate suggested.

It didn't take them long to find the evidence. There was a green metal cabinet, like something belonging to BT, or Openreach, close to the trees at the back of the copse and a very short entry road to it through an adjoining patch of scrub, doubtless for maintenance purposes. The tyre marks in the compressed, fine gravel were quite distinctive.

'Although we had a bit of rain at the weekend,' Foster said, 'these seem quite clear. But we don't know for certain whether they were left by the vehicle Tammy's abductor was using.'

'It would be a pretty fair guess though, wouldn't it?' Kate replied. 'We'd better get SOCO to take a look at them while they're still visible anyway.'

She stared round her for a few moments, noting the country pub and collection of houses to one side of the through road running past the site. 'Also, someone might have spotted something. Maybe the car, or our kidnapper carrying the girl to it? As you just said, it was a sunny summer's evening on Friday and there would have been people about, customers using that pub at least.'

'Trouble is, it's not exactly a well populated area, is it?' Foster went on, arguing against himself.

'Agreed, but there's still a chance someone might have seen something untoward. Sergeant Morris and PC Stevens can make a start, but, as this has to be a full crime investigation now, we'll need more resources. I'll speak to the DCI ASAP and sort out some publicity with Headquarters' press office. If we move fast, they should be able to get a description out pretty quickly to the main media outlets.'

'Best of luck there.'

She made a grimace. 'But there's something else we've got to do first.'

'See the Robinsons again?'

'Exactly. Tell them what we've found and confirm Tammy wore an anklet like the one that's been found.'

'Should be fun,' he replied sarcastically.

'That's not how I would describe it!'

* * *

Tony Robinson was not at home. Kate guessed he was probably out drinking somewhere again. Helen Robinson answered the door to the two detectives and one look at their grim faces told her they had not come with good news.

'She's not . . . not,' she began, clutching at the doorpost for support.

Kate shook her head. 'No, but we need to speak to you for a few moments.'

Sitting once again in the small sitting room, Kate told her about the anklet, but deliberately omitted any mention of the fact that possible blood traces had been found at the scene. She then produced a photograph of the chain she had taken with her mobile phone, the real thing having been retained by the scenes of crime team for forensic examination.

Helen Robinson confirmed that the anklet was identical to the one her daughter wore, then asked the question Kate was dreading she would ask.

'Do you think she's . . . she's dead?'

Kate was careful with her reply. 'At the moment we're dealing with a suspected abduction,' she said without offering an opinion one way or the other, 'and we'll pull out all the stops to find Tammy. What you need to do is try and stay calm and not jump to conclusions. I'll leave you my card, and don't hesitate to ring me if you need to, or if anything comes to mind that you feel might help us with our inquiries.'

'So, what do you really think then?' Foster said to Kate as they got back into their car.

Kate compressed her lips into a thin, hard line. 'I think we've got a dangerous nutter out there who has meticulously planned the snatch of a vulnerable fourteen-year-old kid and, like you said earlier, I am beginning to fear that what started out as a missing person inquiry could well end up as a murder investigation!' she replied with brutal candour. 'I just hope both of us are wrong.'

CHAPTER 5

He had committed murder! He had strangled the young woman without a second's thought. Held her down and throttled the life out of her. The full magnitude of what he had done only really dawned on him when he got back home in the early hours — but not because he had killed someone. It wasn't the first time he'd committed a similar crime, so he didn't feel any actual remorse over it. He was just furious that it had had to happen in the first place, heaping further possible problems on his head.

Killing the young twitcher (he assumed that's what she was) had been unavoidable. What else could he have done? She had seen Tammy's body on the ground and had realised what he was up to. Also, she could not have failed to see his face on such a brilliant moonlit night, so could have identified him later. He'd had to stop her running off and blabbing to the police.

He really should have hidden the body, though. Buried it in the spot he had reserved for Tammy. But he had chickened out at the last minute, spooked by voices he had heard deep in the woods, calling for someone called Sandra, who was probably the girl he had killed. So, he had panicked, left the body there, lying in the undergrowth, and driven off.

Once his victim was discovered, the balloon would go up. Then the hunt would be on, and when Tammy Robinson managed to contact the police, as she surely would, they were bound to put two and two together and connect the two crimes.

That in turn meant a risk to the continuance of the project he had embarked upon. At least for the time being, which was disappointing, as it had had great potential. Mother had put the idea into his head and, as usual, she had come up with something really novel for him to undertake, involving the disciplining of disruptive, anti-social young people and changing their behaviours through a process of carrot and stick — mainly stick, which had pleased him even more — and he had selected Tammy Robinson as his first subject.

But everything was such a mess now, and it was all down to the stupid bitch he had abducted. She had caused it all by attacking him and trying to escape. But after her accident on the stairs, that should have been the end of it. She should have been dead, leaving him with just the simple job of burying her. Instead, he'd ended up having to kill a potential witness and then spend half the night fruitlessly hunting for the schoolgirl in the woods. Pushing through wet undergrowth, probing thickets and hollows with his torch, and tearing his clothes and his legs on thorn bushes and strands of barbed wire from old, abandoned fencing — until he'd heard those voices and taken off like a headless bloody chicken.

He couldn't understand it. He'd been so sure after the accident that she was dead. He had found no trace of a pulse, and she'd stayed limp and unresponsive from the time he'd laid her on the settee in the sitting room upstairs to when he had lifted her out of the boot in the wood. So, how on earth could she have just got up again and run away when his back was turned? It didn't seem feasible. Yet it had happened. He'd considered the possibility that someone might have found her and carted her away, of course, but who and why? There had been no other cars in the car park when he had arrived, and he would have heard the sound of any vehicle turning up in the few minutes he had been away looking for a suitable burial spot. No, he had to accept that he had made a big mistake with the girl. She must have only been concussed from her fall on the stairs and, in his shocked state, he hadn't checked for a pulse properly. He had jumped to the obvious conclusion much too quickly, and, because of that, she was out there somewhere, maybe injured, but still alive and capable of contacting the police. The only comfort he could take from it all was the fact that he had been wearing his hood right up to the moment she had had her fall on the stairs, so, he was ninety-nine point nine percent sure she had never seen his face, and he was also satisfied that the device he had slipped inside his mouth before each and every conversation with her would have rendered his voice completely unrecognisable for any future identification purposes. Consequently, the risk of him being fingered as a result of anything the police "star" witness could tell them had to be zero. He was totally in the clear.

Nevertheless, he didn't tell Mother about it all. She would only have had a go at him, calling him an idiot and a waste of a skin, as she always had when he'd done something wrong. Instead, he went straight back to his bedroom and hid under the duvet until dawn, just like he had done as a child when confronted with what seemed like an insurmountable problem.

Once daylight came, he would tidy everything up and pretend the nightmare he had just endured had never happened. That meant throwing away or burning the clothes he had taken off Tammy and removing all traces of her presence in the cellar and what he called his secret room that adjoined it, plus cleaning out the boot of his car. There was still the cage, of course. He couldn't burn that, and dumping something so big on a council tip, or in a river would be difficult and could easily attract attention unless it was cut into small pieces. Mother would never agree to doing away with it anyway, especially as it would signify an end to the project, which had been so long in the planning and preparation.

He allowed himself a small, nervous smile. No, he would leave the cage where it was, as well as all the equipment he had in his secret room too. After all, there was no suggestion at present that the police knew anything about him, or were likely to descend upon him any time soon. If they did turn up, they would need a warrant to search his house anyway and grounds to apply for it in the first place. Furthermore, he had every intention of restarting the project, using everything again at some time in the very near future. Following all the years of domination by his mother, he had really taken to this project. It had imbued him with a sense of real power and control, plus the thrilling prospect of being able to mete out punishment to those who refused to cooperate, and that feeling felt far too good to simply abandon. Okay so there had been a hitch with the Robinson girl, but he would manage things a lot better next time, once all the fuss about Tammy's abduction had died down.

* * *

Tammy struggled out from under the fallen tree trunk where she had spent the night until after first light and stood there for a moment, swaying unsteadily and peering around her, feeling confused and frightened. She had no idea where she was, how she had got there and, most important of all, who she was. Her memory was virtually blank, in the same way as, unknown to her at that moment, it had been for a time after her abduction several days before. She did have a vague recollection of awakening to find herself lying on the ground by a car of some sort and hearing loud screams, which had prompted her to haul herself up and flee across some rough tarmac and into the woods. She had been terrified, she knew that, but she had no idea why, or what had prompted her to hide herself under the tree, where she had fallen into a deep sleep.

She felt bitterly cold and, staring down at herself, suddenly realised she was wearing nothing more than a skimpy blouse and pants. What had happened to her? Who had brought her to this place and where were they now? But most important of all, why were some of her clothes missing and her legs and feet bloodied and dirty?

Stumbling off through the trees, trying to ignore the shooting pains that travelled up her legs at every other step, she eventually emerged from the wood on to a lane with a line of pollarded willows bordering a rhyne on the far side. Above the drumming of a woodpecker and the constant twittering of songbirds in the wood behind her, she heard the distant murmur of traffic and turned towards it with a sense of relief. After a few faltering steps, she rounded a bend in the lane and glimpsed a car flash past in front of her from right to left and realised she was approaching a crossroads, or T-junction. She tried to spur herself on, but the muscles in her legs would only comply sluggishly with the signals from her brain and it seemed to take for ever to reach the junction. Then, when she finally got there, grabbing at the wooden fingerpost for balance, her legs finally gave way altogether, pitching her face down on the grass verge, completely done.

* * *

The police patrol car was parked in a gateway, facing out towards a small crossroads maybe ten to fifteen yards away. The occasional passing motorist slamming on his or her brakes the moment they glimpsed the blue-and-yellow checked BMW, with its prominent roof strobe, ahead of them, no doubt suspected that the eagle-eyed coppers were either carrying out an early-morning speed check on a road clearly signed *40*, or were lying in wait for some tasty villain they had been tipped off as heading their way in a stolen car.

In fact, PCs George Larriman and Felicity Terry were doing neither. The mobile diner that was always set up at this time in the layby a couple of miles down the road was a regular haunt of the hungry early-turn (6 a.m. to 2 p.m. shift) crews who made up the force's roads policing, or Traffic, department, and the pair were engaged in a lively argument as they finished off their bacon rolls and paper cups of coffee before the resumption of their patrol on the M5 motorway several miles further on.

'I'm telling you,' Larriman said from the front passenger seat, swallowing his final mouthful of roll, 'the reason the police are losing the confidence of the public is because the powers that be are recruiting too many woke tossers from university, instead of ex-military guys and girls with maturity and common sense.'

'That's rubbish,' Terry threw back at him from behind the wheel. 'We need people with the intelligence and clinical thought graduate-entry candidates can bring to the force.'

'Having a degree in media studies doesn't make you more intelligent than anyone else,' Larriman persisted, grinning. 'I mean, look at you. You're an ex-grad, aren't you? What was your degree in?'

'Psychology, if you must know.'

'Exactly my point. What good's that when you're called to a punch-up outside a pub on a Saturday night? Do you try a bit of psychoanalysis on a crowd of drunken yobs who are trying to kick your head in?'

She grinned back. 'Sometimes understanding the human mind and how people react in violent confrontations can help defuse situations like that.'

He forced the bag that had contained his bacon roll into his empty coffee cup and dropped it with the cup she handed to him into a carrier bag on the floor beside him.

'Is that right? Well, next time we get one of those calls, I'll let you march into the bar and try that out on a six-foot thug swinging a broken bottle, while I wait outside.'

For reply she suddenly jerked upright in her seat. 'Bugger me!'

He chortled. 'What here, in this gateway?'

She ignored him and, starting the engine, quickly swung out on to the tarmacked road surface.

'I'll take that as a no then,' he said.

But she didn't answer and was already switching on the roof strobe and swinging across the road towards the verge on the opposite side, which was when he saw what she had already spotted and whistled his astonishment.

The half-naked figure had emerged at the crossroads from what was little more than a country lane, stumbling along the verge as if they were drunk, or seriously injured, and, even before the Traffic car got to them, they collapsed face down on the grass.

Despite being behind the wheel, Felicity Terry was out of her seat and on her knees beside Tammy Robinson before Larriman managed to disentangle his overweight body from his seatbelt and clamber out of the car.

'We're here, love,' Terry said gently to the young girl. 'You're safe now.'

The policewoman's gaze wandered over her, noting with a grimace the bloodstained legs and feet and the abrasions and other inflamed marks on her bare scalp, suggesting her head had been crudely shaved.

In the background, Larriman had assessed the situation and was already on the radio to the police control room, requesting an ambulance.

Tammy tried to get herself up off the ground, but Terry firmly pressed her down. 'Don't try and get up,' she advised. 'How badly are you hurt?'

Tammy raised her head and stared at her, wiping the tears from her eyes with the back of one hand.

'Feel funny,' she said between sniffs. 'Feet really sore.'

Terry nodded sympathetically, seeing the state of them. 'We've got an ambulance on the way, so you just stay put,' she said. 'What's your name, sweetheart?'

There was a scared, haunted look in the big, brown eyes. 'Don't know,' she whispered brokenly. 'Don't know who I am.' Then she promptly passed out.

'I do,' Larriman said grimly at Terry's elbow, and when she turned her head he showed her a printed circulation, bearing a small portrait photograph, which had been attached, with other notices, to a clipboard in the back of the patrol car. 'It's that missing girl, Tammy Robinson.'

Terry's head jerked back towards the girl. 'Tammy Robinson?' she breathed. 'She looks almost unrecognisable without that mass of long, brown hair. What the hell happened to that?'

Larriman grunted. 'Looks like some evil bastard cut it all off,' he said. 'I wonder what else he did to her.'

* * *

Kate had only just walked into her office in CID Tuesday morning when she heard the news.

'They've found Tammy Robinson — injured but alive,' Jamie Foster announced. 'But someone shaved her head.'

Kate stared at him. 'Shaved her . . . what?' she said, dumping her briefcase on her desk.

He shrugged. 'Barefoot and bald as a coot now, it seems.'

Kate's relief was palpable. 'Well, that she's been found alive is brilliant, but why would anyone—?'

'Dunno,' he said. 'Takes all types, I suppose.'

'So, what are her injuries?'

'Nasty bang on the head apparently, lacerations to the soles of her feet — probably from walking barefoot on rough ground — and some nasty cuts to her legs, but apparently nothing else major.'

'Where is she?'

'General Hospital under observation.'

'Where was she found?'

'Walked out of a lane at the back of Holcroft Nature Reserve on the Levels and collapsed in front of a Traffic car. And there's one other concerning thing.'

Kate's eyes narrowed. 'Go on.'

'She was half-naked, wearing just pants and a top — no trousers or skirt and, as I've said, her feet were bare.'

'Any suggestion of sexual assault?'

'We don't know. She's not that compos mentis. Doc has evidently said she may be suffering from concussion due to the bang on the head. Thing is, the crew who found her said that when they spoke to her before she passed out, she had no memory of what had happened to her, or who she was.'

'Amnesia.'

'Seems like it.'

'We'd better get over to the hospital.'

He shook his head. 'I don't think the hospital will let you speak to her. She's still undergoing checks, and they've said they will not allow access until they are satisfied she's well enough to be interviewed. Might be a while yet by the sound of it.'

'We'll go anyway. If only to make sure this *is* our girl and not someone who looks like her.'

* * *

The hospital was at first stubbornly opposed to the detectives seeing their casualty, but, under assurances from Kate that they had no intention of trying to interview her, the duty doctor, Dr Phillips, reluctantly allowed them into the little private room where Tammy was now accommodated.

The young girl was sitting up in bed resting back against a couple of pillows, wearing a white hospital gown. Her face was deathly pale, her eyes closed and her hands clasped lightly together on the top of the bedsheet as if in deathly repose. But for the faint, telltale rise and fall of her chest, she might have resembled nothing more than a recently admitted corpse, or, alternatively, the product of some skilled waxworks sculptor. Familiar equipment, including an oxygen cylinder, and other kit stood on a trolley by her bed, and she seemed to be connected to a drip.

'She's had a CT scan because of her head injury and also blood tests, on which we are currently awaiting results,' the doctor explained. 'The wound to her head appears to be superficial and the consultant, who has already seen her, is satisfied that she does not appear to have suffered any serious injuries, although it is possible she may have experienced a minor concussion from a fall, or a blow. There are some nasty lacerations to her feet and legs, which had to be treated, and she was very dehydrated, but otherwise we are confident she should eventually make a full recovery.'

'She certainly doesn't look the picture of health,' Foster said drily, 'and the officers who found her said she had no idea who she was and that she passed out while they were talking to her.'

Phillips nodded. 'We believe she has experienced some sort of traumatic shock, which has led to a form of amnesia. Hopefully, this will correct itself in time, but on her arrival here she became very agitated and had to be sedated for her own good. She is still under sedation and, for the present, she needs an uninterrupted period of rest. She is expected to remain here under observation for the next three to four days, during which time other tests will be conducted.'

Kate's mouth tightened angrily when she saw the state of Tammy's head, with its complete absence of hair and the ugly abrasions that were clearly visible where the wide bandage that had been wound around her scalp did not completely cover it. Her mind flashed back to another case she had dealt with some years before. Then the victim had been her old foe, the reporter, Debbie Moreton, who had got too close to a ruthless psychopath she was pursuing and had ended up being dumped in a lane, naked and with her head shaved in exactly the same way. Fortunately Tammy had at least been left semi-clothed, escaping the ultimate humiliation, but Kate couldn't help wondering what else her abductor might have done to her that was not visible.

'I'm sure you appreciate that we will need to have her examined to determine if there has been any sexual assault,' she said.

The doctor frowned, then firmly shook his head. 'Out of the question at the moment, I'm afraid.'

Kate nodded. She had expected such a response. 'I will obtain her parents' permission and come back to you.'

He shrugged. 'You'll have to speak to the consultant.'

'Fine. I'll do that. So, how long do you think she's likely to be in this condition?'

The doctor shrugged again. 'Who knows? This isn't my field. We are arranging for a proper psychiatric assessment to be carried out in due course, but it's early days yet and for the moment there's nothing we can do but wait for her to show signs of recovery.'

'And meanwhile, we've got some sadistic psycho loose out there somewhere, just waiting to do the same sort of thing to another poor kid.'

The doctor made a face. 'I'm sorry,' he said. 'Sadly, we live in a very wicked world.'

Kate snorted as they turned and headed for the door. 'Tell me about it, doc,' she retorted grimly, 'and it's getting worse by the day!'

'Poor little bugger,' Foster commented as they left the hospital. 'What sort of arsehole could do something like that to a fourteen-year-old kid?'

Kate sighed irritably. 'We're not likely to be able to find out any time soon by the look of it. I mean, heaven knows how long she's likely to be in the state she is and there could be a lot of valuable information shored up in that little head of hers, which we need to unlock if we are to get anywhere.'

He stared at her for a second. 'That's a bit of a callous attitude, isn't it?'

'Not really. I feel dreadfully sorry for her, of course I do, but we have a scumbag to catch and I have to be pragmatic about things. There's a time and place for sentiment, Jamie, and now isn't it. Talking of which, I suppose we ought to go and break the good news to our odd couple.'

* * *

It seemed like the Robinsons had been eating their lunch when the detectives turned up on their doorstep, as the smell of cooking hung in the air. Helen Robinson paled the moment she opened the door to them, obviously fearing the worst, and her husband swung round in the act of lifting his coat off a peg in the hall when he heard her gasp.

'Tammy's been found, Mrs Robinson,' Kate said quickly, fearing the woman's legs were about to give way. 'She's not badly injured and she's recovering in hospital.'

The woman raised a hand to her chest and briefly closed her eyes. 'Thank God,' she said, then grabbed the edge of the door to steady herself.

Tony Robinson glared at Kate, one arm through the sleeve of his coat. 'I was just going out,' he commented sourly, finishing pulling on his coat. 'So, the silly bitch has turned up at last, has she? Shacked up with some bloke, I bet.'

'Shall we talk inside?' Kate suggested tartly, giving him a withering look.

Helen Robinson took a deep breath and nodded, leading the way to the sitting room, as before, with her husband, still wearing his coat, reluctantly in tow.

'Tammy is not seriously injured, but she is under observation,' Kate said once they were all seated. 'She is suffering from some kind of shock and will need time to get over whatever it is she has been through.' She went on to explain about the fourteen-year-old being found collapsed in the lane at the back of the nature reserve, suffering from amnesia. She deliberately said nothing about the girl's head being shaved or how scantily she was dressed. She was keen to hear what Tony Robinson might have to say and whether he would reveal something that only Tammy's abductor would have known. Regrettably, he didn't.

'So, how the hell did she get there?' Tony Robinson snapped instead, showing no sympathy whatsoever for his daughter's plight. 'And where's she been all this time?'

'We have no idea as yet,' Kate replied.

'No idea? Haven't you woodentops bloody well asked her?'

'We can't at present,' Kate said coldly. 'She's too traumatised to be interviewed and, when she was first found, she didn't even know who she was.'

Helen Robinson dropped a smouldering cigarette into an ashtray on the chair arm and snatched at a half-full bottle of what again looked like brandy from the little table beside her, spilling much of it down the chair and on to the carpet as she tried to fill her glass with shaking hands.

'T-traumatised?' she echoed, taking a gulp of her drink. 'What do you mean?'

'She's had a very bad experience,' Foster explained. 'We don't know what it was, but it's left her in a rather fragile emotional state. We should also tell you that she has an injury to her head, which is apparently not serious, but may account for the way she is—'

'When was she found and who by?' Tony Robinson cut in, still showing no interest in her condition.

'By a police patrol earlier this morning,' Kate said.

'And you're only telling us now?'

'We were unable to see her and positively confirm that it was your daughter until a short time ago.'

'Bloody negligent, that's what that is, and it's not good enough. I'm going to speak to—'

'Oh, *shut up*, you *moron*!' his wife suddenly shrieked at him, losing her control completely. 'Just get out of here and stay out! I don't want you around anymore!'

Her glass was now lying on the floor, but she left it there as her husband jumped to his feet, his face contorted with anger, and strode furiously out of the room, just as he had on the previous occasion. The front door slammed and seconds later a car started up outside, followed by a squeal of tyres as it drove off at speed.

There was silence in the room. Then Helen Robinson gave a faint, wan smile. 'Sorry about that, Detectives. I am truly grateful to you for finding Tammy alive, but I've had enough of everything, and I just can't stand anymore.' She paused, then said in a much more controlled tone, 'When can I see her?'

'We'll leave you the hospital's number,' Kate said, rising to her feet. 'But she is currently sedated. I would suggest you ring them tomorrow morning, but don't expect a lot from Tammy at the moment. You're going to have to be very patient and resilient when you see her. Furthermore, we need your permission for her to have a medical examination.'

'I thought you said she wasn't badly injured?'

'Er, not that sort of examination, Mrs Robinson. We have to make sure she has not been interfered with in any way.'

'Interfered with? Good grief. Not that!'

'We aren't saying she has been. We just need to make sure.'

The distraught woman closed her eyes tightly for a second, as if to shut out some awful vision. 'Then-then it will have to be done,' she whispered. 'But what-what a horrible world we live in.'

Ditto to that, Kate thought as they showed themselves out, and she was not surprised as they left the room to see Mrs Robinson bending over to retrieve her brandy glass from the floor.

* * *

'You might have told me you were going to keep quiet about Tammy's head being shaved and the fact that she was half-naked when she was found,' Foster commented when they were back in the car. 'Good job I cottoned on before I said anything.'

Kate threw him a rueful smile. 'Sorry, but I wanted to see if Tony Robinson might come out with something in an unguarded moment.'

'Which he didn't.'

'Well, I had to try.'

'You actually think he might be a suspect for this job then?'

She shrugged. 'You've seen the way he behaves and, from what we've been told, he and Tammy never got on at all. So, there's no love lost between them, is there?'

'But to kidnap his own daughter and shave all her hair off, maybe as some kind of punishment—'

'We've come across fathers in the past who have done a lot worse than that.'

'True, but I think she'd have known if her abductor was her own father and would have told someone that when she was found?'

'Maybe, but since she's evidently suffering from amnesia she's hardly in a position to tell anyone anything. Furthermore, her abductor could have been masked or she could have been rendered unconscious. Don't forget, we haven't yet established exactly where Tony Robinson was on the night Tammy was taken. It's also possible that he didn't actually do the job himself, but hired someone to do it for him.'

'Oh, come on, Kate!'

She made a rueful grimace. 'Okay, so that's a bit far-fetched, but stranger things have happened and, as far as I'm concerned, everyone is a suspect until we know otherwise. Remember too, whoever did this is a clever bastard, which means we've got to be even cleverer if we're ever going to catch him.'

He nodded slowly. 'Copy that and, on that basis, what's our next clever move?'

'I don't say it's a clever one, but I think we should take a look at the place where Tammy was found. See if there's anything there for us. How big is this Holcroft Nature Reserve?'

He pursed his lips. 'Well, I've done a bit of walking in that area over the years — sort of hobby of mine — and it occupies quite a few acres. Not the biggest of our nature reserves, or the most popular, but still a fair size and a bit difficult to secure as a crime scene, I would say. If we drop back to the nick, I have a map in the office, and I'll show you.'

'Sounds like a plan,' she said, throwing open the door of the CID car. 'And that will give us the chance of grabbing a coffee too.'

Around twenty minutes later, they were back in the CID office and Foster was rummaging through a drawer in his desk, finally producing a battered, discoloured Ordnance Survey map, which he spread out on his desk.

'There's the place,' he said, stabbing a finger at a green shaded area. 'But we don't know Tammy actually came from there. She could have escaped from a car nearby, or been walking along the road all night from another location.'

Kate studied the map for a few seconds, chewing her lip in thought. 'True,' she agreed. 'But we should still check out the site as a priority before any evidence that might be recoverable is compromised by some nature-loving backpacker or destroyed by a change in the weather. So, the next thing is to get some plods together for the search — and a dog if we can. Be an idea to contact the administrative office of the reserve too. See if they can loan us a warden for a few hours. If you get on to the reserve and HQ for the dog, I'll have a word with the inspector downstairs to see if he can let us have a few of his crew.'

He folded up the map again. 'And what do we tell everyone we're looking for?'

She shrugged. 'That's the problem. I haven't the faintest idea.'

CHAPTER 6

It took a while getting even a small search party together and securing the necessary approval from the management of the reserve, not only for one of their rangers to attend, but for the search to proceed in the first place. As a result, it was later in the afternoon before the mix of Uniform and CID officers, plus a dog unit, assembled in a field off the lane from which Tammy Robinson had been seen to emerge. The ranger, a thin, taciturn individual, who reminded Kate of Private Frazer from the TV series *Dad's Army*, turned up, hot and bothered, minutes into Kate's briefing and it was obvious from his muttered comments that he was far from happy about the potential disruption to wildlife the "invasion" of the reserve would cause.

She sensed also that her colleagues were none too happy with the nebulous nature of the search, and the fact that there was no expert police search adviser (or POLSA) present, as would have been the case in one organised as part of a specific major operation. But in fairness, this was not in the same category as a major search operation. They were not looking for a missing child at serious risk; she had already been found. This was just a cursory fact-finding forage, which didn't require the same level of expertise. Nevertheless, critical looks were directed towards Kate more than once during the briefing and she was not even sure Jamie Foster was fully behind her on this one.

As for the reserve itself, the warden's colourful description of the site as being impassable in places, with areas of wet marsh, transversed by streams, bogs and dense thorny thickets, did little to inspire confidence among the search team and brought even Kate close to having second thoughts.

Yet, despite her frustration, and the downbeat influence of the doubters, she stuck to her guns, and her reward came almost immediately. There was a sizeable gap in the wooded edge of the reserve where it joined the lane, which she had earmarked as the ideal starting point for their search on the assumption that, if Tammy had indeed come from the reserve, this would have been her most likely exit point. Support for her theory seemed to jump out at her too the moment they crossed the road and stepped on to the grass verge. The imprints of a pair of bare feet were clearly visible in the soft mud of a narrow track that stabbed off into the woods just inside the opening and even more significant was the fact that the toes were pointing in the direction of the lane.

More footprints could be seen beyond, stretching back in a line deeper into the woods, though the trail petered out a few yards further on when the track disappeared into a tangle of crushed undergrowth that suggested someone had recently forced their way through.

Kate whistled. 'So, she did come out of the reserve,' she breathed.

'Yeah,' Foster agreed, bending down to study some of the footprints, 'and if you look closer, there are black deposits caking the earth in some of the impressions, which could be dried blood.'

'Which fits with what we were told about Tammy's feet being cut,' Kate went on. 'Pity we won't be able to determine the exact part of the reserve she came from, now that the trail appears to have ended.'

'We could try using the dog,' Foster suggested.

Kate wasn't very hopeful but shrugged. 'What have we got to lose?' she said.

The dog handler, Doug Reynolds, seemed to share her pessimism, but nevertheless he guided his Alsatian, Sam, back to one of the deeper footprints just inside the wood and invited him to sniff at it as if it were some kind of choice doggy treat. At first, Sam seemed noticeably disinterested and took to sniffing the air instead, but then, after a few words from his handler, he returned to the footprint and his sniffing routine became more intense. The next instant, the handler was having difficulty holding him back as he took off, panting hard and straining at the leash, his nose close to the ground.

Instructing two of the uniformed officers to remain at the unofficial entrance to the reserve to prevent anyone else from following them and destroying the footprints, Kate directed the remaining members of the team to follow the warden and herself along one side of the track in the direction taken by the handler and Sam.

They soon found the fallen tree under which Tammy had taken refuge for the night and what looked like more blood traces on the ground beneath it.

'Appears she hid here for a time,' Kate said. 'You can see how the grass has been flattened too—'

She broke off at a distant shout, accompanied by excited barking and whining.

'Sounds like Sam's got something,' Foster exclaimed. 'Hope it isn't just a bloody rabbit.'

But it wasn't. Stumbling a few more yards through the flattened undergrowth towards the sounds, they emerged from among the trees into a small car park and found Reynolds and his canine companion waiting for them on the left-hand side of the tarmac, a few feet from the start of another narrow path. Although they had heard the dog barking excitedly a short time before, he was now lying on the ground beside Reynolds, panting and treating them to a lopsided grin.

'What have you got?' Kate asked his master.

Reynolds frowned. 'Well, Sam seemed quite excited when he got here,' he said, glancing down at the dog, which seemed to have lost interest again, 'and he pranced around a bit, frustrated like, looking for a continuation of the trail. But it seems to have ended right at this spot, going by his antics.'

'No more footprints to see anyway,' Kate commented. 'Tarmacked surface has seen to that.'

'No, but there must still have been a scent — I'd trust Sam's nose every time — and, if you look closely, you can just see a couple of sets of muddy tyre marks just before the start of the path there.'

'Only just visible,' Foster agreed, crouching down. 'Maybe one pair as the car drove in and the second pair overlapping them as it reversed out again. Could be a connection.'

Kate nodded, glancing around the car park. 'Good chance of that, I reckon,' she replied. 'I don't see other tyre tracks anywhere and it's a bit of a coincidence that those marks seem to be the only ones here. It's obvious that Tammy was brought to the reserve in a motor by someone. How else would she have got here? It seems she must have somehow got away from her captor and fled from him through the woods, strangely enough choosing the thick undergrowth as her escape route rather than that path there. The burning question is, why did he bring her to somewhere like this in the first place after holding her prisoner for almost four days?'

She looked around at the other faces staring at her, as if seeking an answer, but no one responded, and they didn't get a second chance as another loud cry brought the conversation to an abrupt end. A couple of the uniformed officers had evidently taken the initiative and investigated the path leading off the car park and one now reappeared, waving and calling out excitedly.

'You need to see this, ma'am,' he said. 'We've found a stiff in the bushes just along the path.'

Kate stared at him. 'A what?' she exclaimed.

'A-a dead woman,' he qualified. 'Looks like she's been strangled.'

* * *

Following Kate's radio call to the control room, after her own brief visit to the outer edge of the crime scene to confirm what she had been told, the wheels of the well-practised police investigative machine began to turn and the police surgeon, Dr Jordan Baptiste, a smiling former casualty doctor from Jamaica, soon arrived, followed by the scenes of crime team, whose photographer started taking some early still and video pictures of the scene before it was disturbed. Baptiste went through the formality of certifying life extinct, giving the probable cause of the woman's death as manual strangulation; not that he could really have come to any other conclusion under the circumstances, Kate thought. Then with a cheery wave Baptiste left, still smiling benignly, as if he had just been to a picnic.

It was a good two hours more before the forensic pathologist arrived and Kate was delighted when she saw the big Volvo swing into the car park and pull up a few feet from half a dozen parked police vehicles, immediately recognising the car and who was driving it.

Forensic pathologist, Lydia Summers, a slender, blonde-haired woman in her forties, was well known to Kate and had attended many of her past crime scenes. So much so that, professionally, they had become good friends over the years and had a great deal of respect for each other.

'Congratulations on your promotion, Kate,' Summers said with a smile when she climbed out of the car. 'DI, eh? Not before time. So, what have you got for me here. Something tasty, I'll be bound.'

Kate laughed without humour. 'I don't know about tasty, doc, but maybe part of a nasty jigsaw,' she said, and waited while the pathologist got a large briefcase out of her car, together with a holdall, which Kate knew would contain the protective kit she would need to pull on over her clothes before carrying out her examination. Then, quickly briefing her on the circumstances, Kate walked with her to the strand of yellow *Crime Scene — Do Not Cross* tape drawn across the start of the footpath. A few yards beyond this the SOCO tent covering the body was just visible among the trees, and she nodded to the uniformed police officer manning the security barrier to allow Summers through.

After that, faced with nothing more she could do until either Summers had finished her grisly task, or the newly appointed SIO visited the scene, she decided to stretch her legs and wandered along the reserve's entry road to where it had been sealed off to unauthorised traffic with blue and white police outer perimeter tape.

A uniformed woman police officer was standing there, looking completely bored, and Kate was about to go over to speak to her when she spotted several figures, some with cameras, standing in the road on the other side of the tape. Press, she mused. As usual, they were right on the ball. It was always a mystery to her how quickly they got to hear of things like this, especially when it was miles from anywhere, way out in the country. And she recognised one of them straight away.

Dressed in blue denims and a black leather jacket, this time favouring bright green spiky hair instead of her usual pink colour, but with the familiar facial piercings reminiscent of a punk rocker, she was an all too familiar figure. Debbie Moreton, the one-time crime reporter for the *Bridgwater Clarion* but now a freelancer, had long been a thorn in the side of the force, particularly where Kate was concerned, and she was the last person anyone would have wanted near a crime scene. The journalist's powerful Triumph Bonneville motorcycle was parked on the other side of the road and Kate couldn't help secretly hoping it would be totalled by a passing lorry.

That didn't happen, but what did was the arrival of another familiar and unwelcome personage in a silver Mercedes saloon, which swung into the gateway and stopped while the policewoman checked the card thrust out of the window. Detective Chief Inspector bloody Ricketts, Kate mused, using his own car so he could claim mileage as an essential user.

'Got a murder, have you, Chief Inspector?' one of the reporters shouted, and Ricketts blinked irritably as a camera flashed close to the car window. 'Who's the victim?'

'Is it the missing girl, Tammy Robinson, Chief Inspector?' Debbie Moreton shouted from the other side.

For reply, Ricketts hit the accelerator and drove straight through the gateway even as the policewoman was unhooking one end of the tape from a tree.

'What the hell are the press doing here?' Ricketts snapped out of the window as he drove past Kate towards the car park.

'Their job, I should think, guv,' she replied, pausing by the window as he stopped alongside. 'We've circulated as much as we can about Tammy Robinson's suspected abduction and the downside to that is, once you activate the press, there is the likelihood that they'll become a real pain in the arse.'

He snorted and drove on without a reply and Kate caught up with him as he was climbing out of his car, now parked next to Summers' Volvo.

'So, what have we here then?' he asked tersely, peering at the yellow crime scene tape drawn across the footpath entrance. 'I understand from control room that it's a murder. Not the schoolgirl, is it?'

Kate shook her head. 'No, it's what appears to be a young, female backpacker, probably a twitcher interested in nocturnal bird species. One of my team found her. Looks like she was manually strangled.'

'So, what's the connection to the abduction inquiry?'

'We don't yet know if there is one.'

'So, why were you here in the first place?'

Kate quickly filled him in on the situation. 'Forensic pathologist is already here doing her stuff,' she said, and nodded towards one of two scenes of crime vehicles parked a few yards away. 'SOCO are also on hand waiting to get fully stuck in.'

'Do we know who this dead woman is?'

'Not so far, but once the pathologist has finished, we should be able to check her clothes for ID.'

'What about the schoolgirl, Tammy whatshername? Have you spoken to her yet? She might know who the dead woman is and who killed her.'

'According to the hospital, she's not capable of being interviewed at present due to some sort of traumatic condition and she is currently under sedation anyway. They will let us know when there is any change in the situation.'

'And have you been back to them to see if there has been?'

'Not as yet, no. I'm a little bit busy here at the moment.'

'It looks like it! You still had time to go for a stroll just now.' He gave a short, disparaging snort, adding before she could think of a suitable riposte, 'Not simply dragging our feet, are we, Detective Inspector?'

She met his stare with a cold, hostile one of her own. 'You're the DCI,' she reminded him. 'If you think I am, you're welcome to take over the inquiry yourself.'

'Oh, that won't be necessary,' he replied loftily. 'A major investigation team will be doing that now, in view of the severity of the case and the attendant circumstances, and I gather the superintendent appointed as senior investigation officer is already en route from another job. They might not get here until much later however. So, until then, you're temporarily in charge, heaven help us.'

Kate ignored the nasty dig. 'SIO someone we know?' she asked.

Ricketts couldn't help himself. He rejoiced in knowing more than anyone else, and, in order to impress, he just couldn't keep such things to himself.

'Detective Superintendent Deirdrie Hennessey actually. She has previously been SIO on several of our major inquiries at Highbridge, so, I know her well.'

The hell you do, Kate thought, recalling that Hennessey had brutally trimmed his tail on more than one occasion. But she tried to conceal her delight at the news.

Hennessey hailed from Northern Ireland, where she had previously been a member of the highly respected Royal Ulster Constabulary just before political pressure changed its name. In her late forties now, the sharp-tongued, no-nonsense senior detective had been a good, supportive boss to

Kate in the past when she had worked under her as a DS on several major inquiries. A woman with a keen, analytical mind and a dry, sometimes wicked sense of humour, Hennessey had earned a reputation for herself as a tireless, focused investigator, who had no time for excuses or procrastination and always tackled things head on. Not always strictly according to the rulebook either. The old adage, so often overused in police appraisal reports, "doesn't tolerate fools gladly", was a particularly apt description when applied to Hennessey, and, looking at Ricketts, Kate smiled again, thinking he would be wise to stay out of her way.

Abruptly her musings were interrupted, as Ricketts half-turned and pulled open his car door again, obviously keen to be on his way well clear of the "coalface" when he should by rights have been assuming command. 'Of course,' he added, 'once the superintendent takes on her role, you will be surplus to requirements and have to return to your more mundane duties as DI at this station, letting the major investigation team get on with the job. There will be no further need for you to be involved. So, I don't want to see you poking your nose back in afterwards in order to make some sort of glory name for yourself.'

Climbing back behind the wheel, he slammed the door shut behind him, sneering at her again through the open window. 'I recall you made the point to me on Monday that you are the DI at Highbridge now and you will run your department as you see fit.' He started the engine and slowly pulled away. 'Well, let's see you do it instead of swanning around trying to be the great detective, but remember, I'll be watching you. Make a cock-up and I'll be right there at your career funeral!'

'Nice to know the guv'nor has your back, Kate,' Foster chuckled, coming up behind her as Ricketts drove off.

She watched, tight-lipped and angry, as the DCI's car disappeared round a bend in the entry road. 'One day,' she muttered aloud. 'One day, I'm going to see that pillock fry.'

He gave a wry grin. 'A worthy sentiment, Kate, but before you think of lighting the barbecue you might have to join a pretty long queue.'

* * *

It was some time before the pathologist finished what she had to do, and she met Kate by the police tape, just inside the entrance to the footpath. The SOCO team in their protective overalls were already moving in on the tented scene and Kate saw further flashes of the photographer's camera among the trees. Summers smiled when she saw her old friend already waiting there for her.

'Walk me back to my car, will you, Kate?' she said.

Ducking under the tape and carefully stepping round the additional cordoned-off area where the dog handler had found the tyre tracks, Summers strolled over to her car and began stripping off the protective booties and overalls covering her clothes and dumping them with her large brief-case in the back.

'Well, it was definitely manual strangulation,' she said. 'Quite frenzied, I would suggest, probably through panic. Severe bruising is already starting to manifest itself on her neck. Your SOCOs have found several telltale tracks on the muddy path, which suggests she may have been running away at the time, but whoever was in pursuit doubtless caught up with her, knocked her off her feet on to her back and probably knelt on top of her while he did the deed.'

Kate emitted a low whistle, a likely scenario at once occurring to her. 'She stumbled on to Tammy and her abductor by accident, didn't she?' she breathed, thinking aloud. 'Maybe Tammy screamed for help as he was about to finish her off, and the woman fled, but she wasn't fast enough.'

Summers nodded. 'I don't know much about Tammy,' she said, 'but you may well be right that this was an unfortunate chance encounter. All the signs indicate something like that anyway. The ferocity of the attack almost certainly snapped the deceased's hyoid bone and ruptured her trachea. As I've said already, severe bruising to the neck is apparent, plus conjunctival petechiae in both eyes, which is often associated with asphyxia occasioned by manual strangulation.

'The deceased herself I would put at about twenty-five years of age, and possibly an outdoors type, going by her clothing and the condition of her skin and fingernails. She had quite an expensive-looking camera slung around her neck, so, if I had to hazard a guess, I'd say she was out doing a bit of nocturnal photography and maybe camping somewhere not too far away.'

'Time of death?' Kate asked automatically.

Summers frowned. 'Difficult to say, as I would suggest that she's been lying here for quite a few hours, and the body temperature and ambient temperature of the scene will both have changed over time. But going by present lividity, as well as evidence of rigor mortis and a number of other factors, I would estimate she has been dead for about fourteen to sixteen hours.'

Kate glanced at her watch. 'So, midnight to one a.m.?'

Summers shrugged. 'I'll be able to be a bit more precise once I get her on the slab.'

Kate winced at the picture this conjured up in her mind. 'Any idea what sort of timescale we're talking about?'

'That depends on you. In view of the nature of the death, I should be able to push things through fairly quickly, and I'll confirm a date for the post-mortem by email when I know the body is being released to the mortuary. See you at the PM in due course, eh?'

Kate shook her head. 'It'll probably be the SIO who attends, not me.'

Summers chuckled, knowing Kate's aversion to post-mortems. 'You should insist, Kate,' she replied. 'At least it would give you something to look forward to.'

And climbing into her car, the pathologist was still chuckling as she drove away.

* * *

Detective Superintendent Deirdrie Hennessey arrived shortly after the departure of the forensic pathologist. She looked tired and strained, her hair slightly adrift and her blue trouser suit unusually rumpled, as if she had been wearing it for a long time. She treated Kate to a weary smile as she got out of her car, followed by a stocky red-faced man with light curly hair and a noticeable paunch, dressed in a brown leather jacket and grey flannels.

'Hi Kate,' Hennessey said in her strong Northern Irish accent. 'Sorry I'm a wee bit late for the party, but I've come straight from another big job over at Bristol.' She waved a hand at the man with her. 'I've brought my crime scene manager, Peter Jones, along with me, as he will be coordinating everything from now on.'

Jones gave an equally tired smile and shook hands with Kate.

Hennessey glanced quickly around her. 'No DCI then?'

'Been and gone,' Kate said without saying anything else.

Hennessey made no comment about that, but Kate saw her give a tight, knowing smile. 'Pathologist away too?'

Kate nodded. 'Only just, but the body's still in situ, and I can brief you on her initial findings.'

Hennessey gave no hint of her frustration over missing Summers. 'Sure, that's dead on, and I can catch up with her again if I need to, so I can.'

She turned back to her car and opened the boot, pulling out a similar holdall to the one Summers had brought with her. 'Right, if you give us the SP first, that'll be grand. Then we can take a wee dander to the crime scene, get kitted up and see what's what before it gets dark.'

She glanced at her watch. 'Sure, we might even be in time for a wee cup of tea and a bun at Highbridge afterwards, if we're lucky.'

CHAPTER 7

They were still setting up the major incident room in the police club on the third floor of Highbridge police station when Kate walked in the following morning and found the DCI wandering about like a fish out of water. The skeleton staff knew exactly what they were doing — they had done it many times before — but Ricketts, obviously unaware that Hennessey had attended the crime scene the previous night because no one had told him, needed to feel relevant until the full team had been assembled and the SIO materialised.

Several workstations were already in evidence, and Kate knew that more sophisticated technology would follow, including the computer-based HOLMES or "Home Office Large Major Inquiry System", which was designed as an administrative management and information gathering and recording support for use in the investigation of serious or complex criminal investigations. Less sophisticated, though still necessary, was the whiteboard on an easel that had been placed a few feet from a colour television in front of the club bar, which was now well and truly closed and sealed behind interlocking wooden panels, and on the other side of the television there was a full-sized photocopier. The ubiquitous coffee machine, with a plastic tray full of mugs beside it, occupied a small table in one corner, together with a lidless cardboard box, which on closer inspection would have been found to contain replacement cartridges and packets of dried milk, and at the far end of the room, a glass-panelled office, which was more like a cubicle and was identical to the one in the CID general office below, was now grandly labelled SIO. This large, stuffy, former clubroom, reeking of yesterday's beer, was nothing like the impressive state-of-the-art incident room so often portrayed in films and on television, but it was the real deal, and Kate smiled to herself as she wondered what the general public would make of it all if they were ever to be given a guided tour.

'Something amusing you, Inspector?' Ricketts snapped, staring at her suspiciously.

'Not at all, guv,' she replied. 'What could be amusing about a murder inquiry?'

He grunted. 'By the way, I don't like being referred to as "guv". It's a crude, TV-inspired title and quite inappropriate in today's modern police service. "Sir" is a much more respectful address.'

She raised her eyebrows. '*Sir*, it is then, sir,' she agreed, musing disrespectfully, *As long as it's spelt "cur".*

Ricketts stared at her with a frown, not sure whether the tone in which she had replied was suspect. 'Anyway,' he continued, giving a little self-conscious cough, 'the SIO for the inquiry will be shortly arriving and I am keen to ensure there is an effective handover and a thorough briefing by us on the case when she does.'

Kate felt like questioning his use of the word "us", since he had taken no part in things at all so far, but in the end she couldn't be bothered and left him to dream on, contenting herself with the fact that he would shortly be given a rude awakening.

That awakening came with the sudden appearance of Hennessey, looking a lot more sprightly, dressed this time in a neatly pressed, green trouser suit. Inviting them both into the SIO's office, she carefully installed herself in the swivel chair behind the desk and smiled sweetly at the DCI, much like a rattlesnake looking at its breakfast.

'Morning, ma'am,' Ricketts said, opening proceedings. 'I thought it would be helpful for the DI here to brief you on the case in hand, which she has been initially investigating under my direction—'

Hennessey stopped him with a wave of her hand. 'Thank you, Chief Inspector. But Kate here briefed me at the crime scene yesterday evening.'

'She did *what?*' he exclaimed, forgetting himself. 'But I was not told—'

'Ach, you're all right,' Hennessey cut in, 'and I'm now up to speed anyways, so don't bother your barney. However, you need to know that I will be seconding DI Lewis here to my team for the duration of the inquiry. I must apologise for the short notice, as I know this will mean some reorganisation of your department.'

Ricketts' lower jaw would have hit the floor had it not been connected to the upper half, and for a moment he was completely speechless — but only for a moment.

'Sorry, ma'am, that is out of the question,' he blurted finally. 'I can't leave Highbridge station without a DI—'

'You won't have to,' Hennessey cut in. 'You have a DI at Bridgwater, and he can cover both stations for this limited period, with yourself maintaining . . . what is it I hear you call it? Ach, that's it, a "watching brief".'

'But this is just not practicable.'

Hennessey's eyes narrowed. 'Sure, it's not only practicable, Chief Inspector,' she corrected, 'but it is what is going to happen, so it is. DI Lewis has been involved in this case from the start and she also has considerable local knowledge. It makes absolute sense to keep her on board. Furthermore, a few of the local uniformed officers, together with your DS Foster, who has been very much a part of the initial investigations, will also be joining us. It is, as you know, the usual policy for the local area to provide some personnel to assist the major investigation team on such inquiries.'

'But-but, with respect, this is ridiculous. You'll have already taken my DI and now you're adding the department's only DS. How do you expect Highbridge CID to function?'

'You have two detective sergeants at Bridgwater. One of them can be temporarily transferred to Highbridge to cover DS Foster's absence. Anyway, I have already cleared the arrangements with ACC, Operations and I had a wee chat with your superintendent, Mr Rutherford, a short time ago. He has offered whatever local assistance he can provide. So, everything is arranged, and the secondments will take effect from today.'

Ricketts opened his mouth to protest further, but nothing seemed to come out, and he then lost his chance, as Hennessey stood up with a cold smile and said, 'Thank you for your cooperation, Chief Inspector. It is much appreciated, so it is. Now, I am sure you will want to get these changes on your area's CID sorted out as quickly as possible, so I'll not detain you any further. Good afternoon.'

For a second Ricketts hesitated, as if he was considering standing his ground, but then apparently realising he was on a total loser, out-gunned and out-manoeuvred, he stumbled to his feet, threw Kate a look of absolute venom and promptly left the office without even a polite "au revoir"!

Hennessey made no comment on the exchange between her and the DCI after he had left, and Kate did her best to try to conceal her glee at the outcome, even though she knew she would pay for it with Ricketts when things returned to normal.

The briefing of the whole major investigation team followed in the incident room, which was now up and running, with the regular principal positions on the team identified, including the deputy SIO, which had been filled by a wizened, cynical DI named Fergus Smith, the crime scene manager who Kate had already met, plus the office manager, exhibits officer and a number of other standard posts. Individual "action teams", comprising Uniform and plainclothes officers, were then set up to carry out the specific physical enquiries, interviews and searches that would be required as part of the investigation over time and Kate was well pleased to find herself and Jamie Foster assigned to continue solely on investigating the Tammy Robinson abduction side of the investigation, leaving the rest of their colleagues free to follow up on the murder itself. There was no definite evidence to indicate that the two crimes were connected, but, like Kate, Hennessey nursed a shrewd suspicion on the grounds of probability that they were, which meant that the Robinson case could hold the key to it all. But Kate was acutely conscious of the fact that what they had been allocated was a potential poisoned chalice. They *had* to deliver the goods — failure was not an option — and no one would be more pleased if it all went pear-shaped than Detective Chief Inspector Toby Ricketts!

* * *

Mother was furious with him when she found out what had happened. She had previously assumed everything had gone according to plan and that Tammy Robinson was no longer a problem. At first, he'd been too frightened to tell her the truth. Instead, he had kept quiet about things and had simply gone back to work on Tuesday morning as usual after clearing up the house, trying to pretend to himself that nothing bad had happened and hoping it would all go away. But it hadn't, as it never had after previous faux pas he had made, and when he'd heard the newsflash on the local radio about Tammy Robinson being found and taken to hospital, suffering from some sort of trauma, he'd had to finally admit to Mother that he had fouled up yet again. As he'd expected, she had gone mad, saying some very hurtful things to him, calling him weak, useless and a total excuse for a man.

She'd said he should have made sure the Robinson girl was dead before he'd put her in the car (but he already knew that). Then, when she had escaped, he should have searched the reserve until he had found the little bitch and finished her off once and for all, not just given up and run away with his tail between his legs. What if she had got a look at his face when he'd lifted her out of the car boot? She would be able to identify him to the police, and what would happen to his poor old mother if he was locked up and there was no one left to look after her?

As for the woman he'd killed, just dumping her body in the undergrowth and leaving her there had been really stupid. He'd had a spade with him, hadn't he? So, why hadn't he used it to bury her? Then there would have been less of a risk of her being found. As it was, someone was bound to stumble on to her corpse eventually — another rambler, a dog walker, or maybe even a ranger — and what then? There was every chance that he had left DNA traces at the scene, which could be used to tie him into the murder. He was a bloody idiot and he deserved to get caught!

Still smarting over the tirade of rebukes he had received, he nevertheless knew Mother was right. (Weren't mothers always right?) He had made a pig's ear of everything and he needed to sort out what he could before it was too late. When Mother had calmed down, she had told him what had to be done and, though he knew it would be very risky, he was determined to do what she said and try to make amends for at least one of his mistakes. Then maybe he would be able to sleep at night again . . .

* * *

Kate's mobile rang at lunchtime, as she and Jamie Foster were grabbing a quick bite to eat in the police canteen.

'Detective Inspector Lewis?' a woman's voice said.

When Kate confirmed the fact, there was a slight hesitation, then the caller said, 'This is Mrs Joan Wiseman, er, Gabrielle's mother.'

'Ah, yes, Mrs Wiseman,' Kate replied, pushing her plate to one side, 'what can I do for you?'

'Would it be possible for you to call and see Gabs and me? She's, er, off school at the moment, a bit poorly. Only she has something to tell you.'

Kate felt a quickening of her pulse and threw a glance at Foster. 'That's fine, Mrs Wiseman, we'll be right there.'

'I take it lunch is over?' Foster said, as Kate ended the call and stood up, and he snatched his last corner of sandwich from his plate as he followed her out of the canteen.

Mrs Wiseman answered the door even before the detectives reached it.

'Gabs is in the sitting room,' she said, lowering her voice, 'but she's very upset, so please be gentle with her? She's only thirteen and very unsure of herself.'

Kate nodded. 'Of course,' she replied, 'but could you give us an idea what this is about first?'

'She was ill at school this morning,' Mrs Wiseman explained, 'and she had to be sent home. About an hour ago, she opened up to me, and it seems she's been having bad dreams over something quite nasty that happened to her a few days ago. Apparently, a man exposed himself to her and her friends on a footpath, which runs through a wood opposite the school.'

'Did he indeed?'

'She was too embarrassed to tell my husband or myself about it before and, unbeknown to us, she's been having sleepless nights ever since . . . Thinking about what happened to Tammy Robinson, I felt you ought to be told.'

Kate's expression was grim. 'We should be told about something like this anyway, whether it's connected to Tammy or not,' she said. 'You've done the right thing.'

Gabrielle was slumped in a big armchair, dressed in a T-shirt, jeans and a pair of enormous, fluffy slippers. She was chewing at her nails when they walked in. Her eyes looked red and puffy, and she was trembling a little.

Kate dropped into a chair opposite her, motioning to Foster to take a seat further back by the door, so as not to overwhelm the schoolgirl. Joan Wiseman deposited herself on the arm of her daughter's chair and reached down to grasp her hand.

'Hello again, Gabrielle,' Kate began, giving her an encouraging smile. 'Your mum says you're not feeling very well at the moment and that you're off school?'

There was a hesitant nod.

'Well, I'm sorry to hear that. It's not nice being ill. Now, your mum also tells me that there's something that's been bothering you and keeping you awake at night?'

A quick, heavy-lidded glance across at her.

'Is it about something you've seen?'

Gabrielle didn't answer, but looked up at her mother, as if seeking her permission before saying anything. It reinforced Kate's previous impression of the girl, in that she lacked the precocity that had been attributed to Tammy and which might possibly be also applied to her other friend, Mandy. She was obviously very nervous, and lacking in confidence, more like a typical, naive youngster of eleven or twelve instead of thirteen.

'Tell the police lady what happened,' Joan Wiseman said quietly. 'You're not in any trouble.'

Gabrielle swallowed hard and cleared her throat, studying her slippers and wriggling her toes inside them. 'There was this-this man,' she said. 'He was in the woods by the footpath when I walked by.'

'And which footpath was this?' Kate asked, trying to lead her in gently.

'It's-it's called Ellis Drove and it's opposite the school. Me, Tams and-and Mand sometimes use it to get to school and home afterwards, so we don't have to go the long way round.'

Kate gave her another smile. 'And were Tammy and Mandy with you at the time you saw this man?'

Gabrielle shook her head. 'I was on my own.'

'Can you remember when that was?'

Gabrielle frowned. 'I-I think it was about four thirty last-last Thursday.'

'Did the man speak to you?'

'Yes. He-he said, "Hello, pretty girl," and smiled at me.'

'Was that all?'

She stared into space for a few seconds, then yet again looked at her mother, her face growing redder. 'No.'

'He did something else, did he?'

'Yes, he-he—' She broke off and Kate saw the tears starting to come again.

'Take your time,' Kate said quietly and waited patiently for her to carry on.

Gabrielle sniffed and wiped her nose on her sleeve. 'He-he did something really disgusting.'

Kate got out of her chair and, going across to her, bent down and rested a hand on her knee, squeezing it for a second.

'I think I know what he did, but you have to tell me in your own words. Do you think you can do that?'

Gabrielle nodded and, after more hesitation, blurted, 'His trousers were undone and he-he pulled his thingy out and showed it to me.'

'His willie?'

'Yes.'

Kate's mouth tightened. 'Did he say anything else?'

'He said something like, "Do you like that?".'

'What did you do?'

'I didn't do anything. I was too frightened. Then some people came along the drove and he ran away into the bushes.'

Kate thought for a second, before continuing. 'Had you seen this man before?'

Gabrielle nodded. 'A couple of times. hanging about the footpath, but he's never said anything before. Sometimes he has a little, spotty dog with him on a lead.'

'Was there a car parked nearby that could have been his?'

She shook her head. 'You can't drive a car along the drove. There's rails at each end.'

'Have your friends ever said anything about him to you?'

'Only Tam and Mandy.' She gave a shy, self-conscious smirk. 'They call him "Mr Creepy", cause he's so weird and they say he's always staring at them.'

'Has he exposed himself to them before?'

She hesitated, then nodded. 'They told me he had, but they said they just laughed at him. Tam said she squirted a Coke bottle she was drinking from all over him.'

'What did he do when she did that?'

'She told me he got mad and said he'd fix her one day soon.'

'He actually said those words?'

'Yes. Then she said he just ran off, like he did with me.'

'Do you know when this was?'

She thought for a second. 'About a month ago, I think.'

'And Mandy?'

'I don't know.'

'Could you tell me what this man looks like?'

She blew her nose on a handkerchief her mother provided (not before time) and said, 'He was ever so skinny, with gaps in his teeth, and he had black straggly, dirty-looking hair right down to his shoulders.'

'Was there anything special about him?'

Gabrielle thought again before adding with an excited look in her eyes this time, 'He had a silver ring through one side of his nose and-and a long pink mark down his face.'

'What, like a scar?'

'Yes.

'What was he wearing?'

'I think it was a long grey coat and red trousers.'

'Would you recognise him if you saw him again?'

'I don't know — I think so.'

There was a remarkable change in the young girl now she had unloaded what had obviously been plaguing her for several days and Kate was quite impressed with the description someone of her age had managed to give, but she felt sure she could probably provide more with a little coaching.

'You've done very well,' Kate went on. 'And now, if you and your mum don't mind, I'd like to get all this down in a written statement. Can we do that, do you think?'

Gabrielle looked apprehensive. 'I'm no good at writing.'

Kate laughed. 'Oh, don't you worry about that. I'll do it for you and if it's right you and your mum can then sign it. Okay?'

* * *

'Do you think this character is our man?' Foster said to Kate after they had left.

'Possibly,' Kate replied. 'After all, he did threaten Tammy, according to Gabrielle. So, we have a motive there. But whether he is Tammy's abductor or not, we need to get him off the street anyway for the sake of other children.'

'Fully agree with that, but we have to find out who he is first and that could take quite a bit of legwork.'

'Well, we can make a start by giving this Ellis Drove footpath the once-over and also check out the school when they finish this afternoon.'

'You don't seriously think this flasher will conveniently turn up on cue to help us out, do you?'

'Hardly, but there again, you never know. Anyway, once school is over, I think we should pop and see Mandy Williams at home and ask her why she didn't tell us about Mr Creepy when we were last there.'

* * *

Foster's lack of optimism proved justified. There was no sign of their man during the time the DS concealed himself among the trees by the footpath, and Kate had a similar negative result sitting in the CID car just down from the school when the final bell went and the youngsters poured out.

Giving Mandy Williams enough time to walk home, they called on her minutes after they saw her arrive. Her mother was clearly startled to see them when they rang the front doorbell, but politely showed them into the sitting room as before. Mandy joined them a few minutes later when her mother called upstairs to her. She was still dressed in her school uniform and looked bewildered.

'Mandy,' Kate said, sitting down opposite her. 'Is there something you haven't told me?'

The schoolgirl looked irritable. 'About what?' she retorted, her voice sharp and aggressive.

Her mother, sitting across the room, tutted. 'Come on, Mand,' she said, 'just answer the officer's question, there's a good girl.'

Mandy shrugged. 'There's nothing I haven't told you,' she said confidently.

'How about Mr Creepy?' Foster put in from the chair beside Kate.

Her eyes widened appreciably. 'Who told you about him?' she demanded.

Neither Kate or Foster answered her, but waited for her to say something instead. Seconds later, the truth seemed to dawn on her and the pretty face twisted into an unbecoming sneer. 'That silly bitch, Gabrielle, I bet. She's just a bloody loser.'

'Mandy!' her mother exclaimed, plainly shocked. 'That's not nice.'

Not nice? Kate thought. The remark was a lot worse than not nice, coming as it did from a fourteen-year-old kid. It appeared that Mandy Williams needed substantially more parental discipline than she was getting.

She controlled her natural impulse to snap back at the teenager, instead trying another approach. 'Gabrielle was very upset because of what this man allegedly did a few days ago by exposing himself to her. Did you know about that?'

She shrugged. 'Might have done.'

Kate sharpened her tone, tiring of her insolent bravado. 'Well, did you, or didn't you? She says she told you about what happened.'

'So what? Tam and me thought it was hilarious. She's such a scaredy-cat, is Gabs. Would pee herself if she spotted Father Christmas.'

'Has he ever exposed himself to you?'

'Could have. Creepy is always hanging about near the school, but he's harmless. He's just a sick perv and Tam and me just laugh at him.'

Kate had to grit her teeth. 'Just answer the question, young lady,' she snapped. 'Has he ever exposed himself to you?'

'Okay, okay,' she shouted angrily. 'Once, yes.'

'When was this?'

'A few weeks ago, on Ellis Drove.'

'Can you remember the day and date?'

She glared at Kate. 'No, I can't, okay? But it was the day after the final of the home netball match, I remember that.'

Jenny Williams looked white-faced and shocked. 'But why didn't you tell your father or me about that, Mand? It's a serious matter.'

There came an abrupt change in the schoolgirl's manner with her mother's intervention, and she was immediately on the defensive. 'Tam said not to,' she replied sullenly. 'She said if our friends at school knew we'd reported it, we'd look like scaredy-cat losers ourselves and end up being laughed at.'

'Didn't it occur to you after Tammy disappeared that this man could have been responsible for abducting her?' Foster cut in again.

There were tears in Mandy's eyes now and it was apparent that she had lost all her bravado. 'But-but Tam's been found, hasn't she?' she pleaded. 'They say she's in hospital.'

'Yes,' Kate said brutally. 'Mr Creepy is still out there, though, and if he was behind her kidnapping, he could well do the same thing to another of your friends, and next time things may not turn out so well.'

Mandy was sobbing now and Kate waited while her mother consoled her with a cuddle and smoothed her hair. Then she said, 'What's important now is for us to find this man and we need your help. Have you any idea who he is, or where he lives?'

Mandy pulled away from her mother, dried her eyes on a handkerchief and shook her head. 'He always comes through the woods to the drove and sometimes he has a little dog with him. Tam said she thought he might be living near the old peat works.'

'Could you describe him and say how old you think he is? Would he be as old as my colleague here, for instance?'

She studied Foster for a moment, then said, 'No, not that old. Maybe about forty.'

Kate threw Foster a glance and saw the affronted look on his face.

'He's very thin, has long black hair and he has a pink scar on his face and gappy teeth,' Mandy added, then came out with something Kate didn't know. 'He has a limp too — the left leg, I think.'

'Brilliant!' Kate replied, pleased with her sudden enthusiasm and eye for detail.

'Now, how about we put all this down in a written statement I can write for you?'

Before Mandy could reply, her mother cut in quickly. 'No, I don't think that's a good idea at all, Inspector. I want Mandy kept out of this business until I've had a chance to talk to my husband.'

'But if we bring this man in, we'll need Mandy as a witness to corroborate what Gabrielle has told us, as both the girls are under-age and we would need to show a link.'

'Sorry, but the answer is no. I would have to speak to my husband first anyway. Now, if you're finished, Inspector, I would be grateful if you both left.'

Kate was furious as she walked back to the car. 'No bloody corroboration, no case,' she grated. 'Same old story. We're constantly being criticised for not cutting crime and then when we need a witness to prosecute someone, Joe public refuses to cooperate.'

Foster grunted. 'Don't fret, boss,' he said sourly. 'She wouldn't have been much of a witness anyway if she couldn't even assess someone's age properly. Fancy thinking I was actually over forty? Bloody cheek!'

Despite the way she felt, Kate couldn't help seeing the funny side of that and chortled a reply, which only deepened his scowl.

CHAPTER 8

There was nothing on the descriptive index of the police national computer. Kate found that out when she accessed the system back in the incident room. She then paid a visit downstairs to the office of the local intelligence officer. She found her husband, Hayden, sitting at his desk with a mug of coffee on one side and two Bounty bars on the other. He was peering at the computer screen, but, rather than police crime data, he had accessed a computer game and was engaged in a futuristic battle between rival alien forces.

He swung round guiltily when Kate threw open his door and strode in. 'Ah, Kate,' he said, hastily shutting the screen down, 'I was just, er—'

'I could see what you were doing, Hayd,' she snapped, and flicked idly through the wire tray beside the computer, which appeared to be full of printouts and copies of forms completed by uniformed patrol officers following vehicle and person checks. 'But this force doesn't have an interplanetary task force!'

He made a face. 'I, er, was on a break,' he said. 'Nothing wrong with that.'

She snorted. 'Your whole life is one long break, you lazy prick,' she retorted. 'You've certainly found your ideal niche here.'

'Hey, that's slanderous,' he protested. 'I resent that sort of remark coming from a senior rank.'

'*Resemble it*, more like,' she said. 'Well, now you can do some proper work.' She placed a typed copy of Gabrielle's statement on the desk in front of him. 'Read that, digest it and do some digging for me. The offender the schoolgirl describes doesn't come up on PNC's descriptive index. But I know you keep quite a lot of information here on local faces. So trawl through it and let me know if you hit on anything. Do you think you can manage that — between breaks?'

Then she turned on her heel and walked out, shaking her head and wondering when her husband would ever start working for the benefit of the job rather than himself.

* * *

He had seen on the detective films he'd watched that professional criminals usually liked to reconnoitre target premises before carrying out their crimes, so as to judge the lie of the land and not get caught out by unwelcome surprises. Taking a leaf out of their book, he had decided to do exactly the same thing on the Wednesday evening after work.

They'd said in the local newspaper that Tammy Robinson was being kept in the local hospital under observation after suffering from some sort of traumatic shock, which had led to amnesia, and that she was currently under sedation and not in a fit state to be interviewed by police. The fact that she was not yet well enough to be questioned and had lost her memory into the bargain had to be good news. But as Mother had pointed out, it was unlikely that her traumatic condition would remain permanent and, as far as her amnesia was concerned, her memory could return at any time, which meant he had to silence the bitch before the police got to her and he ran the risk of being identified as her abductor. The thought of carrying out a job like that in a busy hospital ward frightened him to death, but it had to be done and, at least once he'd completed it, he'd be free to carry on with his project exactly as before, but with a new subject.

Before he left home, he dressed casually in a thin anorak over an open-necked blue shirt and matching jeans, with a blue baseball cap pulled down low over his glasses, and a COVID mask tucked into his pocket to slip on before entering the main hospital entrance. A lot of people still wore masks in hospital for fear of picking up viruses, even though the epidemic that had hit the country a few years before was more or less over. Therefore, he didn't think the thing would attract undue attention, while at the same time it would enable him to conceal most of his face from scrutiny and subsequent identification.

He was very nervous when he drove into the hospital car park, but he managed to pull himself together after ten to fifteen minutes sitting quietly in the car watching all the comings and goings. Then, taking a deep breath, he got out and walked across the service road to the front entrance and through the automatic doors into the hospital's main reception area. To his surprise, no one challenged him as he passed the reception desk and entered the corridor beyond, and he noticed that quite a few of the visitors and some of the uniformed staff wore COVID masks, which meant, as he'd thought before, that he wouldn't look out of place. He was also pleased to see that signs to all the main departments, including outpatients, specialist areas, like X-ray, physiotherapy and endoscopy, and the dozen or so wards, were clearly displayed, obviating the need to ask a member of staff for directions. But although the information was unambiguous, that in itself was of little real help to him, since it didn't and couldn't tell him where to find a particular patient, like Tammy Robinson!

He was left with no option but to carry out a laborious foot-slogging check of each ward in turn, starting from the ground floor upwards and using one of a bank of lifts halfway along the main corridor. He made for the clearly signed Intensive Care Unit first, but was prevented from entering it by locked double doors allowing access only with a staff security card. Frustrated, he turned back, trying to reassure himself that the girl was unlikely to be in the ICU anyway, since, according to the newspaper he had read, she was not a critical case but simply being kept in under observation.

Thereafter, however, his search was given an unexpected boost by the discovery that, as far as the rest of the general wards were concerned, he had hit official patient visiting times, and in the to-ing and fro-ing chaos that resulted there was little attention paid to whoever was visiting who. Only once was he asked by a suspicious nurse if she could help him and, using his wits after noting the list of patients on a whiteboard just inside the door, he was able to gain admittance by giving one of the names he had just picked out.

Ironically, it was straight after this that he actually stumbled upon what he was looking for. The uniformed figure sitting on a chair outside the closed door of a side room up ahead immediately gave the game away, and he had the presence of mind to nod to the policeman with a polite, 'Good evening,' as he walked past. The officer looked up briefly from the mobile he was interrogating, but said nothing in reply, simply returning to his web browsing, or whatever else it was he was doing.

His heart was thudding fit to burst as he slipped into an adjacent room, labelled *Toilet*, and stood for a moment behind the locked door, breathing heavily and staring fixedly into the mirror above the wash-hand basin, his hands gripping the rim as tightly as he could in momentary panic.

Damn it! The little bitch had got a police guard. He ought to have known that would be the case. Old Bill was bound to suspect that Tammy's abductor would try to get to her at some stage to shut her up. The policeman could have been stationed there for another patient, of course, except for the fact that the large notice affixed to the door in bold block capitals had borne Tammy Robinson's name and the precise instruction: *No Entry Without Express Police Authority Except for Medical Staff*.

So, he had found her at last, but what good was that if he couldn't get to her? He needed to come up with a plan of when and how to slip past the "bluebottle" sitting outside the door before his luck ran out and he was rumbled.

Quietly leaving the toilet, he was about to head back to the car to do some serious thinking when he spotted a male cleaner in his distinctive scrubs chatting to a female colleague in the half-open doorway of another room, signed *Staff Only*. He was pleased to see that both were wearing COVID masks like himself.

'Heading home, are you?' he heard the woman say.

'Yeah,' came the reply. 'Just got to change out of this gear and I'll be away like a rocket.'

'Lucky you,' came the reply. 'On my break now, but I've still got ages on shift yet.' Then the woman wandered away, pointlessly pushing a wide broom along the floor ahead of her.

But even as her colleague disappeared into the staff room, a daring plan was already being hatched in the mind of Tammy's abductor. It would take a lot of brazen courage, but it could work and, right at that moment, he was pretty short on options. Okay, so he had meant to be carrying out nothing more than a reconnoitre at this stage, but with the main ward still full of visitors coming and going, and the nurses seemingly completely tied up, there wasn't a better time to do what had to be done. Fate had given him a golden opportunity and there was no way he could pass it up.

Tammy's police guard was far enough away on the other side of the corridor, his attention still focused on the mobile, so, casually turning to face a cork noticeboard on the wall behind him, he pretended to read the various health notices displayed on it while he waited for the male cleaner to reappear.

The man didn't take long. He re-emerged just a few minutes later, dressed in leathers and a full-face crash helmet, and headed off along the corridor towards the far end of the ward without giving him a second glance. Quickly side-stepping to the room the cleaner had just left, the intruder slipped through the door into a short corridor that lay beyond. There were two more doors opposite each other at the end, one labelled *Female* and the other *Male*. Taking a chance on the coast being clear, he pushed through the latter and winced as the door banged shut behind him.

He found himself in a larger room than he had anticipated. Shower and toilet cubicles occupied the far end, while wooden benches lined the right-hand wall and perhaps a dozen steel lockers stood against the left. He had feared that any lockers would be securely locked, and he was relieved to see that the doors of several of them had been carelessly left open, a couple with their keys still in the locks. He had no idea which locker belonged to the cleaner who had just left, but it didn't matter anyway, as two of the lockers held the same sort of uniform tunic and trousers he had been wearing, each hanging on a peg.

Closer inspection revealed that one pair was far too small, but the other turned out to be more or less the right size and he quickly pulled the uniform on over his clothes, also slipping on a pair of rubber gloves from a packet he found on the top shelf. Keeping the baseball cap and COVID mask in place, as before, hoping neither would be queried by anyone in the short time he would be visible on the ward, he studied himself briefly in a full-length mirror on the far wall to satisfy himself that he looked the part. Then, taking several deep breaths to steady his nerves, he grabbed one of two plastic buckets and a mop, which had been conveniently left in a corner and headed out into the main corridor.

The ward was still busy with visitors and he was relieved to see that the nursing staff were congregated in the various individual bays, dealing with patients and visitors alike. The policeman was still sitting on his chair in front of the side room, his mobile no longer in sight, and he looked up with a frown when the figure approached and made to go past him into the room.

'Hang on, mate,' he said, climbing to his feet and turning slightly to tap on the notice affixed to the door. 'See what it says there? No admittance.'

'I have to clean,' the man in the cleaner's uniform replied with a shrug. 'Are you saying I can't do my job?'

The policeman thought about that, grinned and said, 'So what's with the hat?'

'My choice,' was the glib answer. 'Speak to the sister if you don't like it. I just do what I'm told to do.'

Another frown. It was plain that the copper was not entirely happy, but at the same time didn't want to cause a ruck with the hospital administration. The sudden bleep of the personal radio attached to his chest made the decision for him. Reluctantly waving the bogus cleaner through, he turned away from him to answer the call.

The other smiled behind the mask and closed the room door behind him. He was in! All he had to do now was finish the job as quietly as possible and get away again before anyone decided to check on the condition of the patient. Then he would be totally in the clear.

Staring across the room at the young girl lying in the bed, he saw that she was fast asleep, a tube connected to one arm from a machine on a trolley beside it. She was obviously still under sedation. He smirked. In one form of sleep straight into a more permanent one, he said to himself. He noticed something else too — a couple of extra pillows left on a chair in a corner. Someone had been very careless and he couldn't have wished for anything better. Setting the bucket and mop down by the chair, he picked up one of the pillows and advanced slowly and as quietly as possible towards the bed, the pillow held out in front of him — and it was as he bent over the sleeping figure with it raised above Tammy's face that her eyes suddenly opened and she stared straight up at him . . .

* * *

Hennessey was in her office when Kate dropped in to tell her about the line they were following after Gabrielle Wiseman's complaint, but she was pipped at the post.

'Just the person,' Hennessey exclaimed, sitting back in her chair and waving her to a seat before she could say anything.

'Hospital have rung to say Tammy Robinson is out of sedation. She's still emotionally fragile, but fully compos mentis and, thankfully, seems to have recovered her memory.'

'I'll get over there to see her right away.'

Hennessey shook her head. 'They've asked us to hold fire until tomorrow. She's not quite up to interviews at the moment. Apparently her parents visited earlier and there was a wee bit of a ruck between her and her da', who was asked to leave.'

'That doesn't surprise me. They don't get on and the man's an arsehole.'

'Aye, I feel inclined to agree with you. What across the water we would call a desperate gobshite. He rang here a short time ago, demanding to know why you didn't tell him and his wife about their wee girl's shaved head before they visited her today. He had some very impolite things to say about you.'

Kate gave a rueful smile. 'I must confess, I was wondering how he would react when he clapped eyes on her,' she replied, 'and the fact that he has reacted the way he has suggests to me that he was genuinely shocked, which means it's unlikely he was involved in her abduction in the first place, otherwise he wouldn't have bothered doing anything.'

'So, this was a test then?'

'Something like that, yes, although to be honest I wasn't that sure he would come back to me on it.'

Hennessey made a face. 'Bit of a callous thing to do to grieving parents, though, wasn't it?'

Kate shrugged, remembering that Foster had said much the same thing to her after they had first seen Tammy themselves. 'Tony Robinson is hardly a grieving parent,' she replied. 'The guy is a selfish, uncaring excuse for a man and I needed to make sure he was not something else too.'

'So, he's no longer a suspect, in your view?'

'Let's say he's a bit less of one, but he's not out of the woods entirely as far as I'm concerned.'

Hennessey nodded, looking disappointed. 'And you've no others in the frame?'

'We might have one possible,' Kate replied, and quickly told her about Gabrielle Wiseman's "flasher".

Hennessey listened carefully to what she had to say, but towards the end of her account commented gloomily, 'Sure, he doesn't sound like the sort of clever, calculating character we are looking for in the abduction of Tammy Robinson.'

Regrettably Kate had to agree with her. 'But we have to follow up on the issue,' she said. 'We can't afford to let something like this go, involving as it does vulnerable children.'

'Of course not,' Hennessey acknowledged, 'so crack on with it anyway and see what comes out of it. And by the way, we've identified our murder victim at the reserve from documents recovered from her coat pockets. Her name was Sandra Hay, she was twenty-four years old and she hailed from Bath. She was one of a group of six college students on some sort of practical wildlife photography trip. She was staying with her boyfriend, Josh Philmore, and the others on a glamping site near the reserve.

'According to Philmore, they had a row and she stormed off with her camera late on Monday night to take some nocturnal pictures, and when she hadn't returned by the early hours they went looking for her. They couldn't find her, so they returned to the glamping site, thinking she might have gone back there. She hadn't, so later that morning, on the Tuesday, they reported her to the nearest nick, which happened to be here at Highbridge.

'We're interviewing the five of them downstairs just now, but at this stage we don't believe any of them had anything to do with her death, though we'll keep an open mind until we've finished with them—'

'Except that you say Hay and her boyfriend had a row,' Kate interjected. 'Could be he followed her into the wood, did the deed and then played the rest.'

'Aye, except they all claim to have been together virtually the whole time, so each one alibis the other.'

'Then it looks like Tammy's abductor has to be in the frame for the murder too?'

'It's the most likely conclusion to be drawn under the circumstances, so it is. But on an interesting note, the group who went to search the reserve all say they heard a car start up and leave at speed shortly after they had been wandering around calling Sandra's name. But by the time they found the car park, it was empty.'

'No sighting of the car then?'

Hennessey shook her head. 'Unfortunately not, but, ironically, from their account of how they got to the car park using a narrow footpath, it seems more than likely that they passed by the very spot where Hay's body had been dumped, although it would have been difficult for them to have spotted a body lying there in the dark, especially when it had been left in thick undergrowth.'

'Back to square one again then.'

'Aye, so it seems, and it means that at the moment your flasher fella is about the only potential lead we've got.'

'Which, if you'll pardon the expression,' Kate replied with a hollow laugh, 'is about as solid a lead as a wet fart in a storm.'

'What a nice poetic analogy,' Hennessey commented drily, giving her a funny look. 'It's obvious you have a quare way with words.'

CHAPTER 9

The scream was loud and piercing, stabbing through the would-be assassin's ears like a knife and sending him staggering backwards, as if it had a physical force all of its own. He very nearly lost his balance, but recovered instantly and, in the grip of panic, virtually threw himself at the door.

The police guard burst through at the same moment, but the panic-stricken killer was in no mood to exchange pleasantries. Slammed back into the door jamb, which expelled half the breath from his body, the policeman buckled up and tottered across the corridor on folding legs as his assailant raced back through the ward, barging staff and visitors aside, before disappearing through the main doors with the fleetness of an Olympic runner.

Even as the ward was trying to come to terms with what had just happened, and the dazed policeman was breathlessly gasping into his personal radio, their quarry was streaking down the stairs to the next floor. By the time hospital security had been alerted and were sealing off all exits, the fugitive was behind the wheel of his car and in a queue heading out of the car park and on to the main road into the gathering dusk . . .

* * *

Kate found the LIO's office empty and Hayden conspicuous by his absence when she went to see how he was getting on with the checks she had asked him to do. She didn't have to go looking for him. Glancing at her watch, she realised he must have already gone home after completing his eight-hour duty.

'Bloody office worker,' she muttered, and she was about to follow his example and head off herself after what had become a very long day when the call came through on her mobile from the control room. Twenty minutes later she was at the hospital and meeting up with the shaken police guard outside the half-open door of Tammy Robinson's room. Inside she could see a nurse and a doctor by the young girl's bed. Tammy was sitting on the edge of the bed and the doctor seemed to be checking her pulse.

'How the hell could this have happened?' Kate demanded quietly, but forcefully, after being given a short briefing on the murder attempt. 'We put this girl under close protection precisely because we thought her abductor might come after her.'

The policeman looked very pale, knowing full well he was in big trouble over the security lapse. 'Cleaners had been in before and this one was wearing the same uniform,' he said defensively. 'How was I to know he wasn't legit? He even had a bloody bucket and mop with him.'

'But you said he was wearing a blue baseball cap. That wasn't part of the uniform, was it?'

The policeman scowled. 'His choice was what he told me,' he replied. 'I'm not hospital staff, so I don't know what they're allowed to wear.'

Kate nodded brusquely, seeing his point and cooling down a little. 'Was she hurt?' she asked.

He shook his head. 'He never actually got to her. He was about to try and smother her with a pillow when I ran in after she screamed.'

'But you must have got a good look at this guy if, as you say, he slammed into you?'

He shook his head again. 'It was all such a blur and he was wearing one of those COVID masks and specs, with the baseball cap pulled down low over his eyes, so not much of his face was visible.' He hesitated. 'All I can say is that he was tall, thinly built, and he had a funny smell.'

'Funny smell? What do you mean?'

Kate glimpsed Deirdrie Hennessey and Jamie Foster striding towards her and turned to meet them.

'Dunno really,' the policeman went on. 'As if he had BO.'

'BO?' Hennessey queried, joining in on the conversation after evidently picking up on its drift.

'Yes, ma'am. Maybe because he was sweating.'

'So, a tall thin man, wearing a blue cap, who might have had BO?' Kate echoed drily. 'Brilliant!'

But Hennessey had lost interest in the interrogation as the doctor had just come out of the room. 'Is Tammy okay?' she asked.

He nodded. 'Very shaken,' he replied. 'But it seems he didn't hurt her. Your officer got there just in time.'

'Can we see her?'

He thought about that for a second, frowning, then nodded. 'Just one of you,' he said. 'But no longer than five minutes, and she needs careful handling. She is still highly emotional, although I have given her something to try and quieten her down a little.'

Hennessey stared at Kate and nodded towards the door. 'Your side of the case,' she said. 'So, you should be the one to have a wee chat with her. We'll wait out here.'

Tammy was back in bed when Kate entered the room. Her eyes followed her as she approached. Kate smiled and sat on the edge of the bed.

'Hi, Tammy,' she said. 'My name's Kate, Kate Lewis. I'm a police officer. We've been very worried about you.'

Tears formed in the big brown eyes and Tammy's mouth quivered. 'He cut off all my hair,' she whispered, not mentioning the attempt on her life. Maybe that was less important to her!

Kate smiled again. 'I know,' she said, 'but it will grow again, honestly. It will take a little time, but it will grow back, as before. You just have to be patient.'

'He put me in a cage.'

Kate stiffened. 'A cage?' she repeated quietly.

'Yes, like the cages you keep dogs in, only . . . only bigger. Said he wanted to punish me — him and his mother.'

'His mother?'

'Yes, he-he kept on about her. Said they were doing all this together.'

'Did you meet her?'

'Never saw her.'

'And why would they want to put you in a cage?'

The schoolgirl shrugged, tears now running in tiny rivulets down her cheeks. 'Don't know. Said . . . said I was an animal and a bad influence, and I had to be punished. Kept . . . kept on about me needing to redeem myself.'

Kate chose her words carefully. 'Did he touch you in any way? Do you know what I mean?'

''Course I know what you mean. I am fourteen.' There was a note of defiance in her tone at this point. Then she shook her head. 'Dunno what he did to me when he cut off my hair, 'cause he drugged me. But I don't think he raped me, or anything like that. I reckon I would know if he had.'

'It might be necessary to have you examined, just to make sure.'

Tammy shook her head firmly. 'No way. I said he didn't and that's that. So, you can forget it.'

Kate didn't pursue the issue any further, knowing that from a forensic point of view it would be a bit late after so many days now anyway. Then, fully aware of the limited time she had left, she tried to home in on some other specifics. 'This cage you talked about, where was it?'

'In a cellar.'

'And where was the cellar?'

'Don't know. There were steps up to a house, that . . . that's all I remember. I fell down them when I tried to . . . to escape. Hurt my head, Then I blacked out.'

'Do you remember being taken in a car to the woods where we found you?'

Tammy nodded a little uncertainly. 'A bit. I was in the boot, I think, and he pulled me out.' She frowned heavily, trying to recollect more. 'A woman screamed. Then I ran away and hid under a tree.'

'Did you see this woman?'

She shook her head, abruptly blurting out, 'He-he tried to kill me just now.'

'Yes, I know. But he won't be allowed to get near you again, I promise. Do you know who this man was, or what he looked like?'

The girl shook her head. 'He wore a black hood all the time before and he had a mask on tonight.'

'Is there anything you remember about him? What about his voice? Could you say whether you'd heard it before?'

Another shake of the head. 'No, it sounded sort of funny, as if he had done something to it so it couldn't be recognised.'

'What sort of voice was it? Did it have an accent?'

'Just a voice.'

'We believe he pretended to be a lad you met on an internet chatroom and that he snatched you when you arranged to meet him at the rec. Is that right?'

She nodded. 'He-he sent me a picture. Said his name was Gerry, but he was not Gerry.'

'Where is this picture?'

'On my mobile.'

'And where is your mobile?'

'He-he took it.'

Inwardly, Kate swore. 'Can you tell me the name of the chatroom you used?'

Tammy frowned and pressed the fingers of one hand into her forehead, as if she was getting confused. 'Can't . . . can't think. Don't want to talk anymore.'

She began twisting the sheets with both hands and repeatedly taking deep breaths. It was plain that she was not far off hyperventilating. Kate realised her time for questions had almost run out, and a sharp authoritative voice from the door then emphasised that fact.

'I think you should finish now, officer. She's had enough.'

Kate nodded to the nurse, but, despite feeling sorry for the schoolgirl, she was conscious of the fact that she still had a job to do, and she steeled herself for a final question. 'Just one last thing, Tammy. If you remember the name of that chatroom, would you ask the nurse for a piece of paper, so you can write it down for me? It's very important.'

'Officer!' the nurse snapped again. 'I said that's it.'

Kate made an irritable grimace at the further intervention. 'Would you do that for me, Tammy?'

'Inspector!'

Tammy shook her head. She was beginning to visibly shake. 'Don't know,' she gasped miserably. 'Don't know.'

Kate sighed. 'Well, you get some sleep now anyway, love,' she said, squeezing her arm reassuringly. 'A police officer will be outside this door all night. Okay?'

'Kate?' the girl called as she got to the door, a renewed strength in her voice. She turned quickly. 'Yes, Tammy?'

'You-you will catch him, won't you?'

Kate hesitated. 'You can bet on it,' she replied with another reassuring smile, but she hoped she sounded a lot more confident than she felt.

Hennessey was waiting tensely outside the room when she left and the hard-bitten detective drew her to the side. 'Well?' she asked. 'What did the wee girl say?'

Kate shrugged and her boss didn't seem particularly impressed when she told her. 'A few pieces of the jigsaw put together then,' Hennessey summarised, 'especially the bit about the cage, but it's a pity we couldn't get the details of that chatroom to follow up on.'

Kate nodded. 'And as for her mobile, her abductor has probably already dumped it in a rhyne somewhere.'

Hennessey grunted. 'Looks like plusses all the way then,' she said sarcastically. 'Anyway, I'll leave you with it. Let me know if one of our eagle-eyed patrols happens to pick up yer man, will you?'

'Yeah,' Kate replied under her breath. 'But I reckon we're fresh out of miracles.'

* * *

He had got away, but only just. Tammy's would-be killer was shaking again when he pulled over into a layby a few miles from the hospital to try to calm himself down. Another bloody cock-up on his part. He seemed to be making a habit of it. He closed his eyes for a few moments and leaned back against the headrest as he tried to marshal his thoughts. Mother would not be at all pleased about this. She would despair of him. And he had been so close to achieving what he'd set out to do too. The little tart had been right there at his mercy and in just a couple of minutes he could have quietly snuffed the life out of her and left again with no one being any the wiser. He'd been so sure she would still be under sedation — that was what the newspaper had said — but she'd obviously been nothing of the sort, only dozing. Just his luck.

On the plus side, at least his face had been covered, so it was unlikely that the copper, or Tammy, would have got a good enough look at him to be able to identify him later, and he had been wearing the rubber gloves he'd found, so there wouldn't be any prints or DNA traces left behind. As for the uniform, he'd screwed it up with the gloves and dumped the lot in a refuse bin in the car park on the way out and any security camera would have had a job connecting the driver of the car that had unhurriedly joined the queue of departing visitors with the murderous attempt that had just been made on a patient's life. Yeah, it seemed like he was in the clear, but it was an empty achievement. Tammy Robinson was still alive and half the county's police force was certain to be out looking for him now. Whatever Mother said, he had to stand up to her and insist on keeping his head down for the time being. That was what he'd intended doing after killing the woman in the woods. But Mother had goaded him into trying to fix Tammy Robinson instead. Only when he was sure he was above suspicion would he resume the project, that's what he'd tell her.

But whatever he said to her, he knew that for himself it would be difficult to hold back even for a short time. Having already tasted the sheer sexual exhilaration he got from the act of dominance and the exercise of punishment, the compulsive itch to start again was still there embedded in him, despite what had just happened. Furthermore, he knew from past experience that that itch would get stronger and stronger, like a kind of heroin addiction, until it would become almost impossible to resist. He had succumbed to it where he'd been living before and, though they had never found the kid he'd snatched, he'd had to move to be on the safe side. His urges did worry him, they always had, but at the same time they gave him something to look forward to . . .

He was so wrapped up in his thoughts that he didn't hear the car and the next instant the flashing red and blue strobe had filled his rear window. Seconds later the flashlight was blazing in his face from beside the driver's door. His heart sank. Even without the strobe, the figure peering into the car from behind the flashlight was unmistakable.

Gritting his teeth, he flicked on the ignition and operated the window mechanism.

'Evening, sir,' the policeman said. 'Mind telling me why you've stopped here?'

He thought quickly. 'Oh, I felt a bit sick, so I thought it best to pull over for a few moments, officer.'

He waited for the anticipated instruction to get out of the car, but to his surprise it never came. Instead, the policeman seemed to start. Then he suddenly leaned further into the car. 'Oh, it's you, sir,' he said with a short laugh. 'I didn't realise who you were at first.'

And it was at this point that recognition dawned for him too. It was the policeman who lived a few doors down from his home and had often exchanged pleasantries with him off-duty when he'd passed him working in his garden on his way to the village store.

'Ray Kendrick, sir,' the other continued. 'How's your mum?'

'Oh, er, still quite poorly,' he replied. 'Old age, you know.'

The policeman nodded. 'No fun getting old, is it?' he said. 'Been somewhere nice today then, have you?'

He thought quickly. 'Er, no, not really. Just to, er, the garage for some fuel.'

'What, the local garage? Open again now, are they? I thought they had closed.'

Bugger it! He'd forgotten about that. 'Er, n-no, the one on the A38 near Axbridge.'

'Crumbs, that's a bit out of your way, isn't it?'

'No, I like the prices and there's a nice shop there Mother likes me to go to.'

A short laugh. 'We all have to do what Mother says, sir, don't we?'

Too bloody true, he mused. Now why don't you piss off and find some innocent motorist to pinch?

'Yes, Ray, and I'd better be getting home to Mother now. She'll be worried.'

The policeman stepped back. 'No problem, sir. It was just a routine check. You have a safe journey home now.'

He started the engine even as the policeman walked back to his car and was careful to pull away as smoothly as possible. Kangaroo petrol was the last thing he wanted to demonstrate under the circumstances.

He started to feel better when he saw that the police car was not following him, but had driven off in the opposite direction and, as he drove the final few miles home, his confidence began to return. It had been just a routine check. Kendrick had said so himself. The policeman hadn't even mentioned the incident at the hospital, so it didn't look like he was engaged in an area search for anyone. Anyway, he had been a fair distance from the hospital there and, thinking about it, it was unlikely a search would have been extended so far out so early on. No, he was still in the clear. The check had been coincidental and he could breathe easily again. But one thing he promised himself. He would pour himself a very large whisky when he got in!

* * *

Kate saw that lights were blazing from the windows when she pulled into the driveway of the little one-bed cottage she shared with Hayden in the village of Burtle.

'Don't bother to pull the curtains then, Hayd!' she muttered as she parked behind his prized, red Mk II Jaguar. Tired and frustrated after the evening's events, she felt a strong, vindictive desire to let one of the rear tyres down, but resisted the temptation.

Hayden was sitting in his accustomed armchair by the fireplace, a bottle of red wine on the coffee table in front of him, and a large full glass in one hand as he studied the classic car magazine spread out on his lap.

He waved his glass at her as she came through the door, spilling some of the contents down his shirt. 'Drink, old girl?' he asked and pointed to another glass beside the bottle.

Kate threw the car keys of her Mazda MX5 on to the half-moon table by the stairs and scowled at him, keen to pick a fight and looking for an excuse.

'You didn't hang about this afternoon then?' she said. 'You were long gone when I went downstairs to see you.'

He smiled affably. 'Office hours, old girl,' he said. 'On at eight and off at four, that's the deal as LIO.'

She dropped on to the settee opposite him and poured herself some wine. 'Pity you never seem to get to work before nine then, isn't it?' she retorted.

He waggled the glass at her in admonishment. 'Now, now,' he said, 'you shouldn't let jealousy get the better of you.'

Her mouth tightened before she even took a sip of her wine. 'So, what happened to those checks you were supposed to be doing for me? No time to do them between canteen trips then?'

He frowned. 'You're wrong,' he said slowly. 'Actually I did do them and I left the results on your desk in the incident room. I can't help it if you can't be bothered to look in your tray before going home.'

She felt embarrassed, but she was determined not to give way, even if she was at fault. 'Well, it just so happens that I was a bit tied up tonight. Someone tried to kill Tammy Robinson in her hospital bed.'

He gaped. 'What, the girl who was kidnapped? Gordon Bennett, is she okay?'

'Only just, and he got away.'

He set his wine glass back down on the coffee table. 'In which case, you might be very interested in what I turned up this afternoon. I left all the details in my note to you.'

Her bad mood was put on hold and she leaned forward eagerly. 'Can you remember what you said?'

He sniffed pompously. 'Of course. I never forget anything I say.'

She gave a sharp hiss of irritation. 'Just tell me, Hayd. Never mind the bullshit.'

He scowled at her use of abusive language, which was a particular hobbyhorse of his, but he chose not to pull her up on it this time. 'Joseph Mixbury, that was his name. Local ne'er do well. In his late thirties. Born in Slough. Nothing known about him until he turned up in this area about five years ago. Got work on the dustcarts for a time, then got sacked for inappropriate behaviour towards a member of the female office staff. So far as I can ascertain, hasn't worked since. Likes to call himself a poet. Lives in a grubby little cottage, courtesy of every social benefit known to man, on the site of a derelict peat works about a mile or so from the village where your misper lives.'

'Does he own the cottage?'

'Hardly. Seems he's just a squatter and the place, by all accounts, is pretty sub-standard anyway.'

'Why does the local authority let him live there?'

He shrugged. 'Nowhere else to put him, I suppose, and as long as he's content to live in squalor they're happy too. You know, out of sight, out of mind.'

'So what about him?'

'Well, he has been checked by police patrols on a number of occasions wandering about the area, sometimes riding an old bike, but more often than not with a little spotty dog on a lead, and mostly in the vicinity of the Windmill Academy school. He's also been seen at the local recreation ground, where your Tammy Robinson was abducted. He was given a hiding there about three months ago by an irate father for chatting up his eleven-year-old daughter, but Mixbury refused to support a complaint of assault against the dad. He has no previous convictions, but, in the light of his known dodgy behaviour and what Gabrielle Wiseman has now said in her statement, I felt he was certainly worth a pull.'

Kate chewed her lip. 'He should have been put on PNC, not just on the local box.'

Hayden held his palms out uppermost, in a gesture of "nothing to do with me". 'Maybe he should have, but there again up until now he's just been the subject of checks, with nothing concrete to suggest anything else. Maybe my predecessor felt we should just keep the info at local level until we had something more positive on him.'

Kate drained three quarters of her glass of wine. 'Well, maybe we have something on him now, but it's still not enough.'

'Do you think he could be Tammy Robinson's kidnapper?'

She shook her head. 'I very much doubt it from what I've already heard about him and what you've just said. Flashers tend to be weak, inadequate characters. Whoever took Tammy is in a completely different mould. But we need to follow up on Joseph Mixbury anyway. Trouble is, we don't want to spook him before we have sufficient evidence, and at present all we have is the uncorroborated word of one child. A friend of Gabrielle who claims he also flashed at her won't play ball.'

'So what *are* you going to do?'

'All I *can* do at this stage — have him watched.'

'That could take for ever, and for a proper round-the-clock surveillance operation you'd need a whole team to do it.'

'True, but I'm not thinking of full surveillance, more of a lower-key one-man observation job and we have to make a start and use what resource we've got available.'

'You won't be able to take anyone from CID or Uniform now. They're really short-staffed because of the current major investigation, and I doubt whether your SIO will agree to anyone being taken off one of her teams for something as relatively minor as this. You'd need to find someone who's buckshee.'

She smiled at him indulgently. 'Exactly, Hayd. You took the words right out of my mouth. Well, if not buckshee, someone who can be spared from a less key role — someone with maturity, good police experience and a keen eye for detail.'

The look of horror on his face was almost comical, as it dawned on him what she was driving at. 'No, no,' he gasped. 'I couldn't possibly . . .'

Her smile grew even broader. 'I'm sure the super will agree that you're the ideal man for the job,' she said. 'After all, you're an experienced CID officer, and now there's direct access to PNC through the incident room we can manage without an LIO for a few days.'

'But-but you know the problems I have with my feet—'

'Exactly, and the exercise will do wonders for them. Now, how about a nice snack before we go to bed? After all, you'll need to be fit and frisky for tomorrow afternoon.'

CHAPTER 10

It was doom and gloom at the Thursday morning major investigation briefing and Hennessey was in an irritable, caustic mood after full details of the incident at the hospital were communicated to the assembled personnel.

'A quare cock-up all round, so it was and I'm no coddin',' she said. 'For someone to be able to get to a victim supposedly under our protection, and then escape without trace within minutes, is unbelievable. Fortunately Tammy Robinson didn't suffer any injury, but it's no' a good look for the force, or ourselves. The public will think the whole inquiry is going arseways and the press will have a field day at the conference, which is the next aggravation on my agenda today.'

'CCTV, ma'am?' queried her bag-carrier, the wizened DI, Fergus Smith.

She shook her head. 'Plenty of that, and we've yet to go through all of it, but it was dusk and the car park was crowded with visitors leaving the hospital after visiting patients. There was a long queue at the barrier and yer man could have been in any one of the cars waiting to get out.'

'Fingerprints at the scene?' someone else asked.

Another shake of the head. 'Seen to be wearing rubber hospital-type gloves with his cleaner's uniform, so it's unlikely he left any prints or DNA evidence behind. We found what we think was his discarded uniform and gloves in a wastebin, but we don't know whether the lab will be able to get anything off the kit and, if they do and the gobshite has no pre-cons, we won't have anything to match it in criminal records anyway.'

'No witness descriptions?' another voice piped up.

Hennessey gave a brief cynical smile. 'Aye, tall and thin, wearing a cleaner's uniform, a blue COVID type mask that covered most of his face and a blue baseball cap pulled down low over his eyes. Should be easy to trace him with a description like that, don't you think?' Then she followed up on the sarcasm by saying almost resignedly, 'Ach, and I'm told he might have had BO.'

Her last remark was met with strangled laughter, which abruptly died when she glared round the room.

'A public appeal has gone out to media outlets,' Kate put in, 'so all we can do now is hope someone comes forward with information.'

'And if they don't?' one pessimist muttered under his breath, a comment that was loud enough to be picked up by Hennessey, and her icy gaze homed in on him. 'In which case, yous can all get off yer fat arses, and do some proper police work, Detective,' she grated, 'instead of faffin' about like a load of buck eejits!'

Closeted in the SIO's office shortly afterwards, Kate and Fergus shared the front page of the local newspaper Hennessey had peeled off from a pile on her desk and tossed across to them. It was the *Bridgwater Clarion* and the news story covering the hospital incident had been attributed to the paper's ex-crime reporter, now independent journalist, Debbie Moreton.

Kate was not surprised by the headline: *THE ONE THAT GOT AWAY — AGAIN!* There then followed a spiteful assassination of Hennessey and the major investigation team and the usual reference to *blundering Keystone Cops*. It didn't end there either. Moreton couldn't leave the piece without a mention of *Defective* (rather than Detective) *Inspector Kate Lewis* and the comment that: *it isn't surprising such a faux pas could occur when the force's very own female version of Don Quixote, Go It Alone Kate, has returned to Highbridge to tilt at windmills and put her own unique blot on the investigation.*

'She obviously likes you, Kate,' Fergus Smith chuckled.

'Yeah,' Kate responded, 'we're old muckers.'

'All the papers adopt the same general theme,' Hennessey cut in. 'The skitters must have really worked their socks off to get the story out by this morning. Chief won't like it, as we're being made to look like eejits. So, gents, we need a result of some sort PDQ. Any ideas? What about this flasher fella of yours, Kate? As you know, I don't think for one moment that he is Tammy Robinson's abductor, but an arrest is an arrest and it would at least show we are doing something.'

Kate seized the opportunity and updated her on Gabrielle Wiseman's complaint, putting forward her suggestion for observations on the suspected flasher, using Hayden for the purpose.

Hennessey raised a suspicious eyebrow. 'And how does our LIO feel about that?' she asked.

'Er, it would be fair to say he's not exactly overjoyed at the prospect,' Kate replied, trying to conceal a smirk.

Hennessey grunted. 'Aye, knowing a wee bit of him, I can see that.'

'But,' Kate went on quickly, 'he's shrewd, perceptive and an experienced copper and former detective. I feel confident he would be a good choice.'

'In view of our manpower situation, it seems to me that he's our *only* choice,' Hennessey said drily, then tutted. 'But I'll speak to your own superintendent, Mr Rutherford, and I'm sure he'll agree to what you're askin'.'

'Hayden *will* be pleased,' Kate said, more than a little tongue in cheek.

* * *

Hayden was certainly *not* pleased and when, a few hours later, in advance of school turnout, he propped himself on a tree stump on the edge of the woods overlooking their target's isolated cottage, he was even less pleased by the fact that it had begun to spit with rain. In front of him a bare, grassy slope led down to a fenced-off patch of land, comprising mainly ruined corrugated iron sheds and pools of evil-looking black water at the cottage's back. The peat extraction enterprise, which had once been set up there, had not been a successful family venture. Too small and lacking enough financial investment or business acumen to make it profitable, it had closed years ago, leaving the father and son who had set it up bankrupted, to the extent that they had decided to abandon their home to flee their creditors. The site was still up for sale, as the marshy land had little value and the cottage had fallen into such a state of disrepair over the years that no developer would even look at it as a potential investment opportunity.

Grabbing a doorstep sandwich from a paper bag in the pocket of his tatty Barbour coat, Hayden sat there scowling his resentment over his current situation and chewing noisily as the rain dribbled from the branches of the tree behind him and found its way down his neck inside his shirt. Kate's instructions still rang in his ears. 'Just watch the place and let us know if and when Mixbury goes walkabout,' she'd said. 'Jamie Foster and me will be about in the area and, if you see our man up to anything, call us.'

Yeah, he mused bitterly, well, for your information, Katie dear, he's unlikely to do any flashing on a day like this and, while you're driving around in a nice dry car, I happen to be sitting on a tree stump in a wood, getting soaked to the skin!

The future looked even less bright too. Hayden had done enough "obos", as they were called in police circles, to know that they tended to be very much hit and miss, and even those that produced a successful result rarely did so on the first day. So, it looked like he was going to be doing what he was doing now for several days at least and, going by the look of the sky, getting wetter each time until he ended up with pneumonia. Then there was the problem with his feet. His size nines were always under strain from the weight they had to carry around and, as they were more used to being supported by a nice, padded chair or mattress, any serious walking was anathema to them.

Pulling a flask from his other pocket, he poured himself a black coffee, laced with a healthy shot of brandy, but he had only just lifted the cup to his lips when he saw the figure suddenly emerge through the front door of the cottage below. Spilling half the contents of the cup down his trousers and jumping to his feet as the hot coffee scalded his leg, he snatched up a pair of binoculars suspended on a cord around his neck, and trained them on the cottage.

It was the target all right — a tall, thin man with shoulder-length black hair, wearing a long, grey coat and red trousers. Exactly Gabrielle's description. And he was about to climb on to a bicycle.

Losing no time in calling up Kate on the dedicated frequency that had been authorised, Hayden shrank back further into the trees as the man on the bicycle pedalled slowly up the hill on a barely discernible track towards him. He passed by seconds later, continuing on the track into the wood in the direction of Ellis Drove and the academy.

Hayden waited until he was out of sight, then crept out of the trees and followed him, walking slowly and carefully to avoid stepping on any of the thin, fallen tree branches that littered the track in places. He couldn't believe his luck. The target had actually shown himself on the very first day. Just do something *please*, he said to himself, so I can nick you and get back to my nice, comfortable office.

In two or three hundred yards the trees thinned, replaced by scrub and other undergrowth. Hayden stopped suddenly as he glimpsed his man just ahead, standing among the bushes on the edge of the wood. At the same moment, the faint sound of a bell, presumably marking the end of the school day, became audible. Matey-boy certainly kept to time, Hayden mused, as he stepped quickly sideways into the trees and crouched down.

Mixbury had leaned his bicycle against a tree, his head turned in the direction of the school, obviously waiting . . .

Silence. What if none of the girls used the drove this time? What if the rain, which had now stopped, had brought parents out instead to pick up their youngsters in their cars? Hayden could feel the tension mounting inside him, and the cramp starting in his legs.

Still no one. He saw Mixbury turn back towards his bicycle. Gordon Bennett, he couldn't give up now, surely? Not when the prospect of that nice, comfortable office for Hayden was just minutes away.

'Hello, sweetheart.'

Hayden stiffened. Mixbury had turned back towards the drove and was talking to a young girl, no more than eleven, with golden plaits, who had suddenly appeared from the direction of the school.

'You couldn't help me, could you?' Mixbury asked. 'You see, I've lost my dog, and I think he's in the wood somewhere. Could you help me find him?'

Hayden's heart was pumping like an old steam engine. The girl was licking a lolly of some sort and she had stopped to stare at Mixbury, a frown on her face.

Then she shook her head. 'My mum said not to talk to strangers,' she said and headed quickly off along the drove.

Hayden gritted his teeth until he heard them crack. So close and yet so far. He couldn't believe it and he watched helplessly as Mixbury tugged his bicycle out from the bush in which it had become entangled and turned back towards the track.

What happened next was totally unexpected. Where the two youngsters came from, Hayden had no idea, but suddenly a girl of about fourteen or fifteen and a boy of roughly the same age were there, confronting Mixbury and shouting abuse at him. The next moment he was cowering under a hail of blows and kicks, screaming in a mixture of pain and terror.

Hayden paused only long enough to shout 'Ellis Drove' into his radio and then he was lumbering up the track and into the melee, trying to separate the girl and the boy from their victim and bellowing that he was a police officer.

How things would have gone had Hayden been left to try to sort it all out on his own, it would be difficult to say, but miraculously running feet announced the arrival of Kate and Foster, who must have been a lot closer than he'd realised, and immediately the teenagers were constrained by stronger arms than theirs.

Mixbury's face was covered in blood from multiple cuts and his nose was also bleeding profusely. Despite this, he was about to totter off unsteadily back into the safety of the woods, when Hayden grabbed hold of him, catching him just before he collapsed in a heap, sobbing like a two-year-old.

The boy, who had already given up the struggle, was having handcuffs applied by Foster, and Kate had the still writhing, spitting girl in an armlock on the ground.

'Enough!' Kate snapped at her, then said grimly, 'You're in big trouble, young lady.'

'Don't care,' Mandy Williams snarled through clenched teeth. 'It was worth it after what he did to Tam.'

'Was it?' Kate replied. 'You may feel differently later, Mandy. Anyway, you're both under arrest for assault occasioning actual bodily harm.'

'And what about him?' the boy shouted. 'He's a bloody perv.'

'Don't worry,' Hayden replied grimly, looking at their battered, bleeding victim, 'he's coming too.'

'Me?' Mixbury exclaimed, recovering a little. 'I'm the one what got assaulted.'

'Yeah,' Hayden agreed, 'but maybe it would have been the other way around if that little girl you accosted had gone with you into the woods to look for your non-existent dog, eh? Anyway, you're nicked!'

* * *

'Holy Mary, yous certainly don't do things by half-measures, so you don't,' Hennessey remarked, after she'd seen the two teenagers being escorted to the detention rooms by Hayden and Jamie Foster and Mixbury being led out the back door of the police station to be taken by the waiting ambulance to the local hospital under uniformed police escort.

Kate smiled without humour. 'Quite a nasty confrontation,' she replied, 'and had we not been there the outcome could have been a lot worse.'

'Was yer man seriously hurt, do you think?' Hennessey went on.

Kate shook her head. 'I had a quick look at him at the scene,' she said. 'He'll have a couple of black eyes, I reckon, and quite a few cuts and bruises, but I believe his injuries will all prove to be superficial.'

'Those two kids obviously mitched off school and were waiting for him.'

'So it appears. I suspect they were hiding in the woods nearby to see if he would turn up. And they have committed a premeditated assault, so they're in a lot of trouble.'

'Aye, that's right enough. And you said the girl — Mandy, isn't it? — claimed the assault was about Tammy Robinson.'

'Yeah, she obviously believed Mixbury was Tammy's abductor because of the pervert he was and persuaded her boyfriend, Danny Frisson, to help her give him a hiding.'

'And do you think Mixbury is yer man?'

'Not now. Having seen the effeminate, wimpish way he behaved when they attacked him, in my opinion he's just a pathetic flasher.'

'Yet you said Hayden heard him invite that wee dote into the woods to look for a lost dog he didn't have?'

Kate made a grimace. 'Yes, that was a bit concerning. It was as if he were graduating towards something more serious than just exposing himself, but we'd have a job proving it, especially as we don't yet know who the little girl was.'

'Looks like we'll have a job proving anything else against him too if, as you say, the Mandy girl won't support a prosecution against him for exposing himself to her. Without that, no corroborative pattern of offending can be established against him to support Gabrielle Wiseman's testimony, which means there would be little chance of a conviction.'

'I think that might change now this has happened. Her mother was the main stumbling block before.'

'Let's hope you're right. Incidentally, I think Hayden did grand.'

Kate smiled with noticeable affection. 'Yes, I'm very proud of him.'

'So, changing the subject, any clever suggestions as to next moves?'

'Well, I need to get the parents of Mandy Williams and her boyfriend here, so we can interview the pair. In view of the circumstances of the offence, the fact that Mixbury was not seriously injured and that his assailants are both juveniles and apparently come from good stable homes, I propose having them reported for summons, so CPS can consider whether a prosecution is appropriate, or not. Then they can be released into the care of Mum or Dad. I'll leave Hayden to take care of that as he'll be the principal officer in the case.'

Hennessey nodded. 'Sounds sensible. And what about Mixbury?'

'Well, he will have to be interviewed when he's released from hospital, but I'd like to search his hovel first to see what dirty secrets he might be hiding there. He wasn't carrying a mobile on him when he was arrested and we need to find that if we can. So, though I appreciate his alleged offences do not appear at this stage to be of any relevance to the major crime inquiry we're dealing with, I feel we are nevertheless duty-bound to take a look at his squat ASAP to ensure we don't miss any other incriminating evidence that might be there.'

'Then you'll need a search warrant.'

'I'll get that organised. We have an amenable magistrate locally we can approach and I'm pretty sure she will approve the application, given the type of offence we're dealing with, as it involves indecency towards children.'

'Aye, and in the meantime it might be an idea to let the Cyber Crime Unit know about this job to give them the opportunity of taking a look at the videos and DVDs you've seized, once SOCO have finished with them. Cyber Crime works closely with the South-West Regional Crime Unit and the

NCA, and one of those agencies might already be working on something that might turn out to be connected to what we've got here. I'll brief my DI, Fergus Smith, so he can follow that up on your behalf.'

She treated Kate to a cynical smile. 'Seeing as we seem to be getting nowhere at present with the major inquiry, it will give him something to do. Anyway, I'll leave you to get on with your potential house search. Enjoy the craic!'

Some craic, Kate mused and, as her boss strode off again, she turned in the opposite direction towards the canteen. She knew Hayden wouldn't be back in the LIO's office, as he would have considered himself temporarily removed from it due to his observation role. She found him, as expected, tucking into a plate of sausages and beans, and he wasn't best pleased to see her, sensing that more work was coming his way.

'The SIO was very pleased with what you did today, Hayd,' she said, dropping into a chair opposite.

He beamed, a piece of sausage frozen aloft on the end of a fork in his podgy hand. 'Oh, just doing my job,' he said modestly. 'But nice of her to notice.'

Kate smiled. 'Yes, so now I want you to sort out the two kids we've got in the detention rooms. Get their parents in, interview them, either with one of the uniformed female officers, or one of the female DCs from our department, then report them for summons and get a file put together for onward transmission to CPS for a decision. Shouldn't take long.'

The sausage fell off his fork into the baked beans as he gaped at her. 'Me?'

She stood up. 'Has to be, I'm afraid. I have to execute a search warrant. You've done all this before anyway, so it should be second nature to you. I'll speak to the custody officer, so he knows what's happening.'

She half-turned on the way to the door. 'Oh, and it needs to be done PDQ, I'm afraid, but finish your tea first. I wouldn't want you to get indigestion.'

CHAPTER 11

He had bottled out of telling Mother what had happened when he got home from the hospital and, to take his mind off things, he'd taken refuge in his secret, locked room. The door to the room was in the cellar, a second door hidden behind some planks placed upright against the wall, which even Tammy hadn't spotted. She had been in there, though, without her knowing anything about it, and traces of the long brown hair he had shaved from her head while she was drugged and unconscious still littered the floor around the leather chair, which occupied pride of place in the centre of the room.

This was his special place, and his all-singing, all-dancing computer was there too, on a small desk in the corner, together with all the specialised kit and paraphernalia he had installed a few months ago to enable him to satisfy his perverted tastes. Had Tammy not escaped, he would have already introduced her to the rest of his punishment regime — his different size canes, whips, handcuffs, neck collars and other kit — but now everything in the room stood idle, waiting for another subject to be selected in her place.

In a peculiar way, despite his fear of being caught doing what he was doing, he refused to acknowledge that it was criminal abuse, and he didn't recognise that he was mentally ill and suffering from a dangerous form of psychosis, justifying his actions to himself as being necessary to achieve the greater good. As a schizophrenic, each of the two aspects of his personality enjoyed an individual existence, as in the Jekyll and Hyde novel by Robert Louis Stevenson. His own Dr Jekyll persona was still strong enough to suppress that of his deviant Mr Hyde for the majority of the time, enabling him to outwardly present himself to others as just an ordinary guy doing an ordinary job. But at the same time, his Mr Hyde was still there, lurking behind his projected mask of respectability, fuelling his inner obsession for dominance over others and the infliction of the punishment he so looked forward to meting out.

A clinical psychologist with knowledge of his past would more likely than not have laid the blame for his psychosis largely on his childhood environment and upbringing, though, in fairness, the condition must always have been there, hidden away within him, waiting to be activated.

He had originally been a sickly, neglected child, brought up in an unstable, often violent, home environment, and the fractious relationship between incompatible parents had eventually resulted in his father walking out on his mother. She, being a spiteful, vengeful woman, seemed to have blamed her son for her abandonment and, because of his clear physical resemblance to his father and the fact that the sight of him constantly reminded her of her former husband, she took out her hatred on him. Beating him with a bamboo cane, locking him in the dark cupboard under the stairs and terrifying and humiliating him at every possible opportunity. She had dominated his life well into adulthood, and even now, a grown man living in a totally different environment in Somerset, he was still under her spell, unable to break free of it.

He had no real friends and had only ever had one girlfriend by the time he reached his late teens. Even then, his mother had not approved of Samantha, and this, coupled

with his own unworldly experience and little natural expertise in the art of courtship, had doomed their relationship to
failure from the start. When, out of frustration, Samantha
had tried to seduce him and found him physically incapable
of responding, she had resorted to scorn and, in a humiliated rage, he had strangled her on the spot and dumped her
body down an old shaft. From that time on, ordinary sex had
become an anathema to him, and it was perhaps inevitable
that he would turn to an alternative but depraved form of
stimulation to give him the satisfaction he had been denied.
This had eventually resulted in the kidnapping and murders
(still unsolved) of two eleven-year-old girls from two different villages over a period of a few months, their bodies, like
that of his girlfriend, never having been found.

The so-called project he and his mother had devised had
promised to provide him with the pleasure he craved, and in
his distorted mind he was able to convince himself that his
motives were not prompted by depravity, but by the laudable
purpose originally espoused by his domineering mother to
improve the behaviour of recalcitrant young girls and turn
them into respectable members of society. The fact that those
girls would never be allowed to rejoin that society afterwards,
as it would mean his criminal activities being exposed to the
police, was another story, which he conveniently overlooked.

For the time being, the shocks he had received from the
debacle at the hospital and the chance encounter he'd had with
the police patrolman afterwards had been enough to hold him
back from continuing with what he had started with Tammy
Robinson. But now, sitting at his desk in the corner of his
secret room, viewing the depraved images his contact on the
Dark Web had just sent him on his laptop, the clamour of
voices in his head, urging him to start again, had become more
and more insistent. Wound up by the degenerate images in
front of him, he could feel his resolve crumbling, and he knew
that it would not be long before he bowed to their persuasion.

He already had a new subject in mind for the even-
tual restart of the programme and the fancy mobile he had

taken from Tammy, which now lay on the desk in front of him, was just the device he needed to get things underway. Especially as she had been silly enough not to protect it with a password . . .

* * *

The cottage looked as if it would not be long before it disappeared into the marsh that surrounded it. The walls were cracked and covered in parasitical climbers that all but completely obscured the cracked downstairs windows. There were numerous tiles missing from the roof, some of which lay on the ground close to the warped front door, now half-buried in the undergrowth, which choked what had once no doubt been a small garden.

Mixbury had been searched prior to being taken to hospital, and a mortice key discovered in his personal property, which he had admitted was his front door key. This had been temporarily seized in advance by Kate to enable Foster and her to gain entry to his house in anticipation of the warrant they needed actually being granted.

Fortunately, crossing fingers seemed to have worked and Kate had been lucky with her application. The chair of the bench had agreed to meet her for the warrant to be sworn in before her without a single quibble and had approved it immediately, despite having long finished at court for the day. Kate only hoped that after all her efforts they would find something worth finding, rather than just Mixbury's spotty dog.

In fact, the little terrier was there all right, and it proved to be a real pain in more ways than one. As soon as they got the door open, it launched itself at them with all the aggression of a Rottweiler, barking, snarling and going for their ankles, which it could just about reach. Foster seemed to attract its fury more than Kate and it managed to tear his socks in two places, drawing blood, before the detective lost patience and, boldly picking the animal up by the scruff of its neck, dumped it in the downstairs toilet and shut the door, only just resisting the temptation to drop it into the toilet bowl and pull the chain!

The house was one of the dirtiest dwellings Kate had ever visited and she had to hold her nose when Foster initially opened the toilet door to incarcerate the dog. The brief view she was afforded was not a pleasant one, as it looked as though the toilet had never ever been cleaned.

The rest of the house was not much better. There was dog excrement on the kitchen floor, used cartons of fast food piled up on the draining board and a sink full of unwashed dishes. In what served as a living room, there was further excrement on the shabby, threadbare carpet, some of it trodden in, and a table laden at one end with female underwear, which had almost certainly been stolen from local washing-lines.

Upstairs there were two bedrooms, one at the back of the cottage filled with old furniture, bicycle parts and an assortment of rusted tools, and the other, the larger of the two, at the front. This was furnished with a rusted iron bed, sporting a collection of rugs and blankets piled on top of a dirty, stained mattress, and a tatty upholstered armchair with a sagging cushion. The chair was set before a small colour television that had seen better days on a wooden table, with an equally old DVD/video player on the floor underneath. Both appliances seemed to have been connected to wall sockets, with an aerial wire disappearing into the ceiling above, so it seemed that they were probably in regular use, and there was a shelf on the wall behind them boasting a collection of videos and DVDs that turned out to be copies of old cowboy films.

That wasn't the only collection in the room, however, and it was Foster who made the discovery. Crammed into a rickety corner cupboard, minus its shelf, was another mix of DVDs and videos, but, when Foster pulled a couple out, he got quite a shock. He emptied the cupboard on to the bed and called Kate over to look at them. There were twelve in all and, like the others, they had glossy covers. But there the resemblance ended and, from the descriptive titles on the front and the graphically illustrated blurbs on the back, it didn't require detailed scrutiny to establish what kind of films they were. Both detectives had seen plenty of pornography in their criminal investigations before, but they could see that what they were looking at now was not simply pornographic. It was much worse than that. It was clear that here the key players were not well-paid porn stars, but young children, filmed as they were tortured, abused and humiliated in the most appalling perverted scenarios.

'He's a bloody paedophile all right,' Foster said, his tone unusually savage. 'And not just a flasher either. This bastard is into serious child abuse, maybe even snuff.'

Kate felt the bile rising in her throat. Like Foster, she had seen many vile things in her police service and had thought there was nothing left that could shock her in relation to the activities of the gutter filth she had to deal with. But this was something else, something that was well beyond vile, and she turned away, sickened to the stomach.

'But where the hell did he get this stuff from around here?' Foster went on. 'The Dark Web? It looks professionally made.'

Kate shook her head. 'If he was using some internet site to get hold of these, he'd have needed access to a computer. We haven't found so much as a laptop or a mobile phone, and, seeing the squalor in which he lives, I doubt he has either.'

'Maybe he's been using an internet café in town? Or even some dodgy video shop?'

'We'd better get SOCO up here pronto anyway,' she said, pulling out her radio, 'and at some stage some poor soul will need to go through all this filth to establish precisely what is on the films evidentially. This place will have to be torn apart too to see what else might be here. And while we're waiting for that to be done, we'd better have a closer look around to see if there's anything obvious that we may have missed.'

But a thorough examination of the house failed to turn up anything of significance and they found no trace of a cellar, or the cage Tammy had spoken about. The cottage was, as it looked, nothing more than a small, dirty, two-bed-roomed hovel, rotten with damp and gradually subsiding into the marsh. As for the overall site, it consisted of a few ruined buildings with the remains of corrugated iron roofs and it didn't take them long to go through them all. But they found nothing but abandoned, rusted equipment that had obviously once been used for the extraction of the peat, some broken furniture and one partially stripped digger almost buried in undergrowth.

SOCO arrived an hour later and after briefing the super-visor, Andrea James, on the situation, Kate left Foster with them, while she returned to the police station to report to Hennessey.

The SIO met her on the stairs. 'Your flasher has been discharged from the hospital,' she said. 'Only superficial inju-ries. He's back in his cell, demanding to be released.'

'That'll be a long time coming,' Kate replied and steered her boss into one of the interview rooms to bring her up to speed on the search of the house and the actions taken.

Hennessey grunted when she finished. 'With the dis-covery of all that pornographic material, this adds a new dimension to the case, so it does, but I don't want you to be side-tracked from the current major inquiry and end up tying yourself down on the Mixbury business. Not when we are already in the middle of investigating a joint murder and child abduction. Is that clear?'

Kate nodded. 'I'll watch points on it,' she promised. 'But we don't yet know what we might turn up with regard to Mixbury.'

Hennessey frowned. 'But you said before that you don't believe Mixbury could have been involved in Tammy Robinson's abduction, or the murder of that young woman either, so what *is* the problem? I can see that there's some-thing else on your mind.'

Kate shook her head. 'I don't have a problem as such. It's just that Tammy Robinson said her abductor put her in a cage, threatening to punish her, and we already know he shaved her head. The porno videos and so forth we recovered from Mixbury's place all appeared to involve child bondage and punishment. It just seems one heck of a coincidence to me.'

'So, what are you saying? That you suspect there's some sort of connection between Mixbury and our abductor?'

Kate shrugged. 'I don't know . . . Maybe, but not directly. Mixbury seems to have an unhealthy interest in sexual perversion, certainly, and though he doesn't appear to have access to a computer or a mobile, he could have used an internet café, or got the stuff from some shady backstreet distributer in the city. However, I still think he's just a voyeur. A nasty bit of work, of course, but not someone capable of dreaming up something as devious and well-planned as the abduction, and not, from what I've seen of him, the type to commit murder.'

'But you're saying he might know someone who is, eh?'

'Something like that, yes, but I have absolutely no evidence to suggest this. I could be barking up entirely the wrong tree. We can only wait to see what Mixbury comes up with when we interview him.'

Hennessey pursed her lips reflectively for a second. Then she said, 'Aye, well, let's get on with it then. I'm just concerned that while we're faffin' about with that gobshite, Tammy Robinson's abductor might already have his eyes on another wee dote we know nothing about.'

Hennessey's concerns about wasting valuable time on Mixbury soon resonated with Kate. As soon as Foster had returned to the station, she set up the first interview, which took place in the presence of the duty solicitor Mixbury had demanded, a well-known local legal aid lawyer named John Bellman, and it did indeed prove to be a complete waste of time.

Apart from making a complaint of unlawful arrest and asking about the welfare of his dog, which he was told had been taken to the dog pound, Mixbury refused to give any proper answers to the questions put to him. In fact, he replied to most with the all too familiar 'No comment' response given by most criminals and, when asked about the pornographic films seized from his home, he denied all knowledge and suggested the police had planted the videos and DVDs themselves. He also denied indecently exposing himself to Gabrielle Wiseman and Mandy Williams — whose mother had since been approached again and had finally agreed to her daughter providing a written statement. In all, they were silly responses that flew in the face of clear evidence, but it was plain that he intended to go down fighting, even if his case was hopeless. As for the suggestion Kate put to him of his possible involvement in the kidnapping of Tammy Robinson and also the murder of Sandra Hay, far from forcing him into an admission of some sort it resulted in a furious denial. It also brought a sharp rebuke from his solicitor, John Bellman, who asked them whether they had evidence pointing to his client's involvement in the more serious crimes and accused them of going on an unacceptable fishing expedition. Bellman followed this up by reminding them that, in view of the lateness of the hour and the lengthy period Mixbury had been in custody, he was legally entitled to a meal and a rest. Forced to give up for the day, they reluctantly returned him to his cell, advising him and his solicitor that he would be held for further questioning.

'Bloody solicitor,' Foster said afterwards. 'I wonder how he can live with himself, defending such a scumbag.'

Kate shrugged. 'He would argue that that's what he's paid for, Jamie,' she reminded him, feeling a bit like a hypocrite, knowing that she had made similar statements in past cases herself when the frustration had got to her. 'Mixbury has a right to fair representation.'

'I'm well aware of that,' he said testily. 'But I keep thinking of the poor innocent kids in those vile films and I have to ask myself who's defending *their* rights?'

Kate sighed. 'Don't beat yourself up over it,' she said. 'It's early days yet and we'll be having another go at him tomorrow. Don't forget, we still have him on possession of indecent images of children and the law says we can hold him without charge for twenty-four hours. Although we've already eaten into that period, after his night in the cells, we still have a few hours left to us. If necessary we'll see if we can get a superintendent's authority to detain him for up to the thirty-six-hour maximum we're allowed, on the basis that he could be a suspect in a murder investigation.'

Foster snorted. 'That really would be stretching things a bit,' he replied, his face set in an angry mask, 'but even if we did get an extension, all he's got to do is to keep on saying "no comment" and we get nowhere, which means any of his other paedo pals he's tied in with will get off scot-free and kids everywhere will go on being abused — or even worse if snuff *is* involved.'

It was clear that Mixbury and what he represented had really got to Foster, and Kate tried to reassure him. 'You saw how he reacted at the interview,' she pointed out. 'Despite his stubborn refusal to answer questions, he knows he's in the shit big time, and he was plainly rattled. As far as we are aware, he has never been arrested and held in custody before, so it will all be new to him, which is in our favour. You know as well as I do that a long night in the pokey can sometimes work wonders on obstinate tongues, and I have a feeling it will this time.'

'Let's hope you're right,' he said.

'I'm always right,' she replied. 'I'm a woman!'

CHAPTER 12

Kate bumped into the duty inspector when she walked through the back door of the police station at around nine the following morning and he looked far from happy.

'Ah, Kate,' he said. 'Just the person.'

'Something up, James?' she asked warily.

'Yeah,' James Evans replied, 'My colleagues and me really want to thank you for the arsehole you left for us in the traps last night.'

Kate's eyes narrowed. 'Why, what's he done?'

The stocky Welshman rubbed a hand across his beard and gave a short, unamused laugh. 'What *hasn't* he done, you mean?' he said. 'You should ask the night custody sergeant that one. For starters, the tosser spent half the night ringing the cell buzzer, screaming and hammering on the door. Then, when the custody sergeant responded, he was like a madman and tried to force his way out of the cell. When he was put back in, he fouled himself, tried to smash up the toilet and had an unsuccessful go at tearing apart his mattress with his teeth before ripping up his clothes. He had to be cleaned up and given a scenes of crime coat to cover himself. Turned out he suffers from claustrophobia and he had some sort of panic attack over being locked up in the slammer.

Eventually the duty doc had to be called to sedate him before he caused himself serious injury.'

Kate raised an eyebrow. 'How is he now?'

'A lot calmer, but demanding to see you.'

She grunted. 'Something to look forward to then. Okay, so let's do it. I need to interview him again anyway. Give me a few minutes.'

Kate found that Jamie Foster had already arrived and was waiting for her in the incident room, drinking a coffee.

He grinned when he saw her. 'I hear it's been an eventful night in the custody suite,' he said. 'Sounds like our man didn't take too much to his accommodation.'

'Something he'd better get used to,' she said grimly. 'He's looking at a lengthy dose of porridge on the child porno charges he faces.'

He dumped his plastic cup in the wastebin. 'At least if we run out of time and he has to be charged, his violent behaviour in the cells should give the court a reason to remand him in custody for his own safety.'

'True, but equally it could give his brief the chance of getting bail on the grounds of his claustrophobia, then ultimately a lesser sentence to put a stop to him being sent down.'

'That's what I like about you,' he retorted. 'Ever the optimist.'

Mixbury was brought into the interview room by two uniformed officers, securely handcuffed and wearing just a long white coat, and he stared with half-closed eyes at the two detectives sitting on the other side of the table as he and his solicitor, John Bellman, sat down opposite them.

Kate went through the usual preliminary procedures, and Mixbury shook his head impatiently. 'Yeah, yeah, yeah,' he said. 'But you can turn that tape off. I want this off the record.'

His solicitor shook his head. 'I can't agree to that,' he said. 'This interview has to be recorded in my client's interests.'

Kate was in agreement with him, and she shook her head firmly. 'No way,' she said. 'We're not playing games with you here.'

Mixbury's face twitched, then he shrugged and sat back in his seat, saying nothing.

For a moment Kate thought he was going to refuse to speak, but finally he raised his handcuffs, wiped a runny nose across one wrist and said almost pleadingly, 'I can't be banged up. It does me 'ead in.'

Kate remained unsympathetic. 'I'm afraid you're going to have to get used to it,' she said. 'You're facing serious child pornography charges.'

'I'm not into child pornography,' he retorted.

'So how come you had twelve films of child abuse in the cupboard at your home?'

'You don't have to say anything,' Bellman interjected.

Mixbury ignored him. 'They're not mine. I, er, found 'em.'

'Where?'

'I strongly advise you not to answer that question,' Bellman cut in again.

Mixbury took no notice of him, but didn't respond to Kate either, then went on in a rush. 'Look, if I play ball with you, will you speak to the beak, so I can get bail?'

Kate heard the solicitor's sharp intake of breath, but before he could say anything she said, 'No can do. I can inform the court that you cooperated with us, but that's all. It will be up to them as to what decision they arrive at. There will be no deals struck here and, as I've already said, you face serious charges, so how things go is really down to you.'

He hesitated and his solicitor quickly took the opportunity to repeat his advice. 'Make no comment, Mr Mixbury.'

The advice fell on deaf ears. 'Okay, okay, I admit I flashed at them two girls. Couldn't 'elp it. I took a funny turn, see, but I didn't touch 'em, honest. Never would. As for the gear you got from my place, them videos and DVDs weren't mine, as I just said.'

'You still had them and possession of such material is illegal,' Foster stated. 'More importantly, from what we saw of them, it was plain that they involved young children being

163

sexually abused and brutalised. Maybe even worse. You know what snuff is, I assume?'

Bellman's indignation was clear. 'That is out of order, officer,' he snapped. 'You have produced absolutely no evidence whatsoever of my client's involvement in the actual abuse of any children.'

Neither Kate nor Foster responded to the rebuke, but Mixbury's face grew even more pale. 'I-I ain't 'ad nuffink to do wiv' murder. I just watched 'em on my TV. I know that's sick an' I feel right ashamed about it, but I ain't no murderer.'

'So how did you get hold of the films in the first place then? From some dodgy website, was it?'

He looked puzzled. 'Website? What you talkin' about?'

Kate tested him. 'The internet — you know, online through your computer, or mobile phone?'

Mixbury released a short guffaw that lacked any trace of humour. 'You 'avin' a laugh, love? Look at me. No job, stuck on the dole an' livin' in a total shit-'ole you wouldn't put pigs in. Can you see me 'avin' a bleedin' computer, or a mobile? Maybe you finks I left 'em in me Roller in the garage wiv' me case of champagne, eh? Do me a favour!'

'Okay, so, forgetting the funnies, where *did* you get them?'

Bellman tried once more. 'Don't answer that, Mr Mixbury.'

'I said I found 'em, didn't I?'

'Oh, come on! What do you take us for?'

'Okay, okay I nicked 'em.'

The solicitor closed his eyes for a second and seemed to shrink in his seat.

'From where?'

'The back of a motor.'

'What motor?'

Mixbury swallowed hard several times and burped loudly, again not answering the question. Then he seemed to go off at a tangent. 'Fing is, about six mumfs ago, I got a job at the Windmill Academy school, 'elpin' the groundsman keep the place tidy and pickin' up all the litter an' that. But I done a stupid fing. I fort the bins in the changin' rooms was overfull and went in there to empty 'em, but then some girls come into the place to use the showers after netball, so I 'id in one of the bogs in case they fort I was in there to spy on 'em.'

'Which, of course, you weren't,' Kate said sarcastically.

'Nah, honest, I weren't. But I got caught comin' out of the place by the groundsman, didn't I? Guy called Merchant. 'E reported me to that crabby ol' bitch in charge and she sacked me on the spot.'

'How unreasonable of her,' Kate acknowledged drily. 'So, how long were you working at the school before you were sacked?'

''Bout a week.'

'You lasted a long time then? Was that before or after you were sacked by the local council for inappropriate behaviour towards one of their female staff?'

'After,' he muttered, carrying on quickly, without making any attempt to defend himself. 'Fing is, there was this old motor that were always parked at the back of the school, which must've been owned by one of the staff, an' next day, I were in town signing on at the dole place when I sees this same motor parked by the side of the road as I were ridin' me bike 'ome. I were still narked over bein' sacked, so I fort I'd put a few scratches on it just to get even. But then I found it were unlocked, an' on the back seat were this bag, all zipped up like . . .' His voice trailed off.

'So you nicked it?'

There was no further intervention from Bellman. He seemed to have given up on his role and had become nothing more than a disillusioned observer.

Mixbury licked his lips, then nodded. 'But when I gets 'ome an' 'as a dekko inside, there was all these porno videos of kids bein' seen to . . .' His voice faltered and he swallowed hard several times, staring at Kate almost desperately. 'I were goin' to frow the lot away, honest, but you got to 'em first.'

'Is that right?' Foster queried. 'So how come they were still in the bedroom cupboard six months after you nicked them?'

'Forgot about 'em, didn't I?'

The detective nodded slowly. 'Oh, right. Silly me, that explains it. You just forgot you had twelve child porno films in your cupboard. Easily done, that, isn't it?'

Mixbury scowled, but yet again didn't answer.

'And where's the bag you found them in?' Kate asked. 'We didn't see a bag at your home.'

'I frew it in a rhyne.'

'That's convenient. And this car you say you stole it from, what type was it?'

'Dunno. Never 'ad a motor in me life. Knows nuffink about 'em.'

'Was it a big car, or a small one?'

'Sort of between the two.'

'Did you get a look at the number?'

'Nah, too busy makin' sure no one were about.'

'What colour was it?'

'Blue, I fink.'

'And was it a saloon, or an estate car? Did it have four seats, or two?'

'A four-seater yeah, and it also 'ad a boot, I remember that.'

'So, a blue four-seater saloon. And that's it? Out of all the cars driving around, how the hell could you be sure this was the car you'd seen parked at the school?'

''Cause, just like that one, the car were blue, and it 'ad a different colour wing to the rest of it on the front passenger side, what was black — as if it 'ad been fixed up.'

'After an accident you mean?'

'Could be. An' there was these fings — stickers, I'd call 'em — in each corner of the back winder, like funny fish shapes, and a cross at the top like you sees in churches.'

Kate pulled out her pocketbook and drew the outline of the Christian symbol of a fish on one page, then, saying aloud what she was doing for the benefit of the tape machine, she showed him the drawing. 'Did the fish shapes look like this?' she asked.

'Yeah,' he said, 'just like that, but they was silver coloured.'

Kate sat back in her seat and studied him fixedly for a second. 'Have you seen this car since?'

He shook his head. 'Nah, I ain't been back to the school, 'cause the 'ead said if ever she saw me there again she'd tell you lot.'

'A sensible warning under the circumstances.'

'Yeah,' he said again, 'but she was a bleedin' hypocrite. I get frown out of the school 'cause I just 'appened to make a-a mistake and she 'as someone workin' there wiv' all them kids what is into child porn. 'Tain't fair.'

Kate raised her eyebrows. He was lying about why he had been sacked, of course, but he did have a point, and now it was up to her and Foster to find the "Christian" owner of the car, who apparently liked to watch little children being abused in pornographic films.

'Thank you for your cooperation, Mr Mixbury,' she said after ending the interview and turning off the tape, and she threw John Bellman an extravagant wink. 'It has been most helpful.'

* * *

Mandy Williams was up early the day after her arrest, but stayed off school, pretending to be sick and unable to face the other kids, knowing it would all have got out by now. She realised that attacking Mixbury had been stupid and had only got herself and her boyfriend, Danny, into big trouble. It had been a spur-of-the-moment thing and she was just relieved they hadn't seriously injured the perv, otherwise things could have been a lot worse. Her mother and father had been furious at the humiliation she had brought on them and her dad in particular said he would never forgive her for what she had done. Fortunately he had had to go to work that morning, but her mother was still downstairs, sobbing continuously over it all, which was something Mandy simply couldn't handle. So she hadn't bothered with breakfast, but had remained in bed, out of the way, passing the time flicking through the messages on her mobile and listening to music on Spotify for an hour.

She was shocked when she picked up the WhatsApp message from Tammy.

Quitting hosp. Had enough. Stuff 'em. Load of losers. Need to see ya. Think I know who guy was who took me. Bit scared. Meet me old pumping station at 4? Don't call.

Mandy's heart was thumping as she sent a reply to say she'd be there. She knew where the pumping station was. She and Tam had met up there several times to share a joint, and once to try some coke they'd got from a bloke outside the school, which had made her sick. But the river was a fair distance from where she lived, so maybe she would have to use her bike.

Coming to that decision, she sat back against the headboard, staring, unseeing, at the wall. Tammy was coming home from the hospital! Her best friend. That was great. But why hadn't she just told the police who the man was if she knew? Why ask her to meet her instead? Maybe she wanted to get her advice first? It was all very mysterious. Then she thought about how she was going to get out of the house without her mother knowing. It wouldn't be easy, but at least she knew that her dad wasn't usually in from the office until seven and she would be back well before then.

She was still trying to work out a plan when her mother called up the stairs, thankfully without a sob in her voice.

'You coming for lunch, Mand? Only, I have to get over to your nan's by two thirty.'

Of course! It was Friday, wasn't it? And her mother always visited her own mum every Friday afternoon in the residential home at Weston-super-Mare, not getting back until round about six. It couldn't have worked out better. Mandy felt a sense of conspiratorial excitement as she pulled on her dressing gown and thumped down the stairs. Had she known what was in store for her that afternoon, she would not have been quite so thrilled.

* * *

Ahmed Choudhry was a keen fisherman and, following his decision to retire from his grocery business in Bradford and move to the Somerset Levels with his wife, Aynoor, several years ago, he had spent many a happy hour on the bank of the river just a mile or so from his cottage in the small village that had become home to them both.

This Friday afternoon was no exception and, taking a shortcut across the fields, he made his way on foot to his regular fishing spot a few yards from the od, disused pumping station at just after three and settled down to set up his rods.

The red-brick buildings of the abandoned workings, with their tiled roofs and boarded-up windows and doors, which cast a long shadow over the stubby grass, had always fascinated him and once, some months ago, he had tried to satisfy his natural curiosity by climbing over the wire fence enclosing them to take a look around, boldly ignoring the *DANGER. KEEP OUT* notice. There hadn't been much to see, but he had found a half-open door in one of the outhouses and some damp, mouldy bedding and a pile of tattered blankets in a corner, suggesting that maybe some itinerant had at one time used the place to escape the bitter cold of the moor in winter. He had also found rusted lager cans and discarded cigarette butts below some graffiti on a wall, including an obscene reference to a school head teacher called Turnbull, which indicated that the place had also been the resort of more youthful visitors. But none of this meant anything to him and, being a sensitive, superstitious soul, who found the atmosphere of the place more than a little spooky, he convinced himself that the pumping station was the haunt of malign spirits who resented trespassers. As a result, he quit the site a lot faster than he had entered it and had never ventured there again.

What Choudhry did not know as he cast his line on that inauspicious Friday, however, was that the pumping station was about to become the set for a drama that had nothing to do with malign spirits, but rather more to do with perverse human devilry, and that he was about to become a key player in this live production, whether he wanted to or not.

But in his blissful ignorance, seduced by the warmth of the afternoon sun and the equally conducive melody of the marshland birds, he was at peace with the world and inevitably he found himself starting to doze. He was completely unaware of the car arriving quietly and pulling in behind a wall on the other side of the pumping station, or the clanking of Mandy Williams' bicycle chain shortly afterwards, as, perspiring profusely from her ride, she rode up the short service road to the pumping station and propped her bicycle against the wall of one of the buildings. But even as his chin dipped lower and lower on his chest, and his thoughts transported him back to the country of his birth and the vast paddy fields of his beloved Punjab, his sudden return to harsh reality was only seconds away . . .

CHAPTER 13

'It's the school, Jamie,' Kate exclaimed excitedly after Mixbury had been returned to his cell. 'It all comes back to the bloody Windmill Academy. What Mixbury has just told us about those porno films has given us the break we've been looking for in the abduction of Tammy Robinson and the murder of Sandra Hay, and it confirms our earlier suspicions. The fact that a member of staff at Tammy Robinson's own school has been into heavy child porn at round about the same time as Tammy was kidnapped and abused is just too much of a coincidence to be a coincidence. It's clear that our suspect is not an internet pervert from somewhere on the other side of the country who just happened to pick Tammy Robinson's name at random off a chatroom site. She was specifically targeted by someone who knew her, knew the area and could plan her abduction well in advance. Someone who was familiar with her habits, what she was like, where she lived, who her friends were. In short, someone *at the school* who saw her virtually every day and who could watch her, listen to her conversations and know what she was doing in her spare time. Probably someone who didn't actually like her and felt she needed, as her captor evidently told her, to be punished.'

'That's if you believe Mixbury's explanation as to how he came by the material,' Foster said, playing devil's advocate. 'His story could be a pack of lies in an effort to get back at the school.'

Kate shook her head. 'He hasn't the intelligence, or the imagination to concoct a story like that, and he didn't falter in what he was saying. No, I believe he was telling the truth. He wants to avoid "stir" and his only hope of doing so is if he can be seen to be cooperating with the police. He wouldn't want to cock everything up by inventing a load of crap.'

Foster nodded slowly. 'You're making a lot of assumptions here, though, don't you think? Even if Mixbury's story is kosher, because someone at the school likes porno movies, reprehensible though that is, it doesn't necessarily follow that they are also likely to be into kidnapping — and, of course, be capable of murder.'

'No, it doesn't, but don't forget, Tammy Robinson said her abductor put her in a cage,' She quickly consulted her pocketbook, flicked back some pages, then carried on. 'She said he told her she was "an animal and needed to be punished". Then he cruelly shaved her head. But as far as we know he didn't sexually assault her, even though he had every opportunity after drugging her.'

Foster frowned, apparently still not entirely convinced.

'Flaming Nora,' she added irritably, showing her frustration, 'think of the films we seized. We didn't go through them all, but it was plain to see that they were all about bondage and *punishment*. This guy, whoever he is, is not interested in raping little girls for the sheer sexual thrill of it. That doesn't do anything for him. He's into inflicting suffering on them, full stop. He's a sadist, pretending — probably as much to himself as his victim — that he's doing what he's doing for the most laudable of motives. What was it he told Tammy she had to do?' She checked her pocketbook again. 'Ah yes, "redeem herself", that was it. What did Mixbury see on the car from which he stole those films? Stickers depicting the sign of a fish, a Christian symbol, together with a cross, symbolising the crucifixion. And what is Christianity all about? Punishment and redemption, that's what. It all fits. We're not just dealing with some run-of-the-mill sexual pervert, Jamie, but a twisted psychotic, who claims to be motivated by a desire to cure wayward children, but in reality gets off on their torture and humiliation.'

He nodded. 'Okay, I see that there *could* be a connection, though your hypothesis is still a bit shaky, especially the link to religion. But assuming for a moment that you're on the right track, how do we progress things? We can hardly go to the school and wander around checking all their cars for Christian symbols. It's a pretty large school, so there must be at least fifteen to twenty teachers and other staff there, and anyway Mixbury nicked the films about six months ago. The car we're looking for could have been disposed of by now. He said it was an old one and already damaged. On top of that, even if we did spot a motor answering that description, we have nothing to prove the films were ever in there to start with, except on the word of a scumbag, who's into child pornography himself and likes to flash his dick at kids whenever he gets the opportunity.'

Kate grimaced. 'I do hate people who use logic to win arguments,' she said.

* * *

Mandy Williams was worn out. It had been a good twenty minutes' ride to the pumping station from home and it was only the second time she had used her bicycle in the past year. She usually met up with Tammy and Gabrielle to walk to school and she had fallen out of love with cycling for pleasure long ago.

She had puzzled again and again over Tam's message during her ride, asking herself why on earth her friend had set up the meet so far away from where they both lived. After all, she could have chosen the rec in the village. That would have been much more appropriate. Maybe she had been worried about being seen there by someone who knew her, but why?

She hadn't done anything wrong. Also, the same thought that had occurred to her when she'd first received the message still niggled at her. If Tam knew who the person was who had snatched her, why hadn't she just told the police? Why go to all the trouble of fixing up this meet? It was all very peculiar. Tam certainly had some explaining to do.

It was a relief to finally climb off the seat of her bicycle. Unused to the exercise, the muscles in her legs were really aching as she wheeled the machine over to the red-brick building in front of her and propped it against the wall. The door of the outhouse where she and Tammy had smoked those joints all those weeks ago stood half-open. Obviously no one had bothered to repair the rusted lock they had broken, and she guessed Tammy was waiting for her inside.

She glimpsed the top of the car poking above the low wall on the other side of the pumping station, but she didn't give it much thought. There was some guy sitting on the riverbank with a fishing rod just down from the building and she assumed it had to be his. He looked to be asleep and she grinned. Not long ago she and Tam would have played a prank on him while he was out of it, but not now. They had more important things to think about.

'Tam?' she called softly. 'It's Mand. I'm here.'

There was no reply. She frowned and tugged on the handle of the outhouse door, which groaned as she pulled it open. Foul, damp air rushed out to meet her and she wrinkled her nose in disgust. It smelled like one of those backstreet toilets. With just one small window to let in the light, it was quite gloomy inside too and it took her eyes a couple of seconds to adjust, but when she peered around her she saw only the pile of abandoned bedding that had been there before and the cans of lager, now buckled, that she and Tam had brought with them on that last visit. Tam was not there.

Mandy scowled and glanced at the luminous dial of her wristwatch. It was five past four. Where the hell was she? She was the one who had set up the meet and got Mandy all the way out here and now there was no sign of her.

Thinking that she could be outside somewhere, Mandy turned to push open the door. But it opened even as her hand reached out towards it, and it wasn't Tammy standing outside, holding it open. It was the sinister figure of a man wearing a black hood.

'Hello, Mandy,' he said. 'How nice to see you.'

It was then that Mandy's lungs filled with air and she screamed and screamed . . .

* * *

Ahmed Choudhry had never considered himself a brave man, but he had a strong sense of community and right and wrong. When the shrill screams suddenly tore through the tranquillity that reigned on the warm, still riverbank, shattering his own personal sense of nirvana, he was virtually propelled to his feet with an altogether different sense of shock that almost sent him pitching off the bank into the river.

Recovering in time, but still not fully awake, he dragged his gaze towards the origin of the screams and saw the two figures struggling violently by the half-open door of the pumping station. One appeared to be a young girl and the other a man dressed in black with something over his head. The girl seemed to have gone berserk, shouting and screaming like someone possessed and wildly lashing out at her aggressor for all she was worth as he tried to hold on to her.

Choudhry didn't hesitate. Plainly the girl was in trouble and it was clear to him now that the thing covering the man's head was actually some sort of hood. Lurching towards the pumping station across the lumpy tufted grass with a loud shout of 'Leave her alone', and almost tripping over in the process, Choudhry snatched up a broken wooden post by the wire fence enclosing the site and ran round to the open gateway. The man saw him at the last minute and his reaction was immediate. Letting go of the girl and leaving her to slump to the ground, sobbing hysterically, he turned and fled across the site to a gap in the far fence. Even as Choudhry got to the gap, he heard a car start up, and the next moment a large blue saloon erupted from behind the wall with a crashing of gears and streaked across some waste ground on to the main road, where it disappeared around a bend.

The girl was sobbing and hyperventilating when Choudhry got back to her, and she screamed at him when he tried to help her to her feet, her eyes wide and staring as she shrank away from him. He could see that she was hysterical and there was clearly nothing he could do to reassure her after what had happened. Grimly, he pulled out his mobile phone and did the only thing he could do: dialled 999.

* * *

Damn! Damn! Damn! He had fouled up yet again. What was wrong with him? At least he hadn't told Mother what he was up to, so he didn't need to explain anything to her. This one had been completely off his own bat. And it would have been a success but for that sodding fisherman. He hadn't noticed him on the riverbank at first, not until he had shouted at him. He must have been sitting there, with his rod and bank stick all set up, well before he himself had arrived.

If only he had decided to wait for the girl inside the outhouse rather than trying to corral her there from outside, he might have been able to shut her up before she went bananas. As it was, in the struggle he had dropped his trusty hypodermic containing the sedative he had obtained from the internet, and he had heard his foot crunch it into the ground. That meant the police would probably find it and, though there shouldn't be any fingerprints on the thing because he always wore gloves when handling it, nevertheless it was still something they had of his, which they could use against him if he was ever put before a court. His only comfort was that, despite it being a loss he could have done without, he had several more hypodermics tucked away, together with enough of the sedative to enable him to carry on with the project if he chose to do so.

Yes, and that was the point, wasn't it? *Was* he going to carry on with it, or ditch the whole thing for good, regardless of what Mother might say? After the number of cockups he had made so far, he feared it was only a question of time before he made the big one that brought him down. He would have to think about it . . . long and hard.

Meanwhile, he just hoped the interfering fisherman hadn't clocked the number of his car as he'd raced away. Maybe he should get rid of the VW altogether? He had already smashed up Tammy Robinson's mobile and dumped it in a rhyne in case the police could trace the message he had sent to Mandy Williams on the device, so it was sensible to think about the car too.

It was an old thing anyway. He had bought it off a dodgy, "five minute" dealer in Bristol as a runabout a few weeks ago while he was making up his mind what sort of car he wanted to go for. Fortunately, he had been careful to conceal his face from view at the time of the purchase. He'd also never registered ownership with the DVLA and, since he'd paid for the car with cash, the dealer hadn't asked him for any personal details, which meant the gold-toothed wide boy hadn't intended notifying the sale from his end either. Annoyingly, the car still had a few months' tax left on it, plus an MOT, which he would have to sacrifice, but such minor issues weren't worth worrying about. Better to lose the tax than risk facing arrest because the car was now on a police watch list. Realistically, he thought that that was most unlikely, since it could only have been visible to the fisherman for just seconds as he sped away and from a distance of something like thirty yards, but he couldn't take the chance and, to be on the safe side, he needed it to disappear for good.

One option was to take it to a lonely spot out on the Levels and torch it, but that was almost certain to attract police interest and, even without the number plates, they'd be able to identify it through the engine and chassis numbers. As he hadn't registered it with the DVLA, they still couldn't trace it directly back to him, but it would set a hare running and he was conscious of the fact that lots of different people had seen him driving about the area in the car, in particular his near neighbour, PC Ray Kendrick, who had been the one to stop him after his attempt on the life of Tammy Robinson at the hospital. What if the copper had made a note of the number as a matter of course before he had spoken to him? No, torching the car was not a good idea at all.

The only other alternative was to take it to a scrap yard — or "authorised treatment facility", as he believed the places were now called. But even that was fraught with danger. By law, he would have to produce the logbook and his driving licence for them to copy, plus proof of address, and they would be required to inform the DVLA that the vehicle had been scrapped. Furthermore, they would have to pay him for the car by cheque or bank transfer. Payment with cash was illegal. He knew that the police regularly checked ATFs, which meant that, even if they only had scant details of their suspect vehicle on record, there was a possibility some eagle-eyed "bluebottle" would make the connection and turn up on his doorstep one day. No, he couldn't afford to take that chance.

But, thinking about it, there *was* another way. There was an Irish Travellers' site out on the moor between Bridgwater and Taunton, with a load of caravans, piles of rubbish and partially broken-up old cars, nestling in a wooded dip, and he had gone there a couple of weeks ago to arrange for them to collect an old washing machine, a clapped-out garden mower and some other bits and pieces from his home. He was pretty sure they wouldn't care who he was, or insist on following DVLA regulations regarding the scrappage of motor vehicles. It would be cash in hand and good riddance to what would soon become a pile of nondescript metal.

Okay, so even that option posed a risk. The police could pay a visit to the Travellers' site and seize the car before it was stripped. But that was unlikely to happen, since he knew from his casual conversations with PC Kendrick in the past that the boys and girls in blue were always reluctant to venture on to such sites. First because of the hostile, obstructive reception they were certain to receive and second the complaints of harassment that would invariably be made against them afterwards. So, in reality, that particular risk was actually minimal and worth taking.

The next step then was a quick trip to the site Saturday morning to dump the car and, after that, a visit to a reputable dealer in Bridgwater to buy a cheap, good-quality second-hand replacement. Unfortunately, he would have to rely on bus transport to get there once he'd got rid of the Passat, but how did the saying go? "Beggars can't be choosers". And in that respect, he was at rock bottom where choice was concerned.

Pleased with the decision he had taken, he sat back in his study and from a drawer in his desk, took out the plastic bag containing some of the hair he had shaved off Tammy Robinson's head. Opening it up, he held it under his nose to smell the faint aroma that remained trapped inside. Pity he had lost Tammy, he thought regretfully. She would have made a first-class subject to experiment on. Then with a sigh, he closed the bag again and returned it to the drawer. Forget Tammy, he told himself firmly. She's beyond your reach now. But there is something you could do with her hair rather than just destroying it. He would have to talk to Mother about that.

* * *

'So the bastard's tried for another one,' Kate breathed, staring around the grassy area in front of the pumping station from outside the perimeter fence, which was now taped off.

Called to the scene by the uniformed patrol who had responded to the incident, she and Foster could scarcely conceal their frustration.

Foster grimaced. 'Doesn't look like he's intending to give up any time soon,' he said, and nodded towards the young girl sitting in the back of the ambulance. 'At least she wasn't harmed in any way, and it could have been a lot worse but for our plucky fisherman.'

Kate nodded. 'Ah, Mr Choudhry, yes, I've told him how grateful we are for his intervention. Pity he didn't get the make or number of the car matey-boy was driving, but as he said, everything happened so suddenly and it was gone in a flash. It does sound like the blue car Mixbury mentioned, though, so it looks like our nutter might still have the same vehicle . . .'

'Unless he just likes the colour blue and he's now driving something else, without the distinctive features we've been given.'

Kate gave him a critical look. 'That's right, go on and spoil it!'

'Hold up,' Foster said for reply. 'Boss is here.'

Kate went to meet Deidrie Hennessey, as she parked on the verge and walked towards them.

'Another attempt then?' the superintendent said, treating Kate to a tired, critical stare.

Kate nodded, watching as the ambulance now pulled away to take Mandy Williams to the hospital. 'It seems our man still has Tammy Robinson's mobile. He sent a WhatsApp message to Mandy on it, purporting to be Tammy, saying she had discharged herself from hospital and needed to meet up with Mandy here. He was waiting for her when she arrived, hooded again and armed with a hypodermic, no doubt containing the same sort of knock-out drug he used on his previous victim. But for the courageous intervention of a local fisherman, a Mr Choudhry, he would almost certainly have taken her, just as he did Tammy.'

Hennessey gave a big sigh. 'Child okay, is she?'

'Yes, shock and some bruises, that's all. Otherwise she seems fine, but she's been taken to hospital for a check-up to make sure. Interestingly, Jamie Foster found a crushed needle where the struggle took place, so I've sent for SOCO again to go over the scene.' She turned at the sound of a vehicle stopping behind them and saw a white Transit van, with the *Forensic Science* banner on the side a few feet away. 'Ah, looks like they're here.'

'Good. No description, I suppose?'

'No, but we could have turned up something on the car he may be using.'

She told her what Mixbury had said, adding, 'It's all conjecture, but I feel sure that the owner of the car from which the porno films were nicked by Mixbury could be our man and that he could be a member of staff at the Windmill Academy.'

Hennessey pondered that for a second or two. 'Be a bit difficult to prove in the circumstances. What are you going to do?'

'I've been thinking about that. It would be no good just barging in there and flinging accusations around with nothing to back them up. The place will be closed now for the weekend anyway, which means we've missed the opportunity. So, I intend circulating it to all patrols over the weekend as a vehicle of interest. If we can get it pulled over by Uniform, ostensibly as a routine check, at least then we'll know the ID of the driver.'

Hennessey looked sceptical. 'And if the owner of the car has already got rid of it?'

Kate flicked her eyebrows instead of shrugging. 'In which case, ma'am,' she said, 'we're back up that gumtree we spoke about before.'

CHAPTER 14

Saturday was a good day for some, but not others. For Tammy Robinson and Mandy Williams it was certainly a good day, as both were discharged from hospital first thing in the morning into the care of their parents. They were both fully aware of the fact that it could easily have been otherwise and they hugged each other in the hospital car park, promising to be friends for ever, before parting to be driven home, Tammy buried in a thick anorak, despite the warmth of the day, with a woolly hat covering her bare head.

It was also a good day for Joseph Mixbury. He attended a special remand hearing in court and, as Kate had predicted, he was released on bail, leaving the dock with a great big grin on his face.

It was not a good day for Kate Lewis and Jamie Foster, however, especially when they saw Mixbury walk free.

'So now we've got nothing,' Foster complained back in the CID general office. 'That scumbag obviously doesn't have to cooperate with us anymore and, if he holds more info than he's given us, he's not likely to share it.'

Kate did her best to shrug it off. 'Nothing we could do,' she said gloomily. 'The guv'nor wouldn't agree to extending his time in custody, so we were stuffed.'

Foster scowled. 'What do we do now then? Count paper-clips in the office, or spring clean the CID cars?'

'Neither,' Kate replied, suddenly chewing her lip with a new thought. 'Something's just occurred to me. Remember Jeremy Greatorex?'

'What, the deputy head?'

'The same. Tammy told us that her abductor kept on about his mother.'

'So?'

'Greatorex mentioned that he was a single man who lived with his mother—'

'And that makes him the abductor and murderer, does it?'

'No, but it's food for thought, isn't it? And don't forget, he said he'd been off sick for a fortnight when we saw him, which would have been well before Tammy Robinson was taken. Being sick would have given him the opportunity to plan and execute the abduction and, as Tammy was one of his pupils, he would have known all about her and her problems. In short, he would have had the means, the opportunity — *and* the motive, if he's not just a deputy head, but a bent one as well.'

'The fact that he lives with his mother just like our perp allegedly does and that he was sick at the time one of his pupils, for whom he had specific safeguarding responsibilities, was abducted doesn't prove anything. It could be just a coincidence.'

'Ah, once again the word coincidence that I hate so much. So, think on this. Why would an educated, professionally successful, middle-aged man with all life's opportunities before him be unmarried and still living with his mother? That sound normal to you? It's a bit like that TV programme, *Sorry*, with Ronnie Corbett, that everyone used to watch.'

Foster grimaced. 'Oh, come on, Kate, that's not right and it's certainly not PC! I'm surprised at you. Even I wouldn't have come out with something like that.'

'Liar! You've said worse than that in the past, and you will have been thinking it now anyway.'

'Whatever! He's entitled to be single and to live with his mother, if that's his choice. It shouldn't make him a suspect for serious crime.'

Kate gave a sheepish smirk. 'Okay, I accept my comment may have been a bit out of order for the purist brigade, but you must admit, he ticks all the boxes, and we can't afford to allow ourselves the luxury of magnanimity when we have a ruthless psycho still on the loose.'

'In which case, how are we supposed to follow up this latest theory of yours? Raid his house without a warrant in search of a blue car and a cellar containing a steel cage? Could be a bit problematic legally.'

'Nothing so drastic, but we need to bear him in mind as a possible suspect and it wouldn't do any harm to pay him another visit on some pretext or other, to give his place a surreptitious once-over.'

He groaned. 'Oh no, not another of your "can I use your toilet" subterfuges?'

She chuckled. 'Can I help it if I have a weak bladder?'

* * *

The owner of the blue VW car had left home early on the Saturday morning and was at the Travellers' site by ten, just as Mixbury was "wheeled" into court. A heavily built, balding man, with a bushy, black beard and a large pot belly that wobbled as he walked, emerged from a caravan the moment the prospective seller drove in and stood squarely in front of the car. Several other men and women appeared from among the rest of the caravans shortly afterwards and stood at a distance, followed by a ragged bunch of inquisitive children, all eyeing the new arrival suspiciously. Obviously, strangers weren't welcome, and a couple of mangy-looking dogs reinforced that fact by prancing up and down, snarling and barking viciously on the overlong ropes that only just about held them back as the driver of the Passat climbed out of the car.

'Yeah?' Beardy queried aggressively. 'An' what do *you* want?'

'How much would you give me for the car?' he asked.

Beardy grunted, his gaze flicking over it. 'Why? Hot, is it?'

'No, I just want to get rid of it and get a better one.'

'Then why not trade it in?'

'I wouldn't get anything for it.'

'Bollocks. Think I'm stupid? Nicked, is it?'

'Can you see me bothering to nick something like this?'

Beardy didn't answer, but took a slow walk around the VW, kicked the tyres a couple of times, then jerked open the driver's door and ran his gaze over the interior. Next, he opened the boot and peered inside. 'Lift the bonnet,' he growled.

The Traveller spent a few minutes under the lid, examining the engine, before slamming it shut and turning to face his visitor.

'How much you lookin'?'

'Three fifty.'

Beardy threw back his head and let out a loud guffaw. A couple of the men standing watching joined in, although, as they were standing some distance away, they couldn't have known what they were laughing at.

'You 'avin' a laugh? Give you fifty. No questions asked.'

'It's worth a lot more than that. Let's say a ton. The catalytic converter must be a good fifty on its own.'

He had no idea whether that was true, or not, but the internet site he'd checked had put the average scrappage cost of a vehicle at £150 to £350, and he wanted to get as much as he could out of the deal.

'Sixty's me final offer. Take it, or leave it.'

The Traveller's gaze was hard and uncompromising and the other sensed that that was it. He sighed and nodded. 'Deal.'

Beardy strode back to his caravan and returned with a wad, peeling off the notes with one big, dirty paw. Then he paused in the act of handing the cash over and said, 'Don't I know you?'

A quick jerk of the head. 'I wouldn't think so.'

A light seemed to come on behind Beardy's dark eyes as he slapped the notes into the other's outstretched palm. 'Yeah, I remember. Never forget a face, me. We got a washin' machine and then an old mower from your place a while back. Picked 'em up from yer, we did.'

'If you say so,' the nervous recipient of the cash replied, anxious to avoid getting into a revealing conversation with the Traveller. 'Couldn't run me back into town, could you?' he asked cheekily.

Another guffaw and the notes were slapped into his outstretched hand. 'Walkin's good for yer,' was the reply. 'Keeps yer fit.'

Then Beardy climbed into the car and drove it across the site, disappearing behind a ramshackle, tin shed.

Reluctantly, his visitor walked out of the site on to the main road and turned towards home. It would be a longish walk, but, as Beardy had said, the exercise was good for him, and at least he had got rid of what could have been an incriminating piece of evidence — or so he thought.

* * *

Blagging a village post office at eleven in the morning had been a big mistake and, as Mickey Joel raced away from the scene with a powerful police patrol car screaming its indignation around a quarter of a mile behind him, he knew he was facing a long stretch in stir if he was caught. He was already out on licence from Wormwood Scrubs after serving nine years for the same thing and although unlike the previous hit, his sawn-off had actually been a handmade load of crap this time, which couldn't have put a hole in anything, the judge was unlikely to see it that way. The terrified postmistress had *believed* the barrel poking out from under his coat had belonged to a real gun and that was enough. So, it was armed robbery and that was that. The old maxim, if you can't do the time, don't do the crime, was particularly galling too, as he'd only managed to get away with about fifty quid in notes before someone had called Old Bill and he'd heard the sirens approaching.

Feeling the tyres of his stolen Jag spinning on the uneven, tarmacked road surface as he took the next bend, he saw the crossroads sign coming up ahead and at the last minute hauled the steering wheel hard over to take the left-hand turn. He only just made it, careering almost out of control along the verge for around twenty yards and narrowly avoiding a plunge into a rhyne, before regaining control, but it turned out to be a good move, and he caught a momentary glimpse of the pulsing roof strobe in his offside mirror as the police Traffic car screamed past on the main road.

He was shaking as he followed the side road along at a much slower speed, searching for somewhere he could dump the car and nick another one. A wayside cottage or farm would have been good. Instead he found the Travellers' site and, after a moment's hesitation, swung into a field a few yards past it, switching off and leaning back against the leather seat as he tried to slow the crazy beating of his heart. He didn't stay there long, however, but headed back along the road on foot, turning into the entrance to the Travellers' site, looking for anything that had a decent set of wheels.

Beardy caught sight of him when the frenzied barking of the dogs gave him away as he was checking out an old Volvo 4x4 parked near the entrance. The big man had his neck in a stranglehold before he even realised he was behind him. At the same moment the warbling note of a siren drowned out the barking of the dogs and a flashing strobe was briefly reflected in the windows of the 4x4, as a police Traffic car raced past the entrance to the site. Seconds later there was a long, scraping, tearing sound as if it had skidded to a halt a few yards further on, no doubt after the crew had spotted the abandoned car. This was followed by the slamming of doors and loud shouts.

'They lookin' for you?' Beardy snarled, quickly glancing back at the site entrance, and before Joel could say anything he swore savagely and propelled him past the caravans to the tin shed behind which he had earlier parked the blue VW Passat.

'I don't want no trouble wiv' the law, you little prick,' Beardy said. 'So you can piss off through that gate and if you ever come back again I'll 'ave you buried 'ere. Got it?'

Joel was not the tough guy he liked to think he was and he was in no position to argue. Nodding furiously, he tore himself free and set off at a run through an open gateway and into the encircling woods, Shanks's pony being infinitely preferable to him than the prospect of either arrest or an early grave. But he wasn't a moment too soon. He had only just disappeared from sight when a second police patrol car swung onto the site and pulled up just inside the entrance.

The uniformed woman constable behind the wheel glanced around the site as she climbed out, closely followed by her male colleague sitting in the front passenger seat.

Beardy put on his most welcoming smile. 'Mornin' officers,' he said, walking towards them. 'Can I 'elp you?'

The male officer appeared unimpressed by his welcoming manner. 'Anyone come in here just now?' he growled.

Beardy shook his head, frowning when he saw the female officer peering into one of the caravans. 'I 'ain't seen no one. 'Ere, what's she doin'?'

PC George Larriman sniffed. 'We need to check out your site.'

'Got a warrant, 'ave you?'

'Don't need one,' Larriman replied. 'We're in immediate pursuit.'

'Pursuit of who?'

'Some arsehole who just blagged a local post office.'

Larriman walked away from him and joined his colleague as she was pushing past a middle-aged woman into the caravan. PC Felicity Terry reappeared almost immediately and moved to the next van while Beardy watched her impotently with a heavy scowl on his face.

After checking all the caravans, the two officers wandered around the site, peering into sheds and parked vehicles as they went, shortly joined by another policeman who walked on to the site from where the first police car had evidently stopped.

'It's the stolen Jag all right, George,' he said to Larriman, jerking a thumb back down the road. 'Scumbag's on his toes somewhere.'

Larriman nodded. 'We'd better circulate him.'

Hand on his personal radio, however, he paused at a shout from Felicity Terry who had taken a look behind the tin shed.

'Get a load of this,' she said as both the male officers walked over to her.

She was peering into the windows of the blue VW Passat that had just cost Beardy fifty pounds.

'Looks like the car that was circulated last night,' she said. 'Blue saloon, with a black bonnet lid and some fish logos on the back window. Seems someone decided to get rid of it PDQ.'

'This yours?' Larriman said to Beardy as he appeared at his elbow.

Beardy hesitated, but, realising he could hardly deny it, he shrugged. 'Geezer dumped it 'ere this morning,' he said. 'Then he just run off.'

'What geezer?'

'No idea. Just a punter.'

'Name? Address?'

'Dunno,' he said, adding sarcastically, 'didn't get 'is inside leg measurement neither.'

'What did he look like?'

'Can't remember.'

'Then you're in a lot of trouble.'

'Ain't I always?'

* * *

Greatorex was certainly surprised to see the two police detectives on his doorstep again, but when Kate asked if he could spare them a few minutes he seemed only too pleased to invite them inside.

189

Seated in the same sitting room as before, Kate noticed Greatorex studying her intently.

'How's the inquiry going?' he said. 'It's brilliant news that Tammy has been found safe. The head, er, Mrs Turnbull was in touch with me the moment she heard. I believe she was taken to hospital. I trust she wasn't injured in any way?'

'Mainly psychological damage, sir,' Kate replied. 'Nothing serious.'

'And do you know why this man the newspapers are talking about took her?'

'Not yet, I'm afraid.'

'And do you have any idea who he could be?'

'Inquiries are continuing, sir, but I'm sure you'll understand we can't go into that at this stage.'

'Of course, of course. I'm just glad Tammy is safe, that's the main thing. Now, I must admit, I'm rather curious as to why you wanted to see me again. After all, I don't think I can add any more to what I've told you before.'

Kate glanced quickly at Foster, then said, 'We've just had the attempted snatch of another girl from the academy, Mr Greatorex, a Mandy Williams.'

'Good Lord! Mandy? That's dreadful.'

'She's okay, though shaken up, but we're trying to establish if there could be a connection somewhere, that's why we've come to see you again.'

'Yes, of course. How can I help you?'

'We believe Mandy is a friend of Tammy Robinson?'

He nodded, still looking quite shocked. 'Yes, er, I believe they are very close friends.' He made a face. 'Certainly Mandy can be a problem, but not in the same way as Tammy, and I think her behaviour is heavily influenced by Tammy.'

'Can you think of an occasion when both girls together might have done something to someone, played a trick on them perhaps, which could have led to them becoming targets?'

He laughed. 'Well, I don't think either of them would have done anything awful enough to warrant that. They can both be insolent and rebellious at times and prone to outbreaks of quite disruptive behaviour, but that's as far as it goes. There's nothing inherently bad about them. They're just teenagers trying it on and seeing how far they can go.'

Kate thought for a moment, then took the plunge. 'Do you think anyone at the school might have felt particularly aggrieved by their behaviour, though? Someone perhaps who had strong religious beliefs and took exception to their attitude and felt they needed to be taught a lesson?'

He smiled at her almost indulgently. 'You mean, did I abduct her, lock her in a cage and cut off all her hair? The answer is no, I did not, and I can't think of anyone else who would have done that either.'

It was the detectives' turn to be caught on the wrong foot and for a moment Kate simply stared at him in astonishment.

Then he added, 'And your next question is bound to be, how did I know all this when the police haven't released that information yet, eh?'

Kate raised both eyebrows and nodded. 'That would certainly have been the next question, sir,' she agreed, clearing her throat. 'So, tell me, how *did* you know, can you explain that?'

Rising to his feet, he crossed to the coffee table and picked up a newspaper lying on top of some magazines. It was not the *Bridgwater Clarion* this time, but something called the *Saturday Record*.

'Got it this morning,' he said, handing the newspaper to Kate. 'It's a freebie. I get it delivered every week. Mother likes to read the human-interest stories. The piece I saw is on page three.'

Mystified, Kate ignored the headline and main story on the front and turned quickly to the relevant page. A photograph of Tony Robinson, adopting a suitably grim expression, glared at her from under the headline, *A FATHER'S ANGUISH*, and underneath was the byline, *Interview of Kidnap Victim's Father*. The piece was attributed to none other than Kate's "favourite" journalist, Debbie Moreton. Kate gritted her teeth and read on, growing angrier by the second. Robinson had revealed everything Tammy must have told him, or his wife, about the abduction, including how the schoolgirl had been tricked, a description of the cage in which she had been held, the fact that all her hair had been shaved off and even details of her captor's threats. No doubt Moreton, in her usual devious, underhand style, had approached him for an exclusive very soon after he had paid a visit to the hospital to see Tammy. Realising there was an opportunity to make a quick buck off the back of his distressed daughter, he had seized it with both hands. Not only did that make him an unprincipled moron but, since virtually nothing had been left out, it meant the whole country would know all there was to know about the abduction and, more importantly, the future interview of any suspect the police arrested would now be totally compromised.

Still burning with suppressed anger, Kate handed the newspaper back to Greatorex and treated him to a tight smile, as he said, 'Oh, and for your information, Inspector, I don't actually have a cellar here. Would that I had. I would be able to store a lot more of the excellent bottles of wine I have in my cocktail cabinet. So, you would have no need to check this out, but if you wish to take a look around please be my guest.'

There was no animosity in his voice, or in his expression, rather something akin to gentle amusement, and Kate nodded wryly. Touché, she mused, but quickly decided that there was no point in carrying out her original plan now. He would hardly have offered her the opportunity to look around the house if he'd had anything to hide. 'I don't think that will be necessary, sir,' she said, 'but thank you for the offer anyway.'

He smiled broadly. 'Is there anything else I can help you with?

'Just a couple more things,' she said. 'Are you aware of anyone at the school with strict Christian beliefs?'

'Not as I've noticed, no. The school operates on semi-Christian principles, but we do not adhere to any specific Christian doctrine and I think our teaching staff are pretty liberal in their views. Why do you ask?'

'I was just wondering what the school's attitude is towards religious discipline,' she said.

'Religious discipline?' he echoed. 'What, you mean the Ten Commandments and all that? Oh, I think those days are over now, don't you? Everything today is about human rights and multiculturalism. You can't breathe for it.'

Kate smiled. 'Thanks for your time, sir,' she said, rising to her feet. 'We'll be in touch if we need to see you again.'

'You didn't ask him about the blue car we circulated,' Foster said as they drove away.

'I thought about it,' she replied, 'but decided that, with the minimal amount of information now known solely to us after Tony Robinson blabbed to the world, we should keep something to ourselves.'

At which point Kate's radio activated and the police control room passed on the news that would have rendered that question unnecessary anyway. The suspect car had been found!

CHAPTER 15

A breakdown truck was recovering the stolen Jaguar from the field just along from the Travellers' site, with a Traffic car in situ blocking the road, when Kate and Foster arrived. The second patrol car was still parked on the site itself and Felicity Terry walked over to her as she climbed out of the CID car.

'We've got a guy who calls himself John Smith in the caravan over there, skipper,' Terry said. 'George Larriman's keeping him company until you can have words in his pearl.'

Kate shook her head. 'John Smith? You've got to be joking.'

Terry laughed. 'That's what he *says* his name is.'

'Then he must be related to all the other John Smiths we regularly come across among the Traveller community,' she commented drily. 'Must be one hell of a big family!'

'Where's this car?' Kate asked. 'We'll take a look at that first.'

Terry led the way to the back of the tin shed and the detectives studied the blue VW Passat parked there with keen interest.

'It's not nicked,' she said. 'We did a check. RO lives in Bristol.'

'It certainly looks like our motor,' Foster said, pointing first at the fish stickers on the back window, then at the black front wing, which stuck out like a sore thumb.

'Yeah,' Kate agreed. 'We'd better get SOCO up here to give it the once-over, then have it transported to the pound for a closer examination. What did *Mr Smith* say about it?'

'Not a lot,' Terry replied. 'He maintained some fella drove in here, abandoned the car and ran off.'

'Just like that?'

'Just like that.'

'Then we'd better have another chat with him, I think.'

Beardy didn't even look up from the fitted, cushioned box under the window when Foster and Kate invited themselves into his caravan. Larriman was sitting on the edge of an unmade bed opposite him. The policeman got up and left at a nod from Kate.

'Nice van, Mr Smith,' Kate said after introducing Foster and herself. 'Had it long, have you?'

Beardy said nothing and didn't even look up.

Kate sighed and took over Larriman's spot on the edge of the bed, leaving Foster to pull out a stool he found in a corner.

'Make yerself at 'ome then, why don't yer?' Beardy said suddenly, casting Foster a hostile glance.

Kate chuckled. 'So, it's Mr Smith, is it?' she asked.

'Yeah, as I told the other lot.'

Kate nodded. 'You and I know that that's a load of crap,' she said, 'but we're not really interested in what your real name is at this stage. We just want to know about the VW Passat at the back of the tin shed.'

Beardy met her gaze without wavering. 'I already told them pigs outside about that. It ain't nuffink to do wiv' me. This guy drove in an' dumped it there this mornin'. Then he run off.'

'What, like the guy who just dumped the Jag in the next field and ran off? Lot of people dumping cars on you today, then doing a runner, aren't there?'

'Jag weren't left 'ere. Field next door don't belong to me.'

'This site doesn't belong to you either, does it? You're all squatters.'

'Gotta live somewhere.'

'And we don't want to make that difficult for you. We just want to know about the VW and the man who was driving it.'

'Told yer. 'E drove it in and run off.'

'Why would he do that?'

''Ow should I know? Maybe 'e just wanted to get rid of it. Motor's rubbish anyway. Only good enough for scrap.'

'How much did you give him for it?'

'Didn't give 'im nuffink. Told you, 'e just dumped it 'ere.'

'Listen, we don't care about the rules on scrapping cars. That's between you and the DVLA. It's the guy in the car we're interested in. Don't make it difficult for yourself.'

'I ain't. Told you the truf.'

'So, what did this guy look like?'

'Didn't get much of a look at 'im.'

'You must have some idea if you saw him run off.'

He grinned. 'Ordinary lookin', wearin' ordinary sort of cloves. 'Ad an ordinary sort of 'aircut too.'

Kate lost patience and jumped to her feet. 'Okay, Mr bloody Smith, I'm through buggering about with you. You're under arrest.'

He looked staggered and his grin vanished. 'Arrested? What for?'

'How about obstruction and assisting an offender wanted in connection with abduction and murder? Do you find that funny?'

As Terry and Larriman were bundling a worried looking Beardy into the back of the Traffic car, Foster said to Kate, 'You won't be able to hold him on that.'

Kate smiled grimly. 'Probably not,' she said, 'but perhaps long enough to loosen his tongue.'

* * *

196

The previous owner of the blue VW Passat left Bridgwater in his newly purchased car at just after three. It was a smart, red, second-hand Volvo 245 estate. The car was pretty ancient, but it had had only two owners and was sold with a full history and a year's guarantee, so he was well satisfied. It had taken some time to fix up the purchase, once he had decided on it, but a credit card downpayment on the vehicle after all the paperwork was completed had secured the interest-free agreement and he had been able to take the car there and then, as it had a six-month MOT certificate and an equivalent valid excise licence.

The man drove straight home from the garage and parked the car in the drive outside his house while he checked over it again to ensure he hadn't missed anything dodgy. He had his head under the bonnet when the voice called to him, and he banged his head on the lid as he stood up to see who was there. It was his policeman neighbour with a Labrador dog on a lead.

'New car then?' Ray Kendrick asked with a grin.

The man forced a smile back, inwardly cursing the "nosy bastard".

'Your old Volkswagen pack up, did it?'

'More or less,' he replied. 'Scrapped it.'

The policeman looked uncomfortable for a moment. 'Sorry about the other night,' he said. 'You know, when I checked you out in the layby. I didn't know it was you. I didn't recognise your car in the dark.'

'Forget it,' he replied. 'Just doing your job. Not at work today then?'

'No, been off for a couple of days, on leave actually. Not back on till next weekend.'

'I expect you needed a break anyway with everything that's going on after that girl was abducted.'

'Don't know much about it. I haven't really been involved.'

'Lucky you. And I see you've got a dog now.'

'Yeah, got him yesterday,' Kendrick replied. 'Name's Fred. Ex-guide dog for the blind. His previous owner popped his clogs, so I took him on, as he was due for retirement anyway.'

The man slammed the bonnet of his car shut and approached Kendrick, holding his hand out to the dog. 'Hi, Fred,' he said.

To his surprise, the dog emitted a low growl and showed its teeth. He stepped back hurriedly.

'Well, I'm blowed,' the policeman exclaimed. 'He's not done that to anyone else. I don't know what's got into him.'

'I'm not really a dog person,' the man said. 'So, don't worry about it.'

Kendrick nodded. 'Well, I'd best be off. Fred needs a long walk. See you later.'

Not if I can bloody help it, he mused, relieved that at least Kendrick would have been on leave when he'd fled the scene of Mandy Williams' attempted abduction, so wouldn't know anything about the incident yet, and that the policeman couldn't remember much about his old car either, which had to be good news.

Had he known what had been happening at the Travellers' site that morning, he would have been a lot less happy.

* * *

It was obvious from the attitude of the man who called himself John Smith that being arrested and locked in a police cell amounted to little more than an inconvenience, even though he knew that the VW car seized from the Travellers' site might be linked to crimes of murder and abduction. He had obviously been a "guest" of the police before and it didn't take long for him to be identified as Frank William Briggs, aged fifty-two, with a host of previous convictions recorded against him, including burglary, theft, ABH, fraud and car ringing, who had only been released from prison eighteen months before after serving a three-year stretch for GBH With Intent.

It became frustratingly clear to both Kate and Foster that Briggs knew the ropes only too well when it came to police interviews and he immediately asked for his solicitor to be called before agreeing to say anything, then answered every question in the same way as Mixbury had done at his first inter-view with 'no comment'. His only admission was that he had, in fact, bought the car for scrap for sixty pounds, but beyond that he remained totally uncooperative. Unlike Mixbury, there proved to be no opportunity for a second crack at him either. After an hour and a half's unproductive questioning, Kate had to accede to his solicitor's demand for him to be to be released without charge. All they had against him was a tenuous offence of operating without an ATF licence and not registering the purchase and disposal of the car with the DVLA — which he would not have had time to do anyway.

Hennessey was less than sympathetic when Kate briefed her on what had happened, and it was apparent that the detective superintendent was under so much pressure from above over the continued lack of progress on the investigation that sympathy for anyone or anything was in short supply.

In the end, frustrated and disillusioned, Kate plumbed for the only outstanding inquiry that remained open to them, and an hour later they pulled up in the CID car outside a neat, detached bungalow in a smart, wooded area between Bristol and Clifton, which the DVLA record gave as the address of the registered owner of the Volkswagen Passat.

The elderly lady who answered the door was dressed in a neat print dress and wore her grey hair in a tight bun, and she initially greeted them both with a welcoming smile, until Kate flashed her warrant card and said who they were.

'Police?' the lady echoed, her hand flying to her mouth. 'What on earth is wrong?'

'Nothing wrong,' Kate reassured her. 'We would just like to speak to Mr Donald Green, if that's possible.'

The woman stared at her for a second, then treated her to a sad smile. 'I'm sorry, my dear,' she said. 'But you are several months too late. My husband died last December.'

Kate started. 'Oh, I'm so sorry,' she said, her embarrass-ment showing.

'Don't be,' the old lady said, 'He's with the Lord now. But can I help in any way? My name's Audrey.'

Kate took a deep breath. 'I don't wish to bother you at a time like this,' she said. 'It's only about a car he used to own.'

To her surprise Audrey Green chuckled. 'Not that awful blue thing with the black bonnet?' she said.

Kate nodded. 'Yes,' she replied, even further taken aback, and she gave the other woman the registration number.

'You'd better come in,' the old lady said, standing to one side.

Seated in a chintzy front room with walls carrying biblical texts and religious pictures, Audrey Green revealed that her husband had been the local minister and had bought the car several years before from a garage near Bath, planning to do it up.

'He liked his old cars,' she said. 'But he never got around to restoring that one. It was a pity, because he said it had low mileage for its age and had a good, reliable engine.' She chuckled. 'About the only thing he did manage to do was to put some little fish stickers on the back window, which I thought looked rather silly, but Don said that, as Christian symbols, they were a sign of his faith, and that was important to him.'

'What happened to the car?' Kate asked.

The woman sighed. 'Don became quite ill a few months before he died and, as I didn't drive, he decided to sell the car so I would have a little bit of money behind me after he'd gone. He put an advertisement in the local newspaper and almost immediately this man came round and offered him five hundred pounds for it.' She frowned. 'I didn't like the man, and I thought the car was worth a lot more than that, but Don was desperate. He knew he was dying, and he said the man's money was as good as anyone else's. He sold him the car there and then and the man drove it away the same day.'

'Do you know who this man was?' Foster asked.

She shook her head. 'No, I'm afraid not.'

'Can you remember what he looked like?' Kate said.

'Well, if I remember correctly, he was shortish and very well educated, with blond hair down to his shoulders, which

I really dislike in a man, and he had one of those thin moustaches, just like the actor, David Niven. I particularly noticed that he was wearing a rather smart, brown checked suit and a yellow bowtie with a yellow handkerchief in the top pocket of his jacket. Oh yes, and he had this gold tooth at the front, which looked quite ridiculous. That's all I can tell you, I'm afraid.'

Kate smiled at her, her admiration apparent. 'You couldn't have been clearer,' she said. 'You have an excellent memory.'

The elderly lady's face flushed with embarrassment. 'Thank you, Inspector,' she said, seemingly incurious as to the reason for the detectives' interest in the car. 'Now, would you like some tea and perhaps a homemade scone?'

Kate hesitated, keen to get on, but not wishing to appear churlish after all the help they had been given by this dear old soul. She nodded. 'That would be very nice,' she replied.

There was a gleam in Kate's eyes as they finally got back into the CID car and Foster immediately picked up on the excited vibes he was getting from her.

'Something she said?' he asked, as he fastened his seatbelt.

'Willie Wigginshaw,' she replied.

'Who?'

'Audrey Green's description of the car buyer fits Willie Wigginshaw down to a T.'

'And who the hell's Willie . . . whatever his name is when he's at home, and how do you know him?'

'You forget my time as DI in Bristol. Willie Wigginshaw is a nasty little villain, who's into a variety of rackets in the city. He comes from a well-to-do family in Bath, but disgraced himself after being cashiered from the RAF for fraud. He also got two years for it and was thrown out of the family. He's now a Bristol low life and runs a dodgy backstreet garage in the city.'

'So let's go see him then.'

'My thoughts exactly.'

* * *

Wigginshaw Motors occupied the corner of a minor cross-roads on the east side of Bristol and comprised a grey, rendered block of a building set back from one of the narrow roads that bordered it on two sides and fronted by a tarmacked forecourt. There were several cars in evidence on the forecourt, late in the afternoon, all with garish *FOR SALE* placards on their roofs, but with no mention of price, and behind these the wide glass doors of the showroom had been hauled back to reveal a couple of gleaming sports tourers.

A short man with thinning, shoulder-length, blond hair, dressed in a brown checked suit and yellow bowtie, as per Mrs Green's description, emerged from a back office the moment the detectives entered the showroom and started looking at one of the tourers.

'Can I help you people?' he drawled. 'You're just in time before we close.'

Then, as Kate turned towards him, his toothy smile abruptly vanished and his eyes narrowed. 'Ah, Detective Inspector Lewis,' he went on smoothly, 'I thought you'd left us in peace for good.'

'Hello, Willie,' Kate said. 'Thanks for the welcome back. Can we have a little chat in your office?'

He shrugged. 'Do I have a choice?'

Wigginshaw's office was not much bigger than Kate's own office in CID. Opposite the door, just in front of the single window, there was an old-fashioned wooden desk, with a bosun's swivel chair behind it, and facing this was a long stool covered by a black leather cushion standing against the partition wall. A laptop occupied the paper-strewn desk and a printer stood on a metal filing cabinet in the corner beside it. The walls carried framed photographs of a variety of flashy-looking sports cars, together with a larger photograph of a much younger Willie Wigginshaw in full RAF uniform, which he obviously had no qualms about displaying even though he had been thrown out of the service in disgrace.

'You're missing a picture there, Willie,' Kate said, pointing at the RAF photograph as he dropped into the swivel chair behind his desk.

He frowned and swivelled round to look. 'What picture?' he said.

'The one with you wearing the uniform you were given in the nick.'

There was a look of alarm on his face and he craned his neck to see past them both into his showroom. 'Hey, steady on, Inspector,' he exclaimed. 'I could have customers in the showroom.' Then he scowled, and asked irritably, 'What is it you want?'

'Just some information, Willie,' Kate replied and placed her mobile phone in front of him on his desk, which showed a rearview photograph of the Volkswagen Passat. 'Remember this car?'

He peered at it. 'Never seen it before.'

Kate's expression hardened. 'I hope you're not going to be awkward, Willie,' she said. 'We know you bought the car off an elderly man, named Donald Green, over near Clifton. Responded to an advertisement, we believe. Gave him five hundred pounds for it. Does that ring a bell?'

He shook his head. 'Can't say that it does, Inspector,' he said.

'Willie,' she said, 'it's me you're talking to, so don't waste my time. My colleague and I are not interested in the fact that you bought, then sold the car on the quiet without registering either transaction with the DVLA. What *we* want to know is who bought it off you.'

'I honestly don't remember that particular vehicle,' he said apologetically. 'Be fair, I can't be expected to remember every car I buy, or sell.'

'You'd remember this one,' Foster put in. 'It had a black bonnet lid and, as the picture shows, fish symbol stickers in the corners of the back windows, plus a Christian cross.'

The dealer made a pretence of wrinkling his brows and trying to think. 'Sorry, old bean,' he replied with a smirk. 'Doesn't trigger anything in the old grey matter, I'm afraid.'

Kate released one of her deliberate sighs and turned back towards the door. She had heard voices in the showroom and had noticed Wigginshaw glancing nervously in that direction.

'What was it really like being in clink, Willie?' she said, raising her voice. 'You got three years for fraud, and a dishonourable discharge from the RAF, didn't you?'

His eyes widened. 'Keep your voice down,' he protested at just above a whisper. 'I'm trying to earn a living here.'

'The car,' Kate continued ruthlessly, retrieving her mobile. 'Who did you sell it to?'

Another quick glance at the door at the sound of a knock, and he waved a hand at the young woman standing there. 'Be with you in a minute, madam,' he called out. 'I'm just finishing off with these two customers. Do have a good look around.'

'That's fine,' a female voice acknowledged politely. 'There's no hurry.'

'The car?' Kate repeated when she heard the talking resume back in the showroom. 'Now!'

'Okay, okay,' Wigginshaw said hastily. 'Come to think of it, I do remember the VW. It was high mileage and in rubbish condition. I just wanted to get rid of the thing. This punter happened to come in very soon after I'd bought it and I seized the opportunity for a quick sale. As it was a sort of in-and-out situation, I, er, just forgot to do the necessary with the DVLA.'

'I'm sure you did. So, who was the buyer?'

'I couldn't tell you. I didn't get his details. But he was a pain in the arse, I can tell you that. Came in on foot and said he wanted something cheap as a runabout, because, living in Bristol, he hadn't needed a car, but was now moving from the city out on to the Somerset Levels.'

Kate's interest was instantly aroused. 'And?'

He swallowed several times. 'He argued about the price. Said it was too much, even though the vehicle was taxed and MOT'd. He claimed he was starting a new job, and it didn't pay a lot.'

'How much was the car priced at?'

'Er, couple of grand, if I remember rightly.'

Kate thought of what Donald Green had been paid and felt a surge of anger, but she forced herself to stay on track. 'Did he say what the job was?'

'He said something about working at a school — groundsman, I think. Yes, that was it, school groundsman.'

Kate glanced quickly at Foster.

'Can you remember what he looked like?'

He shook his head. 'Not really. He was wearing an anorak, woolly hat pulled down low over his ears, big sunglasses and one of those stupid COVID masks everyone seems to be wearing now after the recent pandemic. Beyond that and the fact that he paid me one thousand two hundred in cash, I can't remember much else about him.'

'Did he tell you the name of the school, or where it was?'

''Fraid not,' he said, 'and that's the gospel truth.'

Kate stared at his twitchy face for a moment and then nodded. 'I hope for your sake it is, Willie,' she warned. 'You really wouldn't want me to have to come back again.'

On the way out, Kate was tempted to warn Wigginshaw's new customers, who she saw were trying out the seats of a Vauxhall Astra, that they were about to be had over by an unscrupulous ex-con, but she thought better of it and walked on, out into the sunlight, instead. Though it peeved her to see a couple of naive youngsters about to be ripped off, it wasn't her place to interfere, and it was more than her job was worth anyway. She couldn't solve all the wrongs of the world on her own.

'A groundsman then?' Foster said, as they drove away.

Kate nodded, her excitement now showing. 'And at a school on the Somerset Levels too. That's what Willie said his buyer told him and Willie had no reason to come out with that if it wasn't true. And there's a particular groundsman that seems to fit the bill too. It's been staring us in the face all this time.'

'Tom Merchant at the Windmill Academy,' he summarised. 'But the guy who bought the car said he had just got the job, whereas Merchant said he's been there for years.'

'Maybe, but for some unknown reason Willie could have been making up what the guy is supposed to have said to him. On the other hand, the guy himself could have been telling Willie porkies. We have no way of knowing exactly what the buyer did say. But the fact remains that he fits the sort of profile we're looking for in our abductor. Ex-Royal Navy, which suggests an old-school mentality and a strong belief in respect, order and discipline. Someone who thinks children should be seen and not heard. We know he resented the bad behaviour of the girls at the school and he got really wound up about it when we spoke to him, saying that they should receive some old-fashioned punishment. We know also that Tammy poured sugar into the petrol tank of his mower, and Jeremy Greatorex revealed that Merchant blew a gasket when he found out about it and said she needed a good thrashing. Yet he said nothing to us about something so serious when we saw him and he gave the impression he didn't know who Tammy was. It's all there, Jamie, and we never picked it up.'

He grunted. 'Maybe, but what do we do about it, that's the point? As I've said before, we can't prove anything against anyone. Everything we've got is either just conjecture, or bits of the jigsaw we've pulled out of the box, but cannot yet join up, and Merchant is hardly going to admit to anything voluntarily, is he?'

'So, let's ask him,' she said.

CHAPTER 16

The tied house that Tom Merchant occupied stood on a small plot immediately to the left of the school and it was obvious that it was well looked after. The front garden consisted of neat lines of vegetables and there were apple and pear trees budding against a low brick wall on the opposite side. A recently painted and still tacky wrought-iron gate accessed a gravel path that cut through the vegetables in a perfectly straight line to a smart front door with gilt furniture set within a small, square porch flanked by bay windows.

An attractive plump woman in her early thirties answered Kate's knock on the door and she smiled, seemingly unperturbed by the sight of the two detectives standing there.

'Is Mr Merchant in?' Kate asked, producing her warrant card and introducing them both. 'We'd like a quick word with him, if he's free.'

The woman half-turned and called back down the hall. 'Dad, police for you.'

Merchant appeared behind her in the hallway seconds later, dressed in blue jeans, an open-necked blue shirt and a fawn cardigan. His lean face wore the same lugubrious expression as before and he stared at them with obvious hostility.

'And what do you two want?' he growled. 'Bit late in the day for you to call on people, isn't it? We've already had our supper.'

'Dad!' the young woman exclaimed. 'Don't be so rude. Invite them in.'

Merchant shrugged, but said nothing and disappeared through a doorway.

'Please,' the woman said, looking embarrassed, 'do come in. I'm his daughter, Grace, and I'm sorry he's such a miserable old sod. He's always been the same.'

Kate chuckled at the apt description. 'We *have* met your dad before,' she replied, 'so we didn't expect a royal welcome.'

Grace Merchant led them down the hall into a small, sparsely furnished sitting room. Her father was sitting in a high-backed, winged chair and he hardly looked at them as his daughter showed them in and waved them to a small settee.

'Would you like a cup of tea?' she asked, and cast an angry look at her father when he gave a disparaging snort.

Kate declined on behalf of both of them, and she smiled. 'Then I'll leave you to it,' she said, and threw her father another dagger-sharp glance before leaving the room.

'We wanted to ask you a few more questions, Mr Merchant,' Kate began, 'and we hope you can help us out.'

There was another snort and the hard blue eyes turned towards her. 'Do you?' he said. 'But that depends on whether I want to answer your questions, or not, doesn't it?'

Kate mentally counted to five. 'It's about a car, sir,' she said, 'a blue Volkswagen Passat, with a black bonnet and Christian fish symbols on the back window.' She recited the registration number. 'We believe you previously owned a car of that description?'

To her surprise, there was a short laugh. 'Me? You have to be joking.'

Kate pulled out her mobile and, crossing to the chair in which he was sitting, she showed him the photograph of the car, as she'd shown Wigginshaw. 'This car,' she said impatiently. 'We understand you purchased the car from a dealer in Bristol,' she went on doggedly before returning to her seat.

He pulled out a packet of cigarettes and lit up. 'Then you'd be wrong,' he replied. 'I've never owned the car and that's a fact.'

'The dealer told us he sold it to the groundsman at the school,' she said, gilding the lily unashamedly by suggesting Wigginshaw had named the academy and avoiding Foster's frown of consternation.

'Did he?' Merchant commented. 'Well, I'm the only groundsman at the Windmill Academy and have been for several years, so why would he say that? Who is this clown and why are you so interested in this car anyway?'

Kate didn't answer the first part of his question, but said, 'It's part of the inquiry we are carrying out into the abduction of the young girl we told you about before, named Tammy Robinson.'

He grunted. 'Still on that, are we?' he said. 'I thought she'd been found. So, you suspect me of snatching her, do you?'

There was an ironic half-smile on his face now, as if he found the whole thing cynically amusing.

'No one is accusing you of anything,' Kate said quickly. 'But the car is relevant to our inquiries and we need to establish who owns it.'

He stubbed out his unfinished cigarette on a tin lid on the chair arm and blew a cloud of smoke in her direction as he swivelled round in the chair to face her.

'Is that so, missie,' he said. 'Well, let me enlighten you on the situation. I do not own the car and never have. In fact—' he seemed about to relish what he was going to say — 'I don't own any car, for the simple reason that I don't drive!'

Kate couldn't help herself tensing in the chair. 'You mean you're not able to?'

'No,' he said slowly. 'I'm not allowed to, on account of the fact that I have had two strokes and I suffer from acute diabetes. The DVLA seem to think I could be a danger to other road users, so they took my licence away over two years ago now. Satisfied?'

The bitterness in his tone was very plain.

For a moment Kate was completely thrown, inwardly cursing her negligence for not checking his licence with the DVLA first, which was standard practice before an interview like this. She had been in too much of a rush to confront the man who had become the prime suspect in her mind, and she had screwed up as a result.

Nevertheless, she was quick to recover her composure. 'In which case,' she went on brazenly, 'can I ask you if you have ever seen this car parked at the school, or know who the owner is?'

'Can't help you,' he said sullenly. 'Now, can you just go? I've got nothing more to say to you.'

Foster didn't make any comment about the faux pas as they drove away, but she could tell what he was thinking, and an uncomfortable silence descended on the car for the next few miles. Then suddenly he chuckled. 'That went well anyway,' he remarked. 'What do you think we could have done as an encore?'

'Very funny,' she said. 'You don't have to rub it in.'

'Not trying to,' he replied. 'It's my fault too. I should have thought about checking up on his licence as well. You know the old adage, more haste, less speed. But it does seem strange that, according to your mate, Willie, the character who bought the car revealed that he was moving to the Somerset Levels to take up a job at a school, which was a bit of a daft admission considering what he was planning to do.'

Kate shook her head. 'It was an attempt to get the car's price right down, nothing more. You know, "look mate, I can't afford much. I've just taken on a pretty low-paid job in a school," and he obviously said it was as a groundsman to support his claim. At that stage, getting a cheaper car was his priority, so he had to be as convincing as possible.'

'Then why hide his face the way Willie said he did?'

She shrugged. 'Maybe the crimes he was planning to commit once he was in the job were still at the embryo stage, but he was looking ahead and trying to ensure someone wouldn't be able to identify him and tie him into ownership of the car if that were to be spotted at a future crime scene later? He was being ultra careful and no doubt specifically went to a dodgy dealership like Willie's so he wouldn't have to reveal his identity.'

'A devious bastard then?'

'Haven't we known that from the start?'

'Yeah, and now we've had to rule out the only real suspect we had left it looks like any chance we had of feeling our perp's collar has gone to rat shit.'

* * *

Kate was still furious with herself when she got home that evening — not only about the debacle over Merchant and the driving licence issue, but also the dead end that had once more been reached after all the time and effort that had been put into following up on the history of the VW car. And to make matters worse, there was no Hayden there to comfort her and cool her down. He was out at a meeting of the classic car club he belonged to and she knew from past experience that he would not be back until very late that night.

Not in the mood to cook herself anything for supper, she settled instead for a double cheese sandwich and a glass of red wine, which soon became two, and she was slumped in the corner of the settee in the living room, half-asleep, when the house phone rang at dead on nine o'clock.

'Control room, ma'am,' the voice at the other end announced cheerfully. 'Sorry to ring you this late, but we had a call from a Tom Merchant. He said he wanted to get hold of you, but we told him we weren't allowed to give out police officers' private numbers. He asked if you could ring him instead. I'll give you his number . . .'

Frowning, Kate took down the number and, finishing the last of her glass of wine, she quickly dialled it.

'Kate Lewis,' she said a little tersely when Merchant's growling voice answered.

There was a characteristic grunt from the other end. 'Been thinking since you left.'

'About what exactly?'

'I should have come clean with you, but I was mad that you had even thought I could be somehow involved in the abduction of that kid. I may be a grouchy old sod, but I'm not some pervert who's into kidnapping fourteen-year-old schoolgirls.'

Anticipating that he might have something interesting to say, she said encouragingly, 'Go on.'

He cleared his throat. 'I've always kept myself to myself, never got involved in other folk's business, understand? That's why I didn't say anything to you this afternoon.'

Kate gritted her teeth, feeling her insides tense. Just get on with it, she mused. What is it you want to tell me? But she held herself in check and said nothing, waiting for him to come out with whatever it was he had to say.

'I *have* seen the car you showed me parked in the school grounds,' he said suddenly, adding, 'and what's more, I've seen who's been driving it.'

Kate's throat was dry with excitement, but, before she could ask him the question that was burning a hole in her tongue, he said, 'But if I tell you, it's in the strictest confidence, and I wouldn't want anyone else to know about it. That's the deal.'

'You've got my word on it,' she said in a voice that didn't sound like her own.

So, he cleared his throat and told her. Then he cut the call.

* * *

Kate felt as if she had been physically winded, and the name Merchant had given her went round and round in her head for quite some time. After the humiliating disappointment she had suffered with her interview of the groundsman earlier, the fact that he had, out of the blue, delivered a potential suspect to her on a plate took a bit of digesting. If he was telling the truth, of course, and not simply trying to smear someone he didn't like, or trying to get back at her by feeding her duff information to cause her further embarrassment.

That seemed pretty unlikely, though. Why would he bother? He didn't strike her as the sort of person who liked to play silly games, and what would he get out of it anyway? She was the one who had cocked up, not him, so he had no reason to want to cause her further grief.

But assuming his information was pukka, the question was what to do with it at this time of the night? Common sense dictated that following up on it would have to be left until the morning, and even then it would be necessary to proceed with the greatest caution. It would be stupid to simply barge into the suspect's home and confront him with allegations that could not be substantiated and in respect of which there was no independent evidence. That was where things had gone wrong with Merchant. This time some degree of subtlety would be required. Yet, with the endgame so tantalisingly close, to be just sitting there in her living room pontificating on the situation went completely against the grain. Every fibre of her being screamed at her to *do something* and despite all the problems overt action had cost her in the past — earning her those nicknames "Maverick" or "Go It Alone Kate" — resisting her inner urges as the night wore on became more and more difficult.

She did consider telephoning Foster to make him aware of the new suspect they had in the frame, to discuss things with him, and at one point she actually started to dial his home telephone number on her personal mobile. But then she realised the futility of that and cut the call. They couldn't move in on the suspect until the following day anyway, so there was no point in bothering him at what was now after ten at night, and, since Hayden was out at his club meeting and was unlikely to be home until after 1 a.m., she couldn't even talk to him about it. But there was one thing she could do. She already knew where the suspect lived, so there was nothing to stop her heading out there now to reconnoitre the place and see if she could turn up anything of evidential value in advance of the approach they decided on in the morning. It would be risky, but so was living and, as she'd said to herself so often in the past, if she was careful, what could possibly go wrong?

* * *

Even as Kate made her decision to once again revert to her maverick past, her "person of interest" was in the process of getting ready for bed, and the last thing he had been expecting was the double ring on his doorbell. Muttering his annoyance, he strode down the hall to the front door, clad in his lime-green dressing gown and matching slippers. Who the hell could be calling on him at this late hour? For a second his heart flipped. Not the police, surely? If it was, it could mean they had sussed him out and had come to arrest him. But if that was the case, where was their car? All he could see through the window beside the door was what looked like a small, flat-bed lorry, clearly visible under the streetlight. He felt a lot better as he turned the handle on the door. It was probably some delivery driver who had seen the house lights on and was looking for directions.

But it wasn't, and the balding ruffian with the big, black beard standing on his doorstep had barged him out of the way and was into the hall before he could get the door closed in time.

'Remember me?' the man police now knew as Frank William Briggs snarled at him, holding him up against the wall with one muscular hand gripping him round the throat. 'You owes me some dosh, mister, for that motor what you sold me.'

He stared back at the Traveller, his eyes bulging. 'I don't owe you anything,' he choked. 'It was a straightforward sales transaction. In fact, you gave me a lot less for the car than it was worth.'

'Yeah,' Briggs agreed, 'but then Old Bill turned up and seized it, didn't 'e?'

'Old Bill? The police, you mean?'

Briggs released his grip, but still held him against the wall with his bulk. 'Yer catches on fast, don't yer?' he sneered. 'And on account o' them taking it, I'm down sixty quid.'

'But-but what did the police want with the car?'

'From what I 'ear, it's mixed up in somefink you done. Seems you been a very naughty little prick.'

'I don't know what you mean.'

'Abduction and murder, they called it.'

'That's-that's nonsense.'

Briggs grinned. 'Then you'd better sue 'em 'adn't you? But before you do, I wants the bundle back what I give you — plus expenses.'

'Expenses? What expenses?'

'Damage to my reputation would be a good start. Then there's me mental 'elf to take into account. Shock of bein' nicked an' all that. A couple of grand should do it.'

'A couple of . . . You've got to be joking.'

Briggs' eyes narrowed and his grin disappeared. 'Jokin'? No, I ain't jokin'. See, I never told Old Bill who sold me the car, did I? If I 'ad, you'd be in the nick by now. So, you owes me for that an' all.'

Trapped against the wall, the other made an attempt to stand his ground. 'I owe you nothing and I intend giving you nothing. So, you might as well leave now.'

Briggs shook his head. 'Fing is, I'm what people calls an opportoonist. I makes the most out of what comes up, an' that's what I'm doin' now. See, I don't care what you done and who you done it to. All I'm interested in is makin' some dosh out of it. You give me what I want an' I'll be gone quicker than shit off a shovel. Ovverwise . . .' He paused for effect and deliberately allowed the donkey jacket he was wearing to fall open to reveal a long-bladed knife in a leather sheath that was attached to his belt. 'I might 'ave to be a bit more persuasive like.'

'This is robbery.'

''Course it is, but so what? Now, let's 'ave a look round your gaff and see what you got that I might take a fancy to. Don't worry about me takin' too much. I got a little lorry out front.'

Briggs stepped back slightly, then pushed his reluctant "host" ahead of him along the hall towards an open doorway. 'We'll start down 'ere, I fink. What's in this room then?'

'N-nothing. It's just a sitting room.'

'Well, we'll take a look anyways, eh? Yer never knows what we might find.'

Shortly afterwards, after a visit to both the sitting room and the dining room and with the big pockets of his coat bulging with silver miniatures and other valuable heirlooms, Briggs was in the kitchen and frowning at the door to the cellar.

'What's in there then?'

'Just a cellar full of rubbish.'

'Is that right? So, let's 'ave a dekko, shall we? Bet yer got some nice vino, or a few bottles of a good malt down there.'

It was at that moment that the man in the green dressing gown lost patience and quite coldly and precisely came to the conclusion that he would have to kill his unwelcome visitor. Seeing the steel steak hammer standing on the worktop to the right of the door by the unwashed plate from his evening dinner, he made the decision that that would do the job rather nicely.

* * *

Hayden Lewis had stomach-ache. He conveniently put it down to constipation, refusing to accept the fact that it might have had something to do with the way he had, as usual, pigged himself at the supper provided after the classic car club meeting. But whatever the cause, he decided to take his leave soon after the meal and headed home in his prized, red Mk II Jaguar, to seek sympathy from his long-suffering wife, Kate.

It was well after eleven when he pulled into the driveway of their cottage in the village of Burtle and he was surprised to see that Kate hadn't left the porch light on before going to bed. His surprise turned to astonishment when he found the house was empty and that there were no signs of Kate having even been to bed. At first he assumed she must have been called out on a job, but seeing no note, which she invariably left for him in such instances, unease became worry. Picking up the house phone, he rang the control room to find out, waiting tensely as the operator checked the log.

'A guy named Tom Merchant rang here at eight fifty asking her to ring him back,' the operator said. 'We passed the message on and that was that.'

'Do you know what he wanted?' Hayden asked.

'No idea, mate. We just gave her the message.'

'Can I have the fellow's number?'

'Problem, is there?'

'I sincerely hope not.'

Merchant's phone rang for ages, until finally a man's crabby voice answered. 'Who the hell is this?'

Hayden told him. 'Are you Tom Merchant?'

'Do you realise what time this is?'

Hayden didn't answer, but he was in no mood for niceties. 'My wife has disappeared,' he snapped. 'I need to know what you rang her about.'

'That was confidential.'

'Listen to me,' Hayden warned. 'I am also a police officer and I'm not playing games with you. What was it about?'

There was a rasping cough. 'I knew I should have kept my mouth shut,' Merchant wheezed. 'That bloody wife of yours—'

Hayden didn't let him finish. 'Never mind that!' he shouted, his anger boiling over. 'Just tell me. We're wasting time.'

'Okay, okay,' Merchant acknowledged. 'I told her about a VW car she was interested in that I'd seen parked at the Windmill Academy. I think she suspected that the owner of it might have had something to do with that girl, Tammy Robinson, who was snatched the other day.'

'Anything else? Come on, man. Give me the rest.'

Merchant hesitated. 'I told her who I'd seen driving it. She got pretty excited then and I reckon she must have gone after him.'

'So, who was this man?'

Very reluctantly Merchant told him, then added in a snarl, 'Now leave me alone,' and slammed the phone down.

Hayden was not much further forward. He had some knowledge of the case his wife had been working on, because of his involvement in the surveillance and arrest of Mixbury, but he wasn't fully conversant with the rest of it. Though Merchant had provided him with the information about the VW car and the name of the man he had seen driving it, which had obviously prompted Kate to go off on her reckless venture, he had not been able to tell him the man's address.

Knowing Kate as he did, Hayden guessed that at this time of night she could only be on a lone snooping expedition, probably looking for evidence for a later raid. That meant a call to her mobile would be the last thing she would want, though if she had had any sense she would have already switched her phone to 'silent'. But he couldn't concern himself about that. Her safety was more important than any embarrassment caused to her by the interruption. But as it transpired, he had no impact at all on what she was doing. The automated voice at the other end told him that the phone was probably switched off.

He was getting desperate now. But then, on the verge of getting the control room to ring Jamie Foster at home to seek his help, he spotted Kate's pocketbook lying on the coffee table where she had left it. Aware of how she operated, he snatched it up and flicked through the pages at the back where she usually made non-evidential notes. There was only a slender chance that she had recorded the details he needed, but it was a possibility worth following up on.

Seconds later the name and address jumped out at him and he quickly rang the control room again to ask for a unit to be immediately despatched to the location.

'No can do,' the operator replied. 'All units committed re a multiple on the A38. Will try and get one released, but we're short on the ground at the moment.'

Hayden didn't bother to reply. Stuffing the notebook into his pocket, he grabbed his anorak and car keys and headed for the door.

CHAPTER 17

Briggs had always been a bully, unashamedly using his powerful bulk to intimidate people whenever he chose to, supremely confident in the knowledge that he would always get his own way. He was also extremely greedy and it was his failure to recognise in his limited perception of things that greed and over-confidence could be a bad combination for someone on the wrong side of the law. Coupled with that, the man he was dealing with may not have had his muscular strength and his intimidating bulk, but he was more astute and a lot more dangerous than Briggs would ever be had he survived to old age — which it was preordained he would not.

'There's nothing in the cellar but rubbish, I assure you,' the man in the lime-green dressing gown repeated to his unwelcome visitor, and he turned away from the door instead of opening it.

Briggs leered at him, seeing his reluctance to go any further as proof that he was hiding something special. 'Oh yeah?' he sneered. 'Then let's see, shall we? Open the door.'

'No, I won't. I've told you there's nothing of value down there and I've no intention of venturing into that filthy place in just my PJs and dressing gown.'

The big man lost patience. 'Well, I don't believe you,' he growled and, pushing him roughly out of the way, he pulled open the door, and peered at the steps leading down into the blackness.

'Where's the bleedin' light?'

His reluctant host reached past him and flicked the switch on the wall. A pale flicker reached up from the depths towards them.

Briggs gave a knowing grin and stepped on to the first step, stopping only briefly before beginning the descent, the thud of his heavy leather boots echoing off the walls as he went.

The other waited until the Traveller was two to three steps down and at about the right level below him to inflict the most forceful blow he could. Then he sprang forward on to the steps, whipped the steak hammer out of the pocket of his dressing gown and brought it down with all the strength he could muster on the back of Briggs' head.

He'd expected a cry of pain, or at the very least one of panic as the Traveller pitched headlong down the steps in a tangle of arms and legs, but there was nothing — only the sickening crunch of the vicious blow and the sound of the body rolling over and over until it ended up on its back on the concrete floor.

He sprinted after it at the same moment, and he was astride his victim with the steak hammer held high in the air even as Briggs twitched and began to make a series of choking moans, trying to get up. Without hesitation, he brought the hammer down with even more force again and again on the big man's unprotected face and skull, reducing it to a bloody, shattered mess, and only when he was satisfied that his unwelcome visitor was dead did he climb up off him. Then, without giving the body a second glance, he reascended the stairs, switched off the cellar light and closed the door behind him. Back in the kitchen, he washed the blood off the steak hammer and returned it to its rightful place in a kitchen drawer for its more conventional use later, before heading for the stairs to his bedroom. He would have to get rid of the Traveller's lorry, he thought, perhaps dump it out on the moor somewhere, well away from the house, then think about getting rid of the body. But before that he needed to change out of his bloodstained dressing gown and burn it, which was a pity, because it had been one of his favourites. He did so like the colour lime-green . . .

* * *

Kate got to the village in her nippy MX5 sports car within half an hour to find the place completely dead, with no one about on foot to ask for directions to the house she was looking for. The satnav had got her to the right part of the village, insisting she had reached her destination, but she nevertheless passed the house three times before it dawned on her that the old flat-bed lorry parked under a streetlamp in front of the fourth detached property along was partially obscuring the name and number on the sign at the end of the driveway. On the other side of the road, not quite opposite the house, there was a large square of broken concrete in front of a derelict garage, where the two petrol pumps that had obviously once been there had been taken out and the kiosk treated as a coconut shy by vandals. She pulled on to it, U-turned and reversed back into a spot beside the kiosk, partially masked by its long shadow which the moon's delicate probing fingers could not fully penetrate, and switched off the engine.

Left with a weird silence, broken only by the ticking of the hot engine, she studied what she could see of the house for several minutes. It stood at the end of a gravel driveway, flanked on one side by a prefabricated garage and on the other by a clump of tall trees. Something like sixty feet back from the road, with tall chimneys and a gabled apex roof, it had the look of a creepy semi-Gothic style house from an old horror film. and she shivered as it occurred to her that the psychopath, Norman Bates, in Alfred Hitchcock's *Psycho* would have really loved the place.

All the lights seemed to be on inside, both upstairs and downstairs, glowing dimly through thick net curtains and, almost like a dark omen, she was suddenly treated to the sight of a cloud of bats sweeping out from under the roof's eaves and disappearing into the moonlit marsh on to which the place backed.

Kate didn't wait to see if they would return, but carefully opened her car door and climbed out — only to freeze against a crumbling wall when the front door of the house opened and a figure dressed in what looked like a hooded coat was framed against the interior light. He then disappeared briefly behind the bulk of the lorry, before reappearing round the front and climbing up into the cab. There was a long pause and in the interior light, which had now come on, Kate saw that the figure seemed to be bending over the instrument panel to peer at it, as if he was unfamiliar with it. Then the next moment the headlights came on and the lorry started up with a thunderous roar, suggesting the throttle had been accidentally rammed down. Twice it started to move forward with a grinding of gears, then stalled, until finally it lurched forward and drove off down the road, kangarooing before steadying itself and disappearing round a bend.

Kate stood for a few moments studying the house again. She was non-plussed. Who owned the old lorry and why had it been parked outside the house? Who was the man who had left the place and driven off in it? It was plain that he was unused to driving something like that. Furthermore, where had he been going at this time of night? It was a real mystery. And more important still, was he the suspect in question? Even in the moonlight, she hadn't been able to make out much of him, aside from the fact that he'd seemed to be wearing a dark hoodie with the hood up. But if it had been him, was there anyone else left in the house and how long was he likely to be gone?

She chewed her lip. The lights were still on, but there was no sound, or sign of movement inside. The house looked totally dead. Then she remembered what Tammy Robinson had said about her abductor referring to his mother. Was the old woman wandering about the house, or perhaps asleep upstairs in one of the bedrooms? She had no way of knowing. But the temptation to get a closer look at the place was too strong to resist. She just had to chance it — but she would be very careful and bolt at the first sign of danger.

Cautiously leaving the cover of the wall, Kate returned to her car and collected a torch. Then, switching off her mobile phone as a precaution, she gave a quick glance up and down the road to ensure the coast was clear before quickly sprinting across and into the tarmacked driveway of the house.

She listened intently. She could hear the flutter of something — probably the bats — in the eaves above her head, but otherwise nothing. The silence was profound.

Treading carefully, she made her way round to the back of the property through an open gateway and along a narrow path. She could have tried the front door, but had dismissed the idea out of hand. It was probably locked but, if not, walking brazenly into the lighted hallway posed too much of a risk if someone else happened to be wandering about inside.

There was a large, overgrown garden at the back, choked with shrubs and tall trees. Obviously the householder wasn't much of a gardener. There was also a paved patio, neglected and sprouting clumps of grass.

More fluttering sounds above her head and she froze. The next moment something — a bat, she thought — skimmed the top of her head, practically parting her hair. Her heart gave a sickening lurch. She swallowed hard and pressed on.

She reached a pair of patio doors within feet and tested them. They were both locked. More bats flew overhead and she heard weird squeaking sounds all around her. Beyond the patio doors she found a single door, possibly leading to the kitchen. Again it was securely locked. But alongside it, there was an open window on a loose metal stay and below that a stubby pipe, probably a sink overflow, projecting about ten inches over a grille in the concrete path. She had found her way in!

* * *

Kate discovered that the room into which she had climbed through the open window *was* the kitchen, as she had already guessed. Like the rest of the house, the ceiling light was on, revealing built-in appliances and cupboards under old-fashioned worktops and a Belfast sink with tall, brass taps, which must have dated back to a design that had been in fashion at least thirty or forty years ago.

The house was very still, apart from the scrabbling sounds of the bats in the timbers above. She stared around her for a moment, trying to decide where to go first. She realised she might not have much time. Wherever the man in the lorry had gone, he would no doubt be back and she had no means of knowing how long that would be. He might already be on his way as she stood there and she had no desire to be caught red-handed, especially by a vicious psychopath who had already shown his willingness to commit violence and murder.

Snapping out of her reverie, she started across the kitchen towards a door at the opposite end, through which she could just about make out what appeared to be a lighted hallway beyond. But halfway there, she stopped short, spotting another door to her left between the end of a fitted cabinet and the far wall.

Changing direction, she approached it and lifted the metal latch, expecting to find a pantry or larder on the other side. Instead, she found herself staring down a flight of stone steps dropping away into blackness. At once Tammy Robinson's voice seemed to speak to her from inside her head: *He put me in a cage . . . like the ones you keep dogs in . . . in a cellar . . .*

She felt her skin crawl. A *cellar*. This had to be entrance to that cellar!

She stared into the musty-smelling, Stygian blackness, chewing her lip nervously. Were she to go down there to check, she could easily end up finding herself trapped if the man in the lorry suddenly returned, and, even worse, a cellar invariably meant spiders, the very thought of which, as a committed arachnophobe since childhood, made her skin crawl. But whether she liked it or not, she had no alternative but to check it out. After all, what was the point in coming here in the first place if she wasn't prepared to follow up on things when that was required?

There was a light switch on the wall inside the door and she switched it on, frowning at the pale light that flickered into life, intermittently touching on the uneven stone steps falling away in front of her. Placing one hand flat against the wall to steady herself, she extended the other holding the torch out in front of her — more to ward off cobwebs than to supplement the meagre light already provided — and began the descent, treading warily at every step.

Less than a minute later she was both surprised and relieved to find that the flight was a lot shorter than she had anticipated, but she got a more unpleasant surprise when she reached the bottom. The body was lying just a couple of feet away and her shocked gaze was so concentrated on the steel cage that had suddenly become visible on the other side of the cellar that she almost tripped over it.

The man was plainly dead. With half his face stoved in, his beard matted with blood and only one eye protruding through the gory mess, Kate felt sure that even a detailed clinical examination could not have come to any other conclusion and, after bending over him and carrying out a brief check, she straightened up. She had recognised him, of course. Frank William Briggs, the Traveller she had arrested earlier in possession of the VW Passat. With his size and bushy beard, Briggs was not easily forgettable. What he was doing in the house didn't take too much working out either. It also explained who the owner of the lorry was and why the mystery man, who was obviously Briggs' murderer, had decided to move it somewhere else. It would have looked a little out of place left parked out there in front of the house.

So, Mr Briggs, she mused, you tried to put the squeeze on the man who sold you the car, did you? Didn't work out too well for you, though, did it? She smiled grimly when she glimpsed the knife attached to his belt. That hadn't afforded him much protection either by the look of it, she thought.

Turning away from the body, she stared around the room, but apart from the steel cage and a chair to her left, which seemed to have been angled towards it for some reason, she saw only half a dozen planks propped up against the wall in the opposite corner, a few feet from Briggs' body. Moving closer to the cage, she ran her eyes over it with a sense of satisfaction. Her so-called "Maverick" style had once again paid off. Not only had the identity of the perp she and Foster had been pursuing so relentlessly been established beyond any shadow of doubt, but enough evidence had been secured — the cellar, the cage, the car, the body and the links between the different elements of the case — to put a watertight prosecution together. Once SOCO had had the opportunity of carrying out a thorough sweep of the cellar, she was pretty sure they would have captured enough forensic material to put the "icing on the cake" too.

Whether the ruthless psychopath would be prepared to admit to anything, or not, he'd have a hard job explaining how Briggs had come to be lying in his cellar with his head caved in. This was one twisted scumbag who was going to go down like for ever, she was sure about that. All that remained to be done was to actually effect his arrest, and, with that in mind, she pulled her mobile out of her pocket to ring for backup before the perp himself got back.

Unfortunately it was at that precise moment that things started to go south. First, she discovered that her phone could not get a signal in the cellar and then, even as she was clambering up the stairs to the kitchen to see if she could get a better reception there, she heard what sounded like a heavy door (the front door?) slam, followed by tuneless whistling from somewhere above her head and seconds later the unmistakable clump of hard-soled shoes on the bare tiles of the kitchen floor. He was back already!

* * *

Hayden had never had a flat tyre, or at least, he couldn't remember his beloved Jaguar letting him down that way before, but he got one soon after leaving home, of all places on a country lane miles from anywhere. Inconvenient though this was, he would have changed the wheel himself, but unbeknown to him the same bad luck goblins that were frustrating Kate's exit from the cellar seemed to have decided to pick on him too. Even as he opened the boot of the car, he suddenly remembered with a feeling of helplessness that he had no car jack. It had snapped on him when he was checking the tyres the day before and he had forgotten to order a replacement.

Slumping back against the wing of the car, he did the only thing he could do under the circumstances and once again rang the control room to check whether the unit he had asked for earlier had yet been despatched.

'Negative,' the voice at the other end replied, and he detected a sharper, more stressed note to it than before. 'Unit designated diverted to major fire in Bridgwater. You'll have to sit tight until one is available.'

Then he abruptly cut off, giving Hayden no opportunity to enlighten him to the fact that he was already "sitting tight" — though not in a comfy armchair at home as the operator had probably imagined, but stuck on a lonely country lane in the marshy wilds of nowhere, agonising on the possible plight of the woman he loved more than life itself.

* * *

Kate was conscious of the fact that the tuneless whistling had faded, then ceased altogether, suggesting that the killer was in no hurry to deal with the body in the cellar but had gone off somewhere else in the house, maybe to see to his mother upstairs or to get ready for bed himself.

An ideal opportunity had now presented itself for a rapid exit and, after waiting a few more minutes, she went for it.

The kitchen was clear. No sign of anyone lurking there. She thought about leaving via the same window by which she had entered the house in the first place. But then she discovered that that option was no longer available. The window itself was now firmly closed and locked with the key removed. It appeared that the security lapse had been spotted by the perp and he had inadvertently left his intruder with no choice but to look for another way out. She was pretty sure that all the other windows in the house would have been fitted with similar locks and there was no point in wasting time and risk being caught checking them out, which meant that the front door was her last hope — provided he hadn't locked that too and was walking around with the key in his pocket.

He wasn't. She could see the key sticking out of the lock when she peered through the kitchen door down the well-lit hall. The temptation to sprint for it almost got the better of her, but she forced herself to hold back until she had made absolutely certain that it was safe for her to make her move.

The hall was quite a long one. To her right there was a staircase boasting a solid wood-panelled balustrade, with a cupboard constructed under it, which rose to the upper floor from a point about ten feet back from the front door itself. To her left, there were two rooms, their doors standing open, separated by a pair of tall, wide bookcases, laden with tired-looking hardback volumes. An old-fashioned chandelier with a few fused bulbs hung from the ceiling and the dark green carpet on the floor was worn and rumpled in places. From what she had seen of the place so far, it could certainly have done with some much-needed TLC. But there again, she mused grimly, this particular householder was probably too busy murdering and abducting people to have time for anything else in his leisure hours!

She listened again, but everywhere was very still. Even the bats seemed to have settled down, or had maybe flown off en masse on a nocturnal hunting trip. Where the perp had gone she had no idea and at this particular moment she had no desire to find out.

Very carefully, she left the kitchen and crept towards the front door, unconsciously holding her breath and taking care not to trip over the lumps in the carpet. She passed what she took to be the dining room on her left, glimpsing part of a long table inside, and continued slowly past the bookcases towards what was probably the sitting room — at this point transferring her torch from her right to her left hand, to leave her right hand free to unlock the front door and quietly ease it open.

But she never got there. The noises came suddenly from inside the sitting room just as she reached it. The clink of a glass against a bottle. The next moment she caught a glimpse of movement in the doorway. He was coming out of the room and there was no time to make it to the front door! She almost froze on the spot, but, true to form, her survival instincts automatically kicked in. Springing diagonally across the hall, she practically threw herself up the stairs, out of sight behind the solid, wood-panelled balustrade that ran its length.

But she didn't stay there long. There was no way of knowing where he was going next and every chance that bed might be calling him. Desperately trying to control the rasping breath issuing from her lungs, she scrambled up the treads on all fours like some panicking animal, trying to be as quiet as possible. The stairs turned sharp right at the top, revealing another short flight. As she turned the corner, she heard creaking from the stairs below her and the sound of a slow footfall. Just what she had feared. He was coming up behind her.

She got to the upstairs corridor and stared about her wildly. There were doors opening off on both sides. She selected a room opposite, then saw when she pushed the door open that it was a bathroom and toilet. At the sound of a cough on the stairs below her, she grabbed the handle of the door to the room next to the toilet, took a chance and threw it open.

She was in a large, thickly carpeted bedroom crowded with old-fashioned dark wood furniture. Thick brocade curtains with swags and tails covered the single window directly in front of her. To one side of this, end on towards her, there was a big double bed. The room was illuminated solely by bedside lamps with ornate shades set on each side. Their smoky flickering light created constant shadowy movement around the walls and across the ceiling as if the room had a life of its own.

But it was on the bed that Kate's eyes were riveted. She could see that there was someone lying asleep under the bedspread. The light from the bedside lamps was enough to reveal a thin, pale face, framed by shoulder-length brown hair, which was spread out over the pillow like a fan.

The truth hit Kate straight away. This was the "Mother" figure Tammy Robinson had said her abductor had talked about. The woman who seemed to have been the motivator behind the perp's crimes. It had to be. She swallowed hard. She had walked straight into the bedroom of someone who was as bad as, if not worse than, the psychopath himself, and now she was trapped there.

She waited for the woman to jerk into wakefulness, catch sight of her and release a terrified scream that would bring her unhinged son running, but there was no sign of movement from the bed. Not even a slight rise and fall of the bedclothes of someone apparently in a deep sleep. Strangely, there was no sound of breathing either.

Curious in spite of her predicament, Kate advanced very slowly towards the bed and peered down at the sleeper. Only to immediately shrink back with a sense of shock, her eyes widening and the hairs standing up on the back of her neck.

The figure lying in the bed was not the elderly woman she had anticipated. In fact, it was not a woman at all. It wasn't anything. It was an inanimate *thing*, dressed in a white silk nightdress. The long brown hair she had first noticed appeared to have been stuck around the circumference of the shiny pink scalp with some kind of glue, leaving the crown bare, the face had been heavily rouged, the wide-open eyes treated with eyeshadow and the partially parted lips painted a revolting shade of red. She was staring at something out of a nightmare — a grotesque parody of a human being, created from a plastic mannequin, which had been painstakingly brought to life in the mind of a madman!

Suddenly the walls of the room seemed to close in on Kate. The atmosphere become so poisonous that she had difficulty getting her breath. As she retreated further from the bed, she found herself imagining that the abhorrent thing in the bed had started to smile at her and was lifting its head off the pillow.

In her traumatised state, she failed to hear the door open quietly behind her and hardly felt the sharp prick in her arm as the needle pierced her anorak.

'I see you've met Mother then,' the soft, mocking voice said close to her ear and, as she felt her legs start to give way beneath her, she was caught in the arms of the person standing right behind her. Her last recollection was of staring up into the smiling face of the man she had finally identified as the ruthless child abuser and psychotic killer she had been pursuing so relentlessly. The Windmill Academy's quiet, unassuming English teacher, Emrys Parry!

CHAPTER 18

Hayden had waited on the side of the road for at least twenty minutes, hoping to see headlights approaching, so he could commandeer a lift, but no traffic appeared and the road remained black and deserted. Finally, after working himself up into a real state of anxiety over Kate's safety and getting the same "no units available" response from a control room battling with emergencies on so many different fronts, he telephoned Jamie Foster at home, rousing him from a deep sleep, tired, confused and irritable. But Foster was not the sort of person to take umbrage at being wakened in such a situation and he recovered almost immediately, rising to the occasion. Half an hour later he pulled in behind Hayden's Jaguar in his Honda CRV, looking haggard and dishevelled.

'So, Go It Alone Kate at it again then, is she?' he remarked drily, as Hayden climbed into the car beside him. 'Whatever must she have been thinking?'

Hayden shook his head. 'Don't ask me,' he replied as Foster roared off. 'From what I've been able to find out, she must have realised who the perp was after speaking to Tom Merchant and probably went to take a look at his drum.'

'Let's hope she just looked and didn't go any further,' Foster added grimly. 'If this guy is the one we've been after, she could have got herself into real trouble.'

'Tell me about it,' Hayden said, his strong sense of foreboding mixed with the frustration of having been in this sort of situation with his live-wire other half more than once before.

They spotted Kate's MX5 immediately when they reached the village and drove slowly past the derelict garage. The unmistakable low-slung shape of the car was just visible down the side of the kiosk.

Pulling in by the concrete island where the pumps had once stood, Foster could see that there was no one in the car, but Hayden had exited even before they had stopped and was already checking round it when he joined his colleague.

'No sign of her,' Hayden breathed.

Foster made a hissing noise. 'I thought you said she was just taking a look at the place?' he said.

Hayden snorted. 'When have you ever known Kate to do things by half-measures?' he replied.

Pausing for a moment on the edge of the forecourt to stare across at the house just a few yards down from the garage, they saw that no lights were showing in any of the windows and it was half-hidden in a deep, brooding darkness.

'So now what?' Foster queried. 'The place looks dead to me. Everyone could be in bed at this hour and we can't just go barging in without knowing whether Kate went in there or not. She could be watching the place from another spot — maybe around the back — and we could blow her cover.'

Hayden agonised for several minutes, appreciating that what Foster said made absolute sense. What decision he would have come to in the end, had it been left to him, was uncertain, but at this point it was taken right out of his hands. The peace of the warm, still night was suddenly shattered by a loud blood-curdling scream that rose to a shriek before ending in a choking gurgle. Plainly, the time for deliberation was over. They ran straight for the house.

* * *

Kate regained consciousness slowly and opened her eyes, momentarily confused by her surroundings. She remembered being in that hideous bedroom with the monstrosity leering at her from the double bed and passing out in the arms of the madman who had crept up behind her. But she remembered nothing else and could only assume he had carried her to where she was now.

She was in a small, square room, illuminated by an intermittently flickering naked bulb suspended from the ceiling, minus her anorak and shoes. She was sitting in a black leather chair, a bit like the kind used in a hairdressing salon, though this one was apparently bolted to the floor. Unable to move her wrists, she found that they were secured to the chair arms by leather straps. Long strands of brown hair littered the leather cushion on which she was sitting and her hands instinctively curled up in disgust when she discovered that more strands, which had caught on the studs of the chair arms, had attached themselves to some of her fingers.

As she struggled to free herself, her gaze wandered around her, homing in on a chilling assortment of equipment, including knives of various lengths, steel hooks, pincers, clamps, neck collars and pairs of handcuffs, all suspended from a long, horizontal steel pegboard attached to the right-hand wall, together with some wicked-looking whips and bamboo canes held in place by individual metal holders. On the opposite wall was a fixture of horizontal wall bars, like those often seen in school halls, though these were made of aluminium, with leather straps attached, and had obviously been installed for a much more sinister purpose than as a healthy climbing frame. By twisting her neck as far as she could, she was also just able to see a long enamel bath with an oversized tap above it, in a corner just beyond the wall bars, and tried not to think about what its intended purpose might be.

She shivered. It wasn't necessary to have a top MENSA score to appreciate what sort of place this was. She had seen photographs of similar rooms kitted out like this on the covers of the videos and DVDs seized from Mixbury's home and in the illustrated histories of torture and abuse perpetrated throughout the ages in books she had read and museums she had visited. Tammy Robinson and Mandy Williams would never know how close they had come to suffering the most horrific fate at the hands of a pervert whose abominable tastes were rooted deep in his own insanity.

Through the open doorway in front of her, she could see the familiar steel cage in the far, right-hand corner of a second room lit by another flickering bulb, which she instantly recognised as the cellar where she had discovered the body of Frank William Briggs. She was obviously in some sort of secret, hidden den or chamber adjacent to it, one she must have missed earlier, and it dawned on her that the door to it must have been concealed behind the planks she had noticed stacked against the wall.

It was too late to regret the oversight anyway. She had more important things to think about now than past failures — the most significant of which was getting herself out of the perilous mess she was in. But with her wrists strapped to the chair arms the way they were, it was hard to see how that was possible without the skills of Houdini. Nevertheless, she had to try, and she was still struggling with the straps, desperately trying to stretch them enough to slide her hands out, when the thin, slightly stooped figure, dressed in a rumpled, grey, oversized cardigan and brown corduroy trousers, appeared in the doorway.

Emrys Parry looked just as Kate remembered him from the interview at the school. The same pale, anaemic complexion, weak chin and mop of untidy, ginger curls that flopped unchecked over his forehead and ears. The same tinted, horn-rimmed spectacles from behind which his evasive gaze blinked owlishly at her. The same wet, pathetic persona suggestive of someone with little or no confidence, or strength of character. But first impressions can often be wildly inaccurate, and she now knew that his untidy, offbeat appearance and mild, liberal manner were just a front, cultivated by him to hide his true nature. He may have looked weak and insignificant, a pushover, to those more extrovert than himself, but he was nothing of the sort. He was one of the most dangerous criminals she had ever encountered and she had recklessly given herself to him on a plate.

'Hello, Inspector,' he said quietly and treated her to a mocking smile. 'How nice of you to call to see me. Mother was especially pleased to meet you and to show off her nice new hair, which you've probably guessed was courtesy of Tammy Robinson.'

Kate remembered the long brown hair stuck to the head of the hideous mannequin upstairs, and, with a feeling of revulsion, she found herself rubbing her fingers repeatedly against each other to try to dislodge the strands of hair still attached to them, only just resisting the urge to throw up in front of him.

'Get these straps off my wrists now, or you will find yourself in very serious trouble,' she bluffed.

He chuckled, a high-pitched unnerving sound. 'Theoretically, I'm already in serious trouble,' he replied. 'But now I have you as my guest, I'm sure that problem can soon be resolved.'

His meaning was not lost on her. 'My colleagues know precisely who you are and where I am,' she lied, trying to keep her voice steady, as she carefully resumed her efforts to loosen the straps on her wrists, 'and they will be breaking down your door at any moment.'

He shook his head. 'Oh, I think not, my dear,' he countered indulgently. 'If that was the case, they would have been here by now. No, I think you were on a little snoop of your own, Inspector. Trying to find the evidence you needed to implicate me. Well, unfortunately for you, it seems you have found enough to put me away for ever, which is a pity, as I really do admire you and the courage and tenacity you have shown. Mother warned me that you might turn out to be a problem, and she was right.'

'Mother?' Kate exclaimed. 'That-that thing in the bed, you mean? You're insane. You need help!'

He sighed. 'You really don't understand, do you?' he said. 'I know Mother's gone. It happened quite a few weeks ago now, soon after we arrived here, in fact. She's buried in the garden in the nicest spot I could find. But she is still with me in spirit and we often chat together in her room. She still loves me, you see, and she completely forgives me, as all good mothers should. She knows she pushed me too far for too long, that's why I lost my temper and killed her.'

'Like you murdered that young woman in the woods and tried to kill an innocent fourteen-year-old girl—'

'Innocent?' he spat, his manner no longer mocking, or indulgent. 'Tammy Robinson wasn't innocent. She was a little slut who needed to be taught a lesson. She was the reason all this started, what you might call the catalyst. Her behaviour towards me and the rest of the staff at the school was unpardonable, and Mother and I felt she needed to be punished and brought under control. Our innovative programme to bring about behavioural change in bad-mannered young girls like her was the result, and it would have worked with Tammy too, if it had been allowed to run its course in my corrective facility here—'

'Corrective facility?' Kate cut in contemptuously, and she threw a glance at the implements on the wall just feet away. 'This place, you mean? This is no corrective facility. It's a torture chamber.'

'One man's torture chamber is another man's corrective facility,' he said glibly, 'and both can achieve the same behavioural changes in the end.'

'You didn't set it up to change behaviours,' Kate accused. 'That's just an excuse. You created it solely to satisfy your own sadistic cravings, and there was never any chance of Tammy being released after you were done with her, was there? She would have been murdered and dumped in a bog somewhere — and it would have been the same with Mandy Williams and all the other poor kids you would have snatched afterwards if you'd got the chance. That's it, isn't it?'

He giggled inanely. 'Can I be blamed if one of my subjects succumbs during the treatment process?'

Kate studied him in the manner of someone contemplating an insect, then made a risky decision. She knew her time was running out. For the moment he was enjoying his grandstanding, but it wouldn't last. He would soon tire of it all and then she would be dead. Her wrists were red and bleeding under the straps from her unobtrusive struggles to free herself, but she could at last feel that the straps had stretched a little under her constant straining against the leather. All she needed to do was to loosen them a fraction more. Her hands were quite small, so maybe she could slide them out after a bit more effort, and with them free she would at least be able to make an attempt to defend herself. But to do that she needed to keep him distracted for a while longer and the best way to do that, she reasoned, was to wind him up.

'What turned you into the pathetic scumbag you are?' she sneered. 'Little mummy's boy, were you? You know, a weak girlie type dominated by a nasty old hag even barmier than you are now?'

She saw his body tense and his face harden, suddenly losing its mocking sneer.

'Scared of her, were you?' she went on regardless. 'Did she knock you about when you kept wetting the bed?'

'You have a nasty tongue,' he hissed. 'Just like Tammy. But insults will get you nowhere.'

'What about girls?' Kate persisted, feeling the right-hand strap ease a bit more. 'Did she put you off them too, eh? Give you a complex about it all, so that you were no longer a real man?'

There was a disturbing glint in his dark eyes now. She had touched a nerve and he was starting to quiver with suppressed emotion. 'You little bitch,' he breathed, stepping a couple of paces towards her. 'You know nothing about anything.'

'Still unable to get it up, is that it?' she persisted, pulling hard against the loosened strap on her right wrist. 'Like to screw *me*, would you? But you couldn't do it, could you? You couldn't manage a real woman. That's why you like to torture helpless kids instead.'

'I'm really going to enjoy snuffing you out,' he said. 'It will be a real pleasure.'

She fully expected him to lash out at her, but he stopped and checked himself even as he raised his clenched fist, his anger abruptly fading and a slow smile spreading across his face. Then, without another word, he turned on his heel and walked across to the pegboard with its array of implements.

Now that his back was towards Kate, she quickly took advantage of the fact, straightening the fingers of her right hand and closing them together to reduce the width of the hand. She gave a hard tug and felt it start to slide out, only to jam again on the knuckles. Her heart was racing and her throat was bone dry as she wriggled and twisted her arm and, just as her hand finally came free, he turned round.

She froze, pushing her fingers back under the strap, hoping he wouldn't notice, acutely conscious of the fact that her left hand was still constrained by its strap.

He smiled again and walked towards her. He was holding something by his side that he had selected from his collection and he held it up to show her. It was a peculiar-looking implement, consisting of two small wooden handles with a length of flexible wire between them.

'I expect you know what this is,' he said. 'It's a garotte, a rather crude but effective method of strangulation which has been employed as an executioner's tool all over the world for centuries. I made this one myself, based on the garrottes with which our military silently killed sentries in the Second World War. It's what I intended using to despatch the "little darlings" on my corrective programme, once their redemption had been achieved, but I've not had the chance to use it since Tammy walked out on me.' He smiled. 'Still, you will make an excellent substitute.'

Kate was now really pulling on the strap securing her left hand, which was partially free, but still trapped by the knuckles. 'Kill me,' she gasped hoarsely as she quietly wriggled and twisted her wrist, 'and the police will hunt you down like an animal.'

'And what then?' he sneered. 'We don't have a death penalty in this country anymore. So, it will either be the funny farm for me, or a maximum-security prison with all mod cons provided. It's worth the risk. After all, what have I got to lose?'

He flexed the wire between the two handles experimentally, then gave a rueful smile. 'I would have preferred to have studied your facial expression as you departed this world,' he said, 'but unfortunately the device is best applied from behind, so I shall have to forgo that pleasure. You don't mind, do you?'

But she didn't answer him. Instead, she had tensed in the chair and was staring intently over his shoulder. The heavy, dragging footfalls had been unnaturally slow and ponderous, and they were approaching from the next room. Parry now heard them too. Forgetting Kate, he turned apprehensively to see who was coming. And he didn't have long to wait. The next moment the nightmare figure appeared in the doorway behind him, like some Frankenstein monstrosity, and stood there, swaying unsteadily, dripping blood in the manner of a leaking colander.

After the frenzied blows Frank William Briggs' head had sustained from the steak hammer a short time before, he should have been dead, and even Kate had come to that conclusion after her own earlier examination. But Briggs was evidently a difficult man to kill and it was plain that he had no intention of dying just yet.

His nose and one eye may have been pulverised into nothing, but his gaping mouth still rasped its weakening life force as he loomed closer. His remaining eye now glared like an obscene, bulging, white marble from a gory mess, projecting bits of splintered bone as it swivelled round to fix on Parry with a terrifying intent, the long, serrated knife held in one huge hand glinting coldly in the cellar light.

Parry seemed unable to move. It was as if he had suffered sudden paralysis, and he simply stood there with the garrotte dangling limply from his hand, as Briggs advanced towards him. The Traveller's hand was hidden from Kate's sight by Parry's body, but she saw Briggs' shoulder complete a thrusting action and heard Parry's long, deafening scream as the blade of the knife emerged from his back with a jet of blood that sprayed the floor all around him and over the chair in which she was sitting. The embedded knife that was still clutched in Briggs' hand seemed to be holding Parry up on his feet, but, as the big man pitched backwards on to the floor, the knife was drawn out of Parry's body, leaving him to slowly collapse with a choking, bubbling moan right on top of his killer. A few shakes and quivers, and then Parry joined Briggs on his final journey to hell. As Kate finally pulled her right hand free and started to unbuckle the strap on her left wrist, she heard the welcome crash from upstairs as the front door caved in.

The "cavalry" had arrived — late as usual.

AFTER THE FACT

'The Marquis de Sade would certainly have admired this fella, so he would,' Deidrie Hennessey commented drily, as she glanced around Emrys Parry's secret room.

Kate nodded, her own gaze lingering on the chair in which she had very nearly met her death. 'Well, at least Parry won't now be able to write *his own* memoir from the funny farm he would have been sent to after his trial,' she replied.

'Seems he'd have had a lot to write about too,' Hennessey added. 'I've just heard from South Wales Police that the search we asked them to carry out at his former home in the Rhondda Valley has turned up what they believe to be the remains of two young girls buried in the garden. The gobshite's been at this before — him and his excuse for a mother.'

Kate felt sick to the stomach at the awful news, but she didn't respond. Her mind had floated off elsewhere.

It was a week since the bloodbath in the cellar and Kate and Foster had been virtually "living" at the crime scene ever since, spending long hours there with the investigation team and leaving late each evening. Kate's wrists were still lightly bandaged after the damage she had done to them while trying to free herself from the chair's leather straps, but the wounds seemed to be healing, and Jamie Foster had even jokingly suggested it might be an idea to wear the bandages permanently as a "turn-on" for Hayden.

The bodies of Emrys Parry and Frank William Briggs had now gone, only dark stains remaining where they had been lying. A partly decomposed body, no doubt that of Parry's mother, had also been recovered from a shallow grave in the back garden and, following forensic examination, all three corpses had been removed to the mortuary for the obligatory post-mortems. The scenes of crime teams had completed their painstaking evidence-gathering task both on behalf of the coroner and to enable the preparation of the major crime investigation file that would ultimately lead to the closure of the criminal case on a finding of "Detected, No Proceedings", and they had already packed up their gear and departed at the same time as Jamie Foster and the rest of the crime scene investigators. Now only Kate and Hennessey remained behind in the house, taking a last look round.

Soon only the ghosts would remain. But Kate knew that the memories of what had happened in those shadowy rooms would stay with her, perhaps for the rest of her life, indelibly etched on the walls of her subconscious, with all the other stabbings, drownings, shootings and strangulations she had dealt with in her long career as a detective. The faces of the latest dead would fade a little with time, as other faces came to take their place, but they would never entirely disappear. Instead, they would manifest themselves at night as she slept, forcing themselves into her thoughts and turning her dreams into nightmares. It was the price she had to pay for the career she had chosen to follow and there was no going back. Even if she packed it all in now, the memories would remain. They were the legacy she had inherited.

Then abruptly, Kate was jolted out of her reverie to the realisation that Hennessey was speaking again, and she only just managed to catch the drift of what she was saying.

'Yous cannot help wondering what made Parry flip and turn into the monster he became?' she said. 'To be sure, how does depravity like this start? Was he always a loon, or did something turn his mind?'

Kate shrugged. 'Who knows? He told me that Tammy Robinson was the catalyst for his so-called project. Her bad behaviour was allegedly what got him started — no doubt with more than a little encouragement from his mother, who seemed to be dominating him via that thing on the bed, even after she was dead. But from the discovery of those girls' bodies in Rhondda, it would appear, as you just intimated, that he must have been into this sort of perversion for quite a while, even if the project itself was a recent innovation.'

Hennessey's face was grim. 'Aye, and the worrying question is, how many other wee dotes could he have abused and murdered before without anyone being the wiser?'

'Maybe we will never know, but it does seem incredible that in this day and age he was able to get away with what he was doing for so long without arousing any suspicions whatsoever.'

Hennessey nodded. 'But if no red flags were raised, why should anyone suspect anything was out of kilter with him?' she said. 'I had Fergus carry out some research for the coroner on yer man through the local police, and it drew a total blank. All that's known about him is that he was born in the Rhondda Valley in South Wales and lived in a wee village there all his life until he came here. Neighbours say his da' walked out on his mother when he was a child and that she was a desperate banshee of a woman who dominated and ill-treated him something terrible, though this never got to the ears of the police, or social services.

'That might have turned his mind over time, but there don't seem to have been any obvious signs of abnormal behaviour. Local people say he was quiet, kept himself to himself and was always polite and reserved, treating his mother with surprising reverence, despite her violence towards him. He must have been clever too. He went to university, got a first in English, and then went to teacher training college to get his PGCE. He got a job as a teaching assistant at a primary school in the Valleys, then, about a year or so ago, was selected as a full-time teacher at the Windmill Academy here. On the surface then, a brilliant achiever—'

Kate snorted. 'Yeah,' she cut in, 'and a real dependable role model for every pupil in the school. Pity that underneath the quiet, reserved facade he was also a depraved madman who got off on abusing and murdering kids.'

'At least he will no longer be a threat to anyone, thanks to you,' Hennessey pointed out. 'You did grand, Kate, even if you did break every rule in the book by doing it, which means that, although you richly deserve a commendation, you won't get it. On the other hand,' she added, grinning, 'you won't be investigated by professional standards for breaching police regulations either. The two balance each other out rather neatly.'

Kate gave her a rueful smile. 'Story of my life, ma'am,' she said drily. 'But you know what they say, if you can't take a joke, you shouldn't have joined.'

Hennessey chuckled. 'Too true. Then you won't mind if I leave you to lock up here then? I'm thinking, you might want a last nostalgic look around before you shut the door on it all for good.'

'Nostalgic isn't quite the word I would use for it,' Kate replied with feeling. 'But I can think of a lot of others.'

* * *

Dusk had already fallen by the time Kate followed Hennessey's example and left the house to head home. It had been a creepy experience checking round the place to make sure everywhere was secure before she locked up. The old building seemed to be constantly flexing its sinews, with rafters cracking as they expanded or contracted, and doors rattling under sudden draughts, and she'd found herself constantly glancing behind her as she'd gone from room to room, turning the lights off one after the other. It was almost as if the house was a living breathing thing that was covertly watching her from within itself. Twice she'd thought she sensed a presence in the shadows behind her and once imagined that a shadow had flitted in front of her as she descended the staircase. It was all in her imagination, of course, but, after what she'd been through in this house of horror, it was not surprising that she had found herself seeing or sensing things that weren't there.

It was with a feeling of immense relief that she locked the front door behind her, pocketing the key that would eventually be handed over to Emrys Parry's solicitor, and followed the driveway out to the road where she had left the CID car parked.

It was a clear, breezy night, with a myriad stars and a full moon gracing the black vault of the heavens. As on her previous visit, flocks of bats flitted in large numbers between the tall chimneys and a heavy perfume rose from some of the shrubs bordering the drive, as she brushed against them in passing. She took a deep breath as her feet crunched on the loose gravel. What had been one of the most horrific cases of her career was finally over and it felt good to be going home to lovable, reassuring old Hayden, knowing that, after days of being sent to Coventry by him over what he had considered to be her reckless, solo, snooping expedition, she had at last been forgiven.

She got to the end of the drive and, reaching the car, stood for a few seconds with one hand on the door handle, fumbling for the ignition keys in her pocket. What caused her to glance back at the house was unclear, but when she did so she found herself momentarily rooted to the spot. Whether it was a trick of the moonlight or not, it was impossible to say, but there appeared to be a light glowing in one of the upstairs windows, even though she was sure she had turned everything off before leaving. Not only that, but the thick net curtains seemed to have been pulled back, and silhouetted in the window was what looked like a sinister human figure, a figure that was staring straight at her with a chilling intensity. Then, suddenly distracted by a rustling sound close to the car, she spun round, in time to see a black cat emerge from the bushes and streak across the road a few feet away. When she looked back at the house, it was again in total, brooding darkness. The light was no longer visible in the upper window and the figure had gone. Shaking her head grimly, she promised herself a stiff whisky when she got home and, unlocking the car, she climbed behind the wheel and drove away at speed, leaving skid marks on the road . . .

THE END

˻hen Jasper agreed to publish his mum's
ˑce novel and it became a bestseller.

ɔince then we've grown into the largest independent publisher in the UK. We're extremely proud to publish some of the very best writers in the world, including Joy Ellis, Faith Martin, Caro Ramsay, Helen Forrester, Simon Brett and Robert Goddard. Everyone at Joffe Books loves reading and we never forget that it all begins with the magic of an author telling a story.

We are proud to publish talented first-time authors, as well as established writers whose books we love introducing to a new generation of readers.

We won Trade Publisher of the Year at the Independent Publishing Awards in 2023 and Best Publisher Award in 2024 at the People's Book Prize. We have been shortlisted for Independent Publisher of the Year at the British Book Awards for the last five years, and were shortlisted for the Diversity and Inclusivity Award at the 2022 Independent Publishing Awards. In 2023 we were shortlisted for Publisher of the Year at the RNA Industry Awards, and in 2024 we were shortlisted at the CWA Daggers for the Best Crime and Mystery Publisher.

We built this company with your help, and we love to hear from you, so please email us about absolutely anything bookish at feedback@joffebooks.com.

If you want to receive free books every Friday and hear about all our new releases, join our mailing list here: www.joffebooks.com/freebooks.

And when you tell your friends about us, just remember: it's pronounced Joffe as in coffee or toffee!